MISCONDUCT

Misconduct

BRIDGET VAN DER ZIJPP

VICTORIA UNIVERSITY PRESS

TE WHARE WĀNANGA O TE ŪPOKO O TE IKA A MĀUI

VICTORIA
UNIVERSITY OF WELLINGTON

VICTORIA UNIVERSITY PRESS
Victoria University of Wellington
PO Box 600 Wellington
vuw.ac.nz/vup

National Library of New Zealand Cataloguing-in-Publication Data

Van der Zijpp, Bridget.
Misconduct / Bridget van der Zijpp.
ISBN 978-0-86473-575-1
I. Title.
NZ823.3—dc 22

Printed in Singapore

TO MY MOTHER

1

It wasn't as if she meant to do it, more that opportunity presented itself. It just happened that she was in the pharmacy when he pulled up in his car and entered the café across the road. She did have a certain familiarity with his habits though, so maybe she'd taken her prescription to that particular pharmacy because she knew he often went to that café, she wasn't precisely sure now.

She watched him through the window as he leaned in and chatted to the dreadlocked girl behind the counter. He'd once mentioned the girl's brother owned an independent recording studio and she always had news about the latest releases.

The pharmacist called out that her prescription was ready so she pretended to browse for a new pair of sunglasses. Looking out through a pair of polarised lenses she saw him take up his coffee with one hand and sit down at the table nearest the magazine rack, where he reached back in a long unhurried move and pulled out a music magazine. And it was precisely that moment, precisely that movement, the familiar languor of that stretch, when she found herself hopelessly mortgaged to some kind of pained impulse.

It wasn't quite feasible simply to go across there, sit down opposite him. She would've done it if she knew she could muster a confident smile, something coltish and beguiling, something that would fetch up all that had been lost. But her energy was so skiddy and unsound that a smile might not come out the way she hoped, might in fact appear more like the decoy cheer of a suicide bomber. Besides, she hadn't brushed her hair yet, was wearing a baggy T-shirt she'd also slept in the previous night. It's not like he would look up and go – *oh how lovely*. She knew she had to be more careful. The last time she'd dialled his number he'd surprised her by speaking into the choked silence.

'You have to stop this, Simone,' he'd said. 'I am not the person that can help you.'

She'd watched him closely when he pulled up, though. Saw him look casually around and then hide the keys under the mat. He never liked carrying keys, didn't like their bulge ruining the line of his jeans, and he was such a dreamer he'd often lose them anyway. He didn't even like carrying wallets. He'd just slip an eftpos card into his back pocket where it would get bent and scratched, and eventually stop working. He was careless with his things.

When he left the café he called out something funny to the girl behind the counter and walked out the door still laughing, and the fact of him walking around casually dispensing jokes only emphasised again how unaltered he was, and how incapacitated she'd let herself become by his leaving. He went into the second-hand bookshop next door and joked around for a while with the spluttering guy who runs that place – who's part of a collective of street poets hanging around the multiplex on Friday nights, shouting out poems which always mentioned pissing, or fucking, and often both.

After a couple of minutes he went up the stairs to the biography section. He never read anything else, liking in particular true stories of artistic people – musicians, painters, poets, sculptors, writers, actors – he didn't mind which. Mostly he was looking for stories of the kind of men he liked to think of as kindred spirits – those who were prepared, if necessary, to forsake a grip on the more trivial matters of life for the sake of their art. She knew he'd be there for ages, moving his finger down the row of books, mumbling the titles with his head turned sideways. He was always quite considered about his choice of books, not really enjoying reading, but liking having read, careful to ensure any purchase was worth the investment of his time.

She wasn't in any hurry as she went up to the counter and paid for her prescription, bought as well a pair of cheap wrap-around sunglasses, and a trucker-style hat with *Detroit* written on it. 'Don't bother wrapping those,' she said, 'I'll just wear them.' And then, casual as anything, she crossed the road, got in his car, found the keys, and drove away.

He had a long history of rashness, a store of childhood misadventures he liked to share as bashful anecdotes, always in a light that made him appear helplessly incorrigible. One of his favourites was about the two weeks he'd spent riding around on his bicycle with explosives hidden in his saddlebag. He was twelve and had made some gunpowder from charcoal, sulphur and the saltpetre he'd stolen from his uncle's butchery, and after experimenting with packing various mixtures inside old toilet rolls, he'd found a discarded golden syrup tin and loaded it up, making a truly exciting bomb. He'd carried that tin around for two full weeks before settling on his grandparents' hen house. She now found herself understanding a little of the thrill of anticipation, the appetite for perfectly framing the climactic moment, but unlike him she felt alongside that the braking weight of caution. It was suddenly clear that when everything was at its most basic she had only a little of his ability for bravura, and hardly any of his active disregard for repercussions. For while it was one thing to steal a car, it was another thing completely to be discovered inside it, and she found she urgently needed a plan.

She drove into a supermarket car park close, but not too close, to where she lived and walked home. If she left the car at the supermarket somebody would surely report it eventually. She thought about leaving it in some rough backstreet with the doors open and the keys in the ignition. But what if the police saw it first? It would just be impounded and returned.

At home she curled up on her bed and thought about pushing the car off a cliff. But what if someone saw her? She would have liked to sell it. But who to? The burden of possession was now like a punishment in itself. It wasn't as if she could ask for anybody's help in this.

Burn it, she decided. Drive it behind the disused factory

near the polluted creek at the industrial park, and set it alight. Lay out a line of petrol leading right up to the car, spill the rest all over it, and then stand behind the edge of the building and toss the match to the ground.

The fire walked up to the car, and then consumed it in a ticklish way, almost as if it wasn't all that interested. The actual act of wrecking the car, it turned out, was not so difficult – much easier than the thought of doing it. She'd siphoned most of the petrol out of the tank, but now she thought an explosion might have been more satisfying.

She'd rifled through the glovebox first. There was a bank statement in there. His account was in overdraft. He'd been to Gino's Restaurant. He'd bought something in a record store. He'd bought something in a sushi bar. He'd been to a lingerie shop. And he had paid $69 for something from a company called Adult Enterprises. That amount! Each item a sign he was going about his new life with some kind of unseemly goatish fervour.

A paper bag all scrunched up with pie crumbs inside. Some broken charcoal pencils and an unused new brush. A supermarket receipt including facial toner, cotton buds and a brand of soya milk he detested. Also pesto, maple syrup, pistachio nuts, chocolate, and champagne, as if he was a high-life kind of person all of a sudden. And there was a demand from the tax department for a large sum of money that advised if it wasn't paid soon they would confiscate some property. And a summons for an unpaid fine for running a red light at 12.05am. He would probably be glad to be rid of those.

A brown envelope had his writing scrawled on the back. Some kind of idea, something he wanted to keep to maybe inspire him later.

I had a dream. I looked out the window at night and suddenly realised I could fly. So I took off, in my pjs, and flapped my arms round and round the big oak

*tree. And I could see all the little birds sleeping and a
big moon in the sky. And when I looked back at the
window my mother was standing there yelling at me
to come back and get to bed. And I laughed. And I
flew.*

She pocketed that. He'd often had flying dreams and used
to give her all the details in the morning, even when she was
yawning and her eyes were glazing over. She'd always tell him
flying dreams meant you were happy, even though she'd once
looked it up, standing in a bookshop, and it had said flying
dreams meant you wanted to escape the life you were living.
This particular flying dream, though, probably had more to do
with the guilty thrill of his recent behaviour.

She pocketed the keys as well. All the rest went up in smoke.
While she was walking home she heard a series of very loud
pops, like a distant, extended death rattle. There was a sense of
lucky extrication, now that it was over. By the time she was on
the bus, a fire engine went past with all its sirens going, and a
few minutes after that she saw a police car. She began to worry
the police might find some sort of indictment, a fingerprint or
something. It hadn't occurred to her until then that she might
have committed an actual, imprisonable crime.

But keys – not just car keys, a front door key too. Who in
their right mind would not want to try it out at least once?

2

Once an age has been acknowledged then somehow it must be lived. Simone wanted to stay at home and cultivate her denial, but her friend Lexie insisted her birthday must be celebrated. 'It's not as if it's all about you!' she'd said, and although she'd meant it as a joke her words did have a chastening effect. It had only been a matter of weeks since Lexie's father had accidentally nudged a beehive with his tractor and died alone of anaphylactic shock, and Simone had to concede it might be more than unsociable to refuse her friend.

'Okay only a few people then,' she'd yielded. 'In a bar somewhere. And nobody is allowed to mention the number.'

That night Simone arranged things badly, getting there first. Venturing out alone was difficult enough lately. It was humbling to once have been part of an established couple and then be the one that everybody knew had been cut loose. Rather than sitting conspicuously unaccompanied, she went into the ladies' room, applied some lipgloss, touched up her hair, and tried to avoid looking at herself too closely in the mirror. She'd noticed recently there was something different about her eyes – an evasive, rabbity quality, that she hated to see.

She emerged to find Lexie and her partner Anton had arrived, and as they wrapped her up in big smacking birthday kisses Lexie's eyes began to water. She cried a lot lately, she said. Happy things. Sad things. She couldn't watch the news. Anton had to shield her from any advertisements for hardware, or spy thrillers, or beer, or other things that living men might need. She could hardly bear to look at the hereditary cowlick growing into her son's fringe. And just last week she'd been walking down the footpath when somebody had driven past in a similar car to her father's, not even the same colour, and this too had made tears form. 'But let's not talk about any of that now,' she said.

They were soon joined by tiny Georgia, who'd turned up without either her husband or the new young lover she couldn't stop talking about. Bernie slouched in, carrying the bitter weight of his recent separation. And then Ingrid breezed in, announcing loudly she'd left her husband home to babysit, and none of them bothered to disguise their gratitude.

They ordered rounds of double-strength vodkas. A night out was a rarer thing than it used to be, and a gathering of their oldest friends was all the licence they needed to shrug off some of their adult answerability and resurrect a common inclination towards recklessness – there was some small, time-cramped ambition in the potency of those drinks. They didn't let her get out her wallet. 'The birthday girl never pays,' Ingrid and Lexie said together.

They toasted her.

'Happy birthday.'

'This is the time to do or die,' Georgia announced in her singsong voice.

'To new beginnings,' someone proposed, and they all cheered heartily, and their combined brightness made Simone wonder if they'd had some sort of prior discussion about certain subjects.

When she next looked up she saw Joey, Lexie's brother, standing near the door. She rose, unsure whether to kiss him hello, always finding him unreadable. He seemed to back off a little, so she put her hand lightly on his elbow and introduced him to the three he didn't know. She noticed how Ingrid was unable to lift her eyes away from the tattoos on his forearms, though it was his tallness and his fantastic mess of curly brown hair that Simone always found most immediately striking. Lexie, who was more unpredictable than usual, shouted, 'So you turned up after all, you big hairy blouse.'

He laughed. 'Okay I'll admit to big and hairy, but blouse? Come on, Sis. You can do better.'

Lexie scoffed. 'Big hairy moose, then, will that do ya?'

'Yep,' he said, 'seems more accurate.'

More drinks arrived and Anton began to tell them about sitting on a plane earlier that day, returning from a management meeting, and this big burly bloke had taken the seat next to him. He'd looked down at the size of this bloke's thighs, and the size of his own legs and started to fret that by comparison his own were pathetically weedy and he was thinking it was finally time to get a gym membership. But then somebody came up and asked for the guy's autograph and he realised he was an All Black. 'I felt so relieved,' Anton said. 'I was sitting next to a rugby star and suddenly it wasn't that my legs were wasted, more that his were bloody huge.'

'Sorry to be the one to mention this, mate,' Bernie said, 'but they are kinda puny.'

They were all squeezed around a table in the corner of a small, neighbourhood bar, which gradually started to fill with the loud background hum of other people's chatter, and at a certain point the proprietor dimmed the lights as if he wished to orchestrate the exact moment the real business of the night should proceed. It wasn't long before Georgia started to slur and told everybody she'd had three laser sessions down below and now she only had a landing strip. She did it for her lover, she said. She offered to show it in the ladies' loo but everyone baulked. Except Bernie. He tried to drag her off by the wrist, until Ingrid slapped his hand away and told him to get a grip. He turned instead towards Simone and said, 'Hey, I was wondering, did you hear from Fraser today or anything?'

Georgia gave him a hard shove.

'What?' he said. 'Are we supposed to pretend he never existed?'

'Yes,' said Georgia emphatically, glaring at him.

He took on the look of a man who had once too often attracted the mystifying disapproval of women and moved off towards the bar. Georgia leaned over to give Simone an extravagant hug which lasted so long it began to feel more

14

like she'd fallen on her. Now that she'd got to the stage of providing hugs, she next turned her attention to Lexie, who was potentially in even greater need of what she had to give. Lexie smiled tolerantly as Georgia climbed onto her lap. 'Just what I need,' she said. 'The incredibly sticky monkey-girl.'

A vacated seat was left beside Simone, and Ingrid switched places to take it up. 'Sooo,' she said in a quiet aside, 'How's work?' She sipped her drink, staring at Simone over the rim of her glass.

'Ah,' Simone replied, her voice lowered. 'So you've heard.' There was a time when Ingrid might have been the first person she would've run to with the discomfiting news that, alongside everything else, she'd also lost her job. They used to be the kind of close friends who shared it all, calling or seeing each other almost daily, but over the last few years the intensity of their alliance had drifted a little. Ingrid always seemed to have whole waves of new friends she'd met through her children's kindy or school. There was often an air around them that they considered they were the ones on the conveyor belt forward, and Simone had thought her failure to keep even as much as a job could only give some satisfaction to that. So over the last couple of weeks she'd been pretending she wasn't home whenever Ingrid stopped by, a few times even diving under the window sill to avoid her.

'Any plans?' Ingrid enquired. 'How will you live?'

There was no correct answer to this. 'I dunno. Breaking and entering,' Simone joked, but wished immediately she hadn't used those particular words, surprising herself. That was the trouble with holding down secrets, the pressure of it was precarious, like an overhang of rocks jutting dangerously above causing inappropriate responses. And even though Lexie still had Georgia draped around her, she suddenly looked up and examined Simone's face in a curiously penetrating and sober way. This spooked her. 'Perhaps life on another planet?' she added lightly.

'Well I guess a change is as good as a rest,' Ingrid said with a dry, resigned sigh.

'I'll say. Especially now you're frigging forty!' shouted Georgia, taking a fiendish pleasure in letting the word ring loudly around the room.

From up near the bar Simone felt Joey staring at her but when she glanced up he looked away. She didn't know him well enough to trust her instincts. He was Lexie's younger brother, who'd flown off to Australia many years ago with a skateboard stuffed into his backpack and a surfboard checked into the hold. He'd only recently returned home for his father's funeral but he didn't seem in any hurry to go back to his former life. There was the sense about him that he'd decided now was finally the time to step up but he wasn't quite sure how a genuine dodger like him was supposed to go about doing that. In ways she knew to be unwise she was drawn to him.

A couple of nights ago they'd gone to see a visiting Scandinavian band together, and at the end of the evening she'd driven him back to where he was staying. He didn't invite her in, had kept one hand on the door handle, but had lingered, telling her something of his life in Australia. His story was not one of grand success, but he was self-effacing and touchingly funny and in the half-light of the car she'd begun to think he was quite handsome in an uncontrived way. While he talked she'd wondered what would happen if she touched him, put her hand up to the side of his face. But she was still so ruined by her sore heart she couldn't be the one who acted first. She wanted him to reach across to her. At some point, as if spooked, he'd suddenly said, 'Right I'm off,' and opened the door and more or less leapt out of the car.

'Maybe you could go out with him?' Ingrid suggested, nodding up to the bar where Joey and Bernie were now slouching, having a conversation that Joey didn't look very interested in.

'Joey?' Simone said, heat rising to her face.

'No, not him,' Ingrid retorted, as if for some reason that was totally unfeasible. 'Bernie. He's single now. Doing okay. I heard he bought a yacht the other day.'

'You've got to be joking,' Simone protested. 'Would you?'

They both squinted across the room to where Bernie was

flopped against the bar, with one half of his shirt tucked in and the other dangling out. He looked back around with such a glass-eyed incurious stare that he reminded Simone of a propped up flounder. They'd both known him since university. He was the guy who'd excelled at beer-drinking games and unrequited crushes. His marriage had been a surprise to them all, but less so the news of his separation. He'd bought the yacht, as far as Simone knew, to spite his ex-wife, and without much regard to the effect that would have on his relationship with his children. Never before had he been in any serious contention, and to have him suggested now . . .

They watched as Bernie, noticing them looking, raised his glass in salute and accidentally spilled some of the contents down his shirt. It was only then that Ingrid finally conceded. 'Okay, I'll give that up now,' she said.

Simone went up to the bar and squeezed in beside Joey, ordering another drink and listening in on the desultory conversation he was having with Bernie. They were arguing over whether or not Joe Strummer could have successfully re-formed The Clash if he'd lived, and she could tell Joey was taking an oppositional view just for the sake of it. 'You're such a contrarian,' she said in a voice which came out more accusing than she'd intended.

'No I'm not,' he countered, grinning.

When Bernie staggered off towards the men's room she said, 'So . . . the other night . . . didn't you fancy me?'

Joey took a long considered sip of his beer and looked towards the front door for a moment before saying, 'Sorry, but nah.' She felt herself sway a little, as she stood beside him at the bar. Into a long silence he added, 'It's just you're my sister's friend, and I like to keep my personal life separate.' He'd had trouble getting the words out, and as she chanced a look at his face she noticed one of his eyes wander off on its own and realised he was completely soused.

If she wasn't so drunk herself she might've chosen a smarter way of asking.

The evening ended relatively early. Babysitters, kids to get off to school in the morning. Simone stood on the footpath with Lexie and Anton saying goodnight. Anton kissed her and when she commented on the lambie-ness of his lips Lexie said, 'Go on, give him a good one.' So she and Anton kissed quite dirtily. Then she and Lexie shared a tender, soft kiss, like two forest deer coming together. It was something they could only do if they'd all been drinking.

Joey came lurching out of the bar. 'Ahh, fresh lips,' she said, grabbing him before she had time to think. And then somehow he had one arm around her waist, and one hand on the back of her head, and was dipping her backwards, and kissing her so forcefully she felt weakened and overcome. They parted for a breath, and then he pulled her even tighter and kissed her again. A taxi horn tooted and Lexie yelled at him to hurry up and let the poor girl go. They fell apart and he was gone. She was left wondering if that surprising hunger was for her, or just any girl standing on the footpath.

Back inside the bar Georgia had passed out on a stained couch. Ingrid had already gone but not before she'd taken the time to slip a card into Simone's pocket, at exactly the moment she was beginning to think she'd acquitted herself quite well, with the phone number of an 'excellent counsellor'. Simone foolishly mentioned to Bernie she'd just kissed Lexie and Anton and then Lexie's brother. 'My turn then,' he said, leaning in with that fishy expression on his face. He tried hard, but his tightly searching tongue seemed like a sad, flat violation. A booby prize. She couldn't look at him afterwards. She went up to the bar to order more taxis.

3

A distant relative of Fraser's once came to stay with them for a short time, saying he needed somewhere for a bit of time out. Rick arrived in a state of mind that made it difficult for him to see the bright side of anything, but was too secretive ever to tell them the reason why. One day, when they'd reached their tolerance of him lying on their spare bed, smoking and still wearing the same stinking clothes he'd arrived in, they arranged for him to go on a day trip around the harbour. He lived so far from the ocean back home in Canada that they thought a sea outing might shake him up a little, he might even enjoy it, although it was his general practice not to enjoy anything. They dropped him off down at the wharf on a brilliant day, one of summer's best. It was gloriously sunny, the sea was sparkling glass. When he got back to the house they asked, in the faux-cheerful voices they'd developed around him, how great it was. 'Well,' he replied, 'there was a little cloud on the horizon.'

Simone was just benchmarking herself against Rick – trying to work out how far up the scale of wretchedness she might be, if he was the measure of ten – when the telephone began ringing. Her immediate response was to feel anxious about what news it might bring – but this morning it was Lexie, ringing with an interesting proposition, she said. She told Simone her mother's half-sister, Alice, had been admitted to hospital, having had a severe stroke. 'The thing is,' Lexie said, in a hurried way, as if she wanted to skim quickly over the possible end implications of such an illness, 'it turns out she's probably going to be there for quite some time and she lives out of town and she has this dog and the family were beginning to wonder about a house-sitter and I was thinking . . .'

'Me?' Simone baulked.

'Well I was thinking about that thing you said about trying

another planet,' Lexie replied evenly, and the moment of her intense, penetrating gaze at the party came into Simone's mind.

'That far away, huh,' Simone said. Unsure if she was being paranoid, she wondered what it was Lexie knew, or thought she knew, or was it that she was just uncomfortable about anything with her brother Joey? Simone found herself struggling to voice some credible reason why she couldn't. Since the party all she'd done was spend her mornings idly circling advertisements for jobs she didn't want and knew she wouldn't do anything about, and her afternoons lying on the couch in front of moronic television programmes thinking she ought to be a better person.

'It's at the beach,' Lexie added, by way of enticement.

'The beach?'

'Yes, lovely sandy beach. And you like dogs don't you? Remember, you always wanted one.'

She'd once told Lexie that when she was eight or nine she'd so desperately wanted a dog for company that she used to take the family cat out for rides on her bike, stuffing it down the front of her windbreaker and zipping it in so just its head was sticking out. Overall the cat was a highly reluctant companion and really would have preferred a warm lap somewhere inside the house, but Lexie had been amused and quite often brought it up.

'Well yes,' Simone had to admit. 'I like *some* dogs, but . . .'

'But?'

'But . . . it's winter.'

'Yes but not for much longer, and less so there.'

'And I can't just up and leave.'

'Because . . . ?'

It had taken her twenty-four hours of energy-consuming resistance to decide she would do it. Poor old lady. Poor old dog. They need me, she thought. And Lexie so rarely asks for favours. She began to be seduced by the idea of a lovely, distant solitude. It had been some weeks since she'd taken Fraser's car, and as far as she knew he was unaware she'd been inside his new house, but still she had a constant half-expectation she'd open the door and find Fraser on her doorstep demanding an explanation. Or even the police. And while she thought she'd probably stopped all that behaviour her conviction was only as strong as that of a newly reformed addict. Better she took these devil hands away.

'Will you be able to drive me there?' she was forced to ask Lexie, not having got around to revealing to her, or anyone, she'd also lost her licence for six months.

The gay couple who'd recently moved in next door mentioned they had a friend returning from overseas who could be interested in subletting her house, so she offered them a lease on her car as well. The next day she hired a skip and started throwing away things she didn't need and didn't want to come back to. Once she started she found she didn't need much at all. She began to be concerned one skip wasn't going to be enough but then overnight half the contents disappeared. At first she was confused and worried by this, felt absurdly deserted by her own possessions, but a willingness to deny such feelings just encouraged her to throw out more until there were only bare-essential furniture and a couple of suitcases of clothes left.

'Sorry about the scowling tiger in the back seat,' Lexie said when she arrived to pick her up. She was referring to her son Billy – whose plan to spend the day watching cricket with his dad had been wrecked when Anton was suddenly called in to work. Instead he was sitting in the car with a grisly little pinched face, holding tight to his right to feel aggrieved.

They lifted Simone's suitcases into the boot and as Lexie slid into the front seat she said cheerily to Billy, 'Righto then. It's a three-hour drive so let's see how long you can keep that up for, shall we?'

As they headed off down the motorway Simone started to recall all those things she'd got rid of, and it occurred to her she might have been rash. She tried not to think of the odd pieces of crockery she'd always liked, the 1970s lamp she'd found cobwebbed into the rafters of Fraser's parents' garage, the little blue rug she'd once knitted for his old cat to sleep on.

Having negotiated their way out of the city, Lexie slipped the car into overdrive and said in a loaded way, 'Sooo, Joey seemed to enjoy himself at the party.'

Simone looked straight ahead, trying to frame a suitable question, but before she could say anything Billy leaned in from the back seat and said, 'The party?'

Lexie reminded him about Simone's birthday.

'Why wasn't I allowed?' he demanded.

'Because it was a grown-ups' party,' Lexie replied.

'I still could've come.'

'Not to a bar you couldn't!'

'That's not fair,' he said, adding 'you suck' under his breath as he slumped back in his seat. Simone looked across at Lexie, but if she'd heard at all she'd decided not to react, and was focusing on the road ahead with a brittle composure.

Simone stared out the window, at the passing countryside, at the cows and thistles and peacefully grazing sheep. She would've liked to bring the conversation back around to Joey, but wasn't confident she could assemble the sufficiently detached tone she needed. After a while she began to feel the weight of Billy's unhappy sighs, and she tried to distract him with a game of twenty questions. But she made the first round too easy by thinking of a famous cricketer, a known hero of his. He guessed it in three questions and then said he was bored with that game already. As a second measure she took a bag of Liquorice Allsorts out of her handbag and passed them over to him. He took two and passed them back, saying with an almost feral menace that he didn't really like that kind.

When he was a toddler he'd once said to her, 'You are my favourite uncle!' He used to squeal with uncomplicated delight at the sight of her. But now, aged nine, he'd worked out she knew virtually nothing about sports, science, astronauts, skateboards, heavy machinery, or even dinosaurs. In particular, she didn't know how to compete satisfactorily at PlayStation and was therefore practically redundant. Mostly she'd ignore his indifference, sometimes ruffling his hair and pinching his cheeks just to get a rise from him. But lately she'd become aware of something else in his face as well. Some recent thing. Some vague dawning that her aloneness, her lack of attachments, was badly managed for somebody of his parents' generation. Somehow, and he probably wasn't even sure why, he considered this made her fair game.

Now she made a big show of rolling down the window and tossing out the whole bag of lollies, feeling what she knew to be a childishly perverse satisfaction.

They had instructions to collect Aunt Alice's dog from *The Wind in the Willows Farmcare*. The driveway leading up from the road was rough and unwelcoming, and when they reached the top it was apparent from the lack of pride in the front yard that this probably wasn't a top-notch outfit. Also there were no willows.

The kennels had a lock on the gate and a sign forbidding unauthorised entry so Simone and Lexie trekked up to the house leaving Billy in the car with his Game Boy, on the verge of exceeding his previous best score. Beyond the glass front door they could see a woman slouching on a chair watching television. She got up and shuffled to the door in her slippers and trackpants, with one eye still on the screen. Lexie explained they'd come to pick up the dog and the woman sighed and reached for a set of keys hanging on a rack near the door.

Lexie and Simone screwed up their faces at the acrid smell of neglect inside the kennels.

'We take them for walks every day,' the woman said defensively. 'My husband takes them down the back of the farm with his quad bike. They get a good runaround. They love it. And we feed them quality food,' she added, without enthusiasm, as if she knew they were thinking she was lying, that they just left the dogs in the stinking cages while they lazily collected their fees.

Aunt Alice's dog was lying dolefully in the back of a pen. 'Did they tell you what its name was?' asked Lexie.

'Tag on his collar says Inspector Clouseau.'

Lexie and Simone exchanged a glance. 'Her idea of a joke?' Simone asked.

'Probably. A lot of Mum's side have a sense of humour straight off the Goons,' Lexie replied.

The woman pulled back a bolt and the dog rose to his feet. She handed Simone the lead. 'There's the fee to be paid, for the care 'n' all,' she announced, her eyes daring them to challenge her. Lexie pulled a cheque book out of her bag and wrote out the amount she asked.

'Come, Inspector,' Simone commanded in a firm voice, giving Lexie a sidelong smile. She led him out through the gate and as soon as he had his paws on the grass he tried to show his gratitude by attempting to lick her on the knees. Now that she could see him more clearly he looked like some kind of sheep dog, with his mottled grey and white coat, and big brown eyes. Talking eyes. Eyes which now beamed up at her with an endearing gonzo eagerness.

When Billy realised the dog was going in the back seat with him he suggested that maybe it could go in the boot. He groaned when Lexie told him sharply to get over it.

'Pooh, it stinks,' he said as they drove out of the yard. 'It's panting in my face.' Lexie suggested he open the window.

When Lexie first mentioned the dog, Simone hadn't thought much about what that would mean. She'd imagined, for some reason, a palsied old black lab. But she took one look in the side-view mirror at that big fruitcake of a face leaning out the window behind her, with his ears flapping, and his big pink tongue floundering in the wind, and she knew she was in danger of falling in love.

'Mum,' Billy said, 'now it's got its bum in my face.'

Lexie suggested he ask it nicely not to, and Simone giggled – causing Billy to mutter 'I hate you' without being specific.

Further down the road they passed a long stream of

vintage cars, which seemed to be on their way to some kind of convention. The passengers were all sitting high in the wind with big dandy scarves tied around their hats and knotted under their chins. Billy refused to look up from his game, but the dog let out an excited yip.

At last, after their three-hour trip from the city, they wove down a hill, past a shopping village, and along a beach road which alternated sluttish plaster mansions with humble, groggy baches. They travelled on, nearly to the end, where the sections became more spartan and isolated, then they turned off the main road into a short dead-end street of five houses, huddled together between the forest and the sea, like a clan.

Alice's house was the last in the street – a little weatherboard settlers' cottage, painted a fading yellow, and nestled in a crowded garden which looked as if it had been planted a hundred years ago and hardly touched since. It was a lush bird haven, where early plantings like camellias and lavender and hydrangeas fought like snooty colonials for their right of place amongst the ferns and native flax.

The jumbled exuberance of the garden did little to prepare them for what they found inside the house. Poor Alice hadn't expected to collapse in the local supermarket and be taken to the hospital. She'd left food out on the bench, rubbish in the bin. And much, much more. Billy breathed in a whiff of trapped rot, declared this the worst day ever, and refused to step inside. Lexie suggested he take the dog for a walk on the beach while they cleaned up.

'Sorry, I didn't know it would be so batty,' Lexie said, as they looked around, opening windows and wondering where to start. The entire house was a mess of hoarded miscellany – unwound wool from old cardigans, jars of buttons, unlidded and dried up glue, cut-up old clothes, Agee jars, clippings from magazines, shells and driftwood, broken crockery, feathers, bones, and dried flowers. And dolls. Not just a few dolls. Plastic and porcelain, baby dolls to Kewpies, rag dolls, knitted dolls, and even Barbie dolls. Not always whole dolls either, sometimes just their heads, or their dislocated limbs, or even just eyes.

'She must have gone a bit insane,' Lexie surmised, but Simone was beginning to think it wasn't that at all. There was something deliberate about it, a certain dippy optimism in the way everything appeared to be waiting for purpose.

They found themselves standing by some photos hanging in the hallway. 'Who are these people?' Simone asked.

'I'm not too sure,' Lexie said. 'I hardly knew her really. Mum's father married twice and Alice was one of the daughters from the first marriage. Mum didn't even find out about his other family until she was sixteen and they didn't get curious enough to meet each other until much later.'

She pointed to a photo of a bridal couple. 'This must be her with her husband. She looks a bit like Mum there.' It was set in a garden and looked to be postwar, perhaps fifties. There was nothing striking about them as a couple, except that they both seemed to be laughing at a pair of geese which were wandering out of the left side of the shot. Lexie picked out another and said she thought that was their son, she'd only met him once when she was ten. It was a photo of a man with gingery hair in a thin brown suit, his eyes didn't quite seem to be focused.

'Where's he?'

'In London apparently. Too busy to come back.'

'Some son. What does he do?'

'I don't know actually. Looks like an accountant or a lawyer or something.'

'Or maybe an undertaker.'

Simone stared for a while at another photograph. It was of a young woman, she thought Alice, pushing a baby carriage through a paddock. She was wearing big men's gumboots, the carriage was loaded with flax, and interested cows were following her. Tucked into the frame was a fading Polaroid of her at some kind of country fair holding up a small trophy. Lexie leaned in to look as well. 'I'd forgotten about that. Guess what she sent me for Christmas one year.'

'Flax bags?'

'No. You could never guess. A set of Wombles made out of kumara.'

'Carved out of kumara?'

'No, no. Just some knobbly kumara that she dressed up in little tartan jackets and hats and wire glasses. They were kind of cool. I played with them until they went all spongy, and then dressed my dolls in the clothes.'

There was another photograph nearby of a young boy. He was dressed as an Indian chief, complete with a feather headdress, and a fringed and beaded shirt. He was pointing his bow and arrow towards the lens and Simone supposed Alice must have made his outfit too. Poor Alice. How could she have known her son would turn out to be so ungrateful?

One of Lexie's errant tears slid down her face and she quickly brushed it away. They began work together in the kitchen with Lexie sweeping things into a rubbish sack, while Simone rinsed dishes under the tap. 'So do you think you'll be all right here?' Lexie asked, sounding dubious.

Simone had no idea. She found she couldn't admit to Lexie that she was quite grateful for all the crowded surfaces and toppling piles. This was a place where she could feel free to completely let herself go for a while.

'What will you do to keep busy?' Lexie wanted to know. She opened a cupboard door and screamed as a frightened mouse scampered across her foot and beneath the sink. 'Christ,' she said, 'I'm so sorry about all this.'

'Well, on the bright side there's plenty of company.'

'And probably a good little listener too,' Lexie agreed, and after a few moments added, 'Well at least this place might keep you out of trouble anyway.'

Simone looked across at her but she was engaged in tipping some grotesquely furry fruit out of a bowl into the rubbish. Did she mean anything by that? 'Hmmm, I'll say,' she managed, falling only slightly short of the droll resilience she'd attempted.

She had the increasing sense that Lexie did know something but was holding back. The two of them had never been much good at traversing truly difficult ground. Their friendship had its roots in things far less loaded. Back in their flatting days if one of them asked if they'd made a drunken fool of themselves at a party, say, then the other could be relied on to reply, no, of course not, you were hilarious. If one of them got into strife at work, the other would tell them their boss was a dick anyway. And if either of them had any boyfriend trouble then the other would agree he was a jerk and then pretend it hadn't been said after a patch-up. The truth could always be propped up a little if necessary, and bad behaviour was almost always normalised by boasting you could do much better yourself. They could make light of anything.

Lexie was her oldest friend, as generous and unjudging and quick to laugh as anybody could be, but her grief was still apparent. Simone knew about the sudden death of a father. She knew about all the things you had to come to terms with. She knew how long it took. But Lexie's father's death, all alone in a paddock, had been particularly resounding in its strangely innocent brutality. And while outwardly Lexie liked to appear quite capably resolved, the shock of his death made her barely able to speak of it. Her sadness around the loss was almost pure in its painful legitimacy, and anything Simone might be experiencing was a notch down on the scale – only the lower-order struggle with the dank, self-hating, miserable fact that Fraser made a *choice* to go. There are no ceremonies, no gathering of relatives, no bittersweet speeches, no aunties arriving with casseroles for that one, only the haunt of the words used in the final conversation. But if Lexie had effectively managed to keep it together then Simone didn't feel she had the right to talk of falling apart.

Lexie picked up a dishcloth and began rubbing at fingerprints on the refrigerator door. 'I know I keep saying sorry but I'm a bit worried about what I've dumped you into here,' she confessed.

'Oh, don't worry,' Simone said airily, gesturing towards all the clutter, 'I've always suspected I might've had a talent for dressing kumara. Up until this exact point in time it may only have been a matter of lack of opportunity.'

'Goodie. When shall we expect the first of your humorous creations then?' Lexie asked.

'Shut up! Do you think there's a café nearby? A library?'

'Maybe a tea rooms, it's that kind of town. Somewhere around here you'll find the perfect Eccles cake.'

'I'll be set then,' Simone smiled.

4

Simone opened her eyes to find herself fully clothed on the daybed in the sun room. The dog was at her side, thwacking his tail on the ground, panting into her face with the expression of an impatient tour guide keen to get the party moving.

The night before she'd washed down the bacon and egg pie they'd bought on the way down with some punishing cooking sherry she'd found on a kitchen shelf. At some stage she'd staggered into the bedroom but hadn't wanted to lie down in the personal sag that had been left in the bed by Alice. She pulled the door shut – closing out all those spooky shoes with their worn-in soles, all those stale clothes in the closet, and the half-empty pill bottles on the dresser. Instead she'd collapsed, still in her clothes, under a pile of scratchy ex-army blankets she'd found in the linen cupboard.

The restless, boiling ordeal that had been her sleep had left her feeling exhausted and sucked dry, cotton-mouthed. Even her skin felt thirsty. She badly wanted coffee but there was none in the cupboards. The beach was over the sand hills at the end of the street, not far. Perhaps there might be a small shop or something.

Discouraging squalls of wind were slicing around the house but when she opened the door to assess their strength the dog squeezed past and leapt onto the path with a joyous skip, oblivious to any disincentive. He lifted his leg on the nearest bush, and then bounded back to offer up a share of his enthusiasm. For a moment she envied his natural happiness, wishing it could come so simply to her.

The closest she'd ever come to having a dog was a few years ago now, when she and Fraser decided to get a puppy. But as they were driving out to the farm to look at the litter Fraser had begun to mutter under his breath.

'What?' she'd enquired.

'Nothing.'

'No, what?'

He had paused for a long moment and then finally said, 'It's just that it's such a big commitment.'

At least he'd had the clarity to look a little sheepish as he said it. Only a few hours earlier, after they'd seen the ad in the paper and rang to make the appointment, they'd danced around the house in their socks, in a state of silly excitement. They'd talked of names, she'd suggested things like Fifi and Snookums and Buffy just to rile him and he had pretended to fall for it saying, 'We're not having some stupid little ball of fluff. Our dog ought to have a ballsy name. He will be . . .' and here he had apishly puffed out his chest before finally declaring, 'Brutus!'

'Doofus,' she'd sung, leaping onto his back and toppling them both over onto the bed.

In the car she hadn't wanted to ask about his change of heart. She was too scared of where such a conversation could lead. She'd suggested he pull into the next farm gate and turn around. 'Are you sure?' he'd asked, and in his voice she could almost hear his relief begin to collapse against a surge of genuine regret. They never talked about it again, but for a long time after that every little puppy became, for her, a symbol of ruined expectations.

The cluster of five houses on Alice's street was like a stranded backlot, closed off from the rest of the community by the dunes, a tangle of trees, and a big green paddock of munching sheep. There was a shabby, lived-in look about them, rather than holiday homes. The gardens were well kept, had been fussed over. Tablecloths and tea towels flapped on the lines, there were gumboots and brollies and wheelbarrows on the front porches, and a little further down she could see two pairs of saggy old y-fronts pegged next to an airing tuxedo jacket. As she walked along she began to feel watched. Out of the corner of her eye she thought she saw blinds flex, curtain edges twitch.

In front of her the dog suddenly took off after a ginger

cat, chasing it across one of the gardens. The cat fled towards the aluminium conservatory tacked on to the front of the last house, and looked behind as it vaulted through the top window. It landed on the shoulder of somebody sitting in a chair beneath and they leapt up in fright, arms flailing out, knocking over a budgie stand with a loud clatter. There was a flash of black hair as the person rushed from the conservatory into the interior of the house. The dog came scampering out of the garden and raced on ahead to raise his back leg on a signpost specifying the times dogs were permitted at the beach. Simone stole down the street after him, hearing the bird's outraged squawking ringing out from behind like an accusation – loudly announcing her to the neighbourhood as the incompetent new guardian of the local lout.

She followed the dog down a path between two dunes and emerged to find the beach was long and desolate, strewn with grisly tangles of seaweed, although not enough of them to weigh down the shifting sands which flew up at her in demonic twists. In the distance she identified a wooden boardwalk and headed towards it, pulling up her collar and burying her hands in her pockets as she trudged downwind. The gusts lifting up off the surf were so cold they made her teeth hurt, but the dog was undaunted, sniffing happily around piles of driftwood. He selected a likely looking stick and dropped it a few yards in front of her with a hopeful look, but her hands were warm inside her coat. As she walked along he did it again and again, looking at her more desperately each time, until she began to think he was taking on the look of a crack addict urgently needing a fix. Finally she picked up the stick and threw it into the shallows and he raced after it like some madly heroic lifesaver.

At the end of the boardwalk there was an old corrugated-iron building that had undergone a conversion at some stage. *The Shed – Café and Supplies . . . open daily until 6pm.* She tied the dog's lead to a balcony post and as she pushed through the front door she was greeted by a pleasant waft of roasting coffee that, at that moment, felt particularly well earned.

The only other customers were five elderly women, sitting around a table in the corner with their heads all bent in towards each other, swapping some kind of irresistible gossip. There were a few shelves of basic grocery provisions, some frozen goods, fresh vegetables, newspapers and magazines, and while Simone gathered up what she needed she heard an announcer on the radio say tomorrow's charity car-boot sale was postponed.

At the counter Simone ordered a coffee, but the woman was not overly friendly and accepted the order without speaking. When she turned to use the espresso machine Simone noticed her hair was woven into a thick black plait, but then the woman suddenly spun around, as if she had some kind of unnatural sight, and started yelling at the other customers. 'Hey, if you wanna sit there all day you buy your coffee from me!'

The startled group began gathering up their things, and the one holding a Thermos from which she'd been slyly topping up her friends' cups said peevishly, 'We've been coming here every week for years, but don't think we'll be coming back. It's not been the same since you arrived.'

For a confused moment Simone thought she was the one that had drawn this remark.

'And your coffee is foul, and too strong,' another added spitefully.

They all marched out and the woman muttered, 'Do I look like I care? Old bags.' She had quite a husky European accent, which Simone couldn't identify, and it intensified the impression there was something very difficult about her. She might have been a little younger than Simone, or perhaps even a little bit older. It was hard to tell.

Simone took up her coffee and found a table near the window, feeling obliged to try and make herself as small and invisible as possible. The coffee was excellent though – strong and murky and svelte – and after a few sips Simone felt her pulse start to quicken. This will do, she thought.

*

33

In her childhood, whenever her family arrived at the seaside, no matter how lovely the day, no matter how sparkling the sea, her father would open the car door, stand with his hands on his hips, and say, 'This place is a dump! Shall we go?' Then he'd pretend to get back into the car and she'd have to beg and plead for him to stay. But as she struggled back, picking her way through the slagheaps of seaweed, she wondered if here, in this inhospitable place, she would ever have done any begging.

When she was very near the house she came across an elderly couple. The man, whose thin cotton pyjamas were flapping around his legs, was being shepherded up the street by the woman. She was more sensibly, if oddly, attired in a fur coat that may once have been luxurious but was now mangy and balding. When she noticed Simone looking at what they were wearing she called out in a playful voice, 'Oh don't mind us, sweetie, we're what happened to Gatsby's crowd after the partying was over!'

She held out her hand, with the generous, sure smile of somebody who had probably been very beautiful once. 'I'm Clara,' she said, 'and this is my husband Charlie. We're your neighbours, I think. You're the house-sitter? And Alice? How is she? Do you know?'

Simone introduced herself and told them as much as she knew.

'Oh. I was hoping you'd have some good news for me,' Clara said, glancing at her husband who had bent to ruffle under the dog's ears while it sniffed with focused interest at his pyjama crotch. 'These days I prefer to hear about miracle cures and astonishing recoveries.'

'Look,' her husband said, 'Inspector Morse is back.'

'Wrong detective, darling. It's silly old Clouseau, remember?'

Up until that moment Simone hadn't been sure if the tag on the dog's collar might've been a joke, so it was good to have some authentication of the name. The dog moved off to nose around the flowerbeds and Charlie straightened himself up.

Looking directly at Simone for the first time, he said, 'Are you here about the subdivision?'

'Sorry?'

'Across the road. The government's planning to put in a huge shopping centre. There'll be cars going in and out all hours of the day and night.'

Simone looked over at the sheep grazing in the paddock and wondered where all these cars were supposed to come from.

'Oh, don't worry,' Clara said, patting his arm reassuringly. 'I think the government's decided not to go ahead with that for now.'

'Terrible wind today,' Charlie tried again, this time without confidence. Simone hoped he was talking about the weather, and was relieved when Clara began chatting away about how it wasn't normally this dramatic.

'We'd hate you to get the wrong impression,' she said. 'Although every time there's a storm these days the voice of doom comes out. I have to keep reminding them about the floods we had ten years ago, and then there was that tornado that ripped through the pumpkin sheds up the coast road. Lots of people lost windows and things that year.'

'Because of the pumpkins?' This seemed so unlikely that for a moment Simone wondered if they were a couple who took pleasure in disarming people by flicking off extravagant claims at every opportunity.

'Oh no,' Clara said, laughing at herself. 'Imagine that! A pumpkin flying in through the window. I think I'd die of fright, wouldn't you? No, it was just the usual sort of storm damage. Wind and trees and things. The pumpkins got washed out to sea but they did stink the beach up for quite a while.'

The dog was sniffing around with one ear half-cocked, as if he had a vested interest in them all getting along. Charlie started picking at a frayed patch on his pyjama sleeve and Simone said she'd better get going.

'Have you met the others yet?' Clara enquired.

'The others?'

'The others on the street.'

'No.'

'Well, I expect you will in time.'

Her husband started to wander off towards their house, the seat of his pyjamas hanging baggily behind him. Simone looked away. She didn't want to watch his retreat, as he seemed to be carrying about him a sense of his own sad reduction, the opposite of pride. She went to move off but Clara gently touched her on the arm and said in a quieter voice, 'Sorry to ask this but if you see Charlie wandering about, could you just turn him towards home for me. Tell him off a bit if you feel like it. He never remembers the next time he sees you.'

5

The essential difference between cats and dogs is that a cat will listen to the weather outside and if it hears the wind bending the trees it will simply burrow deeper under the blankets. The stronger the wind, the tighter the curl of the cat. A dog, on the other hand, will listen to the snapping and cracking of trees, and think there's an adventure just waiting to happen. Waiting. Panting. Scratching. Simone found dogs were very hard to deny.

On her second morning she was only a few steps up the street, just past the house where Clara and Charlie lived, when she heard a voice. 'Hello, hello,' a white-haired woman called out, emerging from one of the houses as if she'd been on watch. 'On the way to the shop again are you? I'm Mrs Galloway, and you must be Simone. I've heard all about you. How are you? Come over here, will you, I'm trying to stay out of that nasty wind.'

Even before Mrs Galloway asked Simone to bring her back a carton of milk, she knew she'd be asked to do something. From the way she occupied the doorway, the way she exuded a sense of personal significance, this appeared to be somebody used to getting other people to do her bidding.

'And if you're going to the shop every morning you might ask the others sometimes too,' Mrs Galloway suggested. She had her purse in her hand, was holding it out in front of her and fiddling inside it. 'That would be a kind thing to do, wouldn't it. They need a little help now and then.' One by one she put some coins into Simone's hand, like she was handing over a gratuity.

'Oh, and speaking of that, we're missing Alice dreadfully down at the gallery,' she said hopefully. She wasn't particularly tall, not even up to Simone's height, but so strong-faced that she had a broad, indomitable quality. She might've been somewhere in her seventies but her skin had the look of being expensively cared for, and even at this early hour her feet were packed into sober shoes, her hair had a firm structured lift, and the most minor movement released a drift of floral scent. It all contributed to the impression that she liked to maintain a strict hold on personal standards, did not countenance slovenliness of any kind. That and her matter-of-fact assumption made Simone feel much less than her years. She didn't wish to volunteer for whatever was being suggested. It seemed best to say little.

Mrs Galloway said, 'Oh well,' waving her hand in a disappointed way, as if to dismiss her.

Simone didn't really know how to be forty. It seemed so much older than thirty-nine, and even that seemed too old for her. Before she'd left her job she'd heard one of the presenters discussing his thirty-sixth birthday in the newsroom, and it had come as a shock to her. She'd always assumed she was younger than the newsreaders with their managed hair, and those voices that dripped reliability and assurance. It was unsettling to realise that wasn't the case any more. She didn't think she'd mind as much if she had her life more together. She'd read an article in a magazine about how you were supposed to change at forty. You weren't supposed to lust openly after fine-boned young men like Orlando Bloom. You should never go to bed without attending to your skin first. You ought to move up to the next generation of moisturiser. You needed to get your teeth whitened. You were best to avoid the latest fashions. You should give up on G-strings. It didn't exactly say so, but it implied a switch over into some kind of wisdom and discretion, and more depressingly, moderation.

The beach seemed changed at first, and she thought if anything it was even more rugged than the day before – huge messy surf lunging and dumping, gritty flurries blasting across her, blue-black clouds speeding around overhead on important business. Maybe her whole time here would consist of this, fighting to stay upright.

Just as she was entering the café a gust caught the door and banged it hard back against the wall. She had to push against the wind to get it shut again. The woman behind the counter said, 'Look what blows in. What you want? Same coffee as yesterday?'

Simone nodded and sat down at a table by the window where she could keep an eye on Clouseau who was sheltering from the wind against an upturned dinghy. Two seagulls stood hunched and watching him from the café railing like a couple of edgy bouncers.

The woman placed the coffee down without speaking and then went back behind the counter and resumed buttering some bread, making it clear she wasn't interested in any conversation. Overall Simone considered this better than the alternative. When Fraser had left, her initial response had been to make a dash into a travel agent and book herself a holiday she intended to be some sort of fast-track to renewal. Not feeling very capable of making choices, she'd quickly picked Vanuatu only because they happened to have a special that week. She'd liked the look of the long, white, empty stretch of sand in the resort poster. But she got badly sunburnt on the first day, significantly limiting her options, and then whenever she sat down in the hotel restaurant the lovely local women, with hibiscus flowers tucked behind their ears, would drift towards her table. 'Aww, you on your own?' they would always ask in their simple, good-natured way. 'Aww, such a pity isn't it,' they would add sadly. And because she was stitched together so delicately, she couldn't stop reluctant tears from spilling out of her eyes and onto the table in front of her. That only made the women more solicitous, hovering around her with their plates like kindly nurses on a suicide watch. Even the slightly uncomfortable feeling of being actively ignored by the only other body in the room was better than that.

On her way out she purchased the milk, finding that despite her great show of generosity Mrs Galloway hadn't quite given her enough money. The woman waited until Simone reached the exit before she spoke again. 'And try not to break the door this time,' she called out. Glancing back, Simone saw she was smiling to herself.

Walking away from the café she pulled the hood of her jacket up and tightened the cords, tying them tightly under her chin and not really caring how stupid that might look, and it registered suddenly, what was different about the shoreline – there was no seaweed. It had all been sucked away overnight as if the tide was demonstrating its might. It can give, and it can take away. It can be nice, and it can be ruthless. There was something admirable in how shifting and pitiless this place was. A feeling came over her – she was unbound, liberated from her usual element. She could shake off her past here. She could reinvent herself, if she wanted to. She made up her mind she wouldn't be sorry. She wouldn't utter his name, ever. That word would not be on her lips when she woke in the mornings. She would never again write those six letters in the steam on the glass wall of the shower as she wept under the flow.

When she got back to the street a portly old man in a homespun jersey was raking between the rows of a vegetable patch, in the same garden where she'd seen the tuxedo jacket on the line. He looked up and waved, and one glimpse at his willing, lonely face told her that he too had been waiting out in the dreadful weather for her.

'Bit of a rough day today, eh Simone,' he said.

Had her name been whispered over every fence in this street?

'Got something for you,' he said, and he went over and collected a lettuce off his front porch and handed it to her. It was the best-looking lettuce she'd ever seen – so green and wide and frilly it almost looked like something you could pop on your head and wear to the races. 'Hydroponics. That's the secret. Grow anything you want indoors all year round. Still think some things grow best out in the dirt though,' he said, indicating the garden behind him.

'Well it's a long time since I've seen one as good as that,' she said as he put it into her hands.

'It's my pleasure,' he replied, and from behind his ear he

pulled a rolled cigarette which was so skimpy she guessed he must be on a tight budget. 'By the way did I tell you about my trip on the bus the other day?'

She shook her head politely, wondering if she shouldn't have tried to get away more quickly.

He lit his cigarette and started his story on the exhale: 'Well, I sat meself down opposite an old gal that lives a bit further up the hill. She carries a bit of weight, that one, always takes up one and a half of those seats. Anyway she had a big bag of peaches on her lap. Must've been visiting someone with a tree. And suddenly the bus lurched and all the peaches spilled out everywhere. Well this old duck wasn't going to let them get away – only when she bent down to pick them up the poor old thing accidentally farted, if you'll pardon my French. Do you know what the bus driver said then?'

He took a long draw on his cigarette and Simone shook her head, trying not to look at the dog, which was now inside the vegetable patch lifting its leg on the silverbeet.

'He said – that's the way, lady. If you can't catch 'em, shoot 'em!'

She laughed, and he laughed too, a big cheerful open-mouthed laugh, which gave off the smell of nicotine and strong tea. It occurred to her that peaches were probably out of season but she allowed him the small liberty.

'Well, better get back to the office,' he said reaching for his hoe. Still chuckling he added, 'They call me Toss, by the way. Although sometimes they call me other things.'

When she handed over the milk a moment later, Mrs Galloway glanced at the lettuce under her arm and said, 'He's a real character, that one, I can tell you.'

Simone walked home with the vague sense she was like a fish on a line, being slowly reeled in.

As she went to bed later that night she could hear the storm worsening. In the far distance the sea was relentlessly punishing the shore. The trees around the house were seething too, cracking and hoarse, as if they had much to discuss.

6

Clouseau woke her with a sudden howl, but there was something else too, she thought sleepily, some kind of metallic bang outside that may have started him off. She opened her eyes and found she was lying neatly on the daybed, in exactly the same position she'd fallen asleep in. Sheets were not twisted around her neck. The bed was not sweaty with unwanted dreams. For the past few months her dream-state had become a hatchery for fears and anxieties that continued to swarm around her on waking. But was this something she could call progress? Still she was reluctant to throw off the blankets, the tip of her nose felt frozen. She reached out, pulled back the curtain and saw the ground was white. There was no movement, not wind, not a leaf rustle – everything was chilled to the point of tranquillity. The grass was transformed into shards of ice, spiderwebs into crystalline bunting. It was as if the gods had decided to still the world for a morning to give them time to think how to go on with it.

Surely this was weird? This was a seaside village, people came here for the moderate climate, didn't they? She turned on the radio in the kitchen and the announcers reported excitedly that two fronts had met to create freak weather conditions. They were bubbling over with news of unfortunate mishaps and power cuts in outlying areas. They warned people about broken pipes and slippery paths. They spent a couple of minutes feigning sincere concern for the 'elderly and the infirm'. And from there it occurred to them to wonder about the plight of the poor cattle and sheep. Underneath she could tell they were thinking this was a great day for radio. It was a disappointment to have to report that the weather office had advised both the fronts had passed over already and it would be sunny for the rest of the week.

Voices outside her window drew her out to find her neighbours having a discussion in the chill of the street. Mrs Galloway was presiding, and as soon as she caught sight of Simone she urgently beckoned her over.

'Clara fell!' she exclaimed, her breath steaming. 'I saw it from the kitchen window. Saw her chasing after Charlie. She's hurt her arm. I was making porridge, I never normally have it but when it's as cold as this . . . and I saw it out the window.'

'Are you all right?' Simone asked, turning to Clara, who looked pale and fragile, holding her wrist to her chest with her good arm. She began to say something but Charlie who stood beside her, still in his pyjamas but this time with a dressing gown too, spoke for her. 'She's going to be fine,' he told Simone. 'But the authorities will be here soon to collect the bodies.'

'Oh, Sausage,' Mrs Galloway said, with a little uncomfortable laugh. 'It's not as bad as all that.'

Toss moved up to Simone's elbow. 'There's a bit more to the story,' he said conspiratorially, nodding behind him, where a car was resting against a tree, its front fender crumpled. This then was the source of the noise that caused Clouseau to howl.

Mrs Galloway gave Toss a glance which hinted at disloyalty. 'I was taking Clara and Charlie to the medical centre. The car skidded around a bit,' she said.

Simone heard Toss snort and realised Mrs Galloway may have been downplaying things. Looking around she noticed Mrs Galloway's letter box lay splintered on the ground. 'I'm not used to it, you see,' she said. 'Ice.'

'It's the climate change that causes it – global warming and all that,' Toss announced.

'But shouldn't that make it hotter?' Mrs Galloway retorted impatiently. 'Not cause things to freeze up.'

'Floods, tornados, tsunamis. All sorts of things caused by disrupted weather patterns. There's more to come yet,' Toss promised, without the least doubt. 'Weather bombs.'

'Why are they making us stand around like this?' Charlie asked. 'I haven't got time for this. I've got things to do.' While

Simone had initially thought Charlie could have been joking, mentioning the bodies, now she saw that there was a basic unhappy schism in his understanding. As the rest of them discussed how to get his wife to the medical centre he kept up an abstract chorus of mumbling, minor concerns.

The problem now was transport. Clara and Charlie didn't have a car, and nor did Toss (on account of a couple of little accidents last year, he said, wanting to continue but being cut off by Mrs Galloway) which only left Zita, who lived at the end of the street, with a working car. On this morning though, even that short walk seemed like a risky passage for all these vulnerable hips, and Simone found herself being clung to as they all took their unsure steps towards Zita's front door. They'd assumed so quickly she was someone they could rely on. But then nowadays every significant weather event tended to create the atmosphere of a public drill for the truly apocalyptic future constantly being foreshadowed – and as they made their way down the street it occurred to Simone that they were possibly clinging as much to a lust for her prospective usefulness, as to her person. Would they have the same enthusiasm if they had an inkling of her recent undertakings? 'Soon mate, soon,' Toss could be heard saying as Charlie mentioned, again, his need to go home.

Zita's house turned out to be the one where Clouseau had chased the cat. Mrs Galloway knocked on the door and shortly afterwards a window in the conservatory opened and a tiny old woman leaned her head out. 'Goodness, what a mob!' she said, peering at them through smeary black-rimmed glasses. She seemed so chalky and frail it might have been dangerous for her to step outside her home at all. After Mrs Galloway explained the situation, she said they were welcome to take her car, but she ought not to drive.

Mrs Galloway turned to Simone. 'You can drive it can't you?'

Simone hesitated and before she could even begin to explain Mrs Galloway sighed and said, 'Well I suppose it's down to me.'

Somebody asked if that was wise and Mrs Galloway responded by saying briskly, 'Needs must,' and a small straightening of her back gave away how much she enjoyed thinking of herself as the dependable one. Not even her abrupt meeting with a tree could dint her sense of superior efficiency this morning. There was no escape for Simone. She was more or less ordered to get Charlie to his bed while they were gone and when Clara became anxious and started to protest, Mrs Galloway, with all the heft of the head of civil defence, insisted it would have to do.

Simone took the confused and unhappy Charlie home and helped him into bed, grateful he was at least already wearing his pyjamas. In the unfamiliar kitchen she made him a cup of tea, then settled in a chair beside the bed to keep him company. He consumed the tea by slurping it noisily off the teaspoon. For him there was nothing but the immediate relief of the tea. He was childlike in his movements and his face had now collapsed into an incurious dismay, with his eyes vacated and his jaw hanging slackly between sips. The events of the morning might have taken a toll.

She glanced at a photo on the bedside table, showing Charlie at about forty. He was holding up a double bass and laughing into the lens, looking like the kind of person you could count on for playfulness and trouble.

He finished his tea and she took the cup from him and put it on the side table. He slid further down into the bed, and then the questions started.

'Where is Clara?' he asked.

'She had to go to the medical centre.'

'But when is she getting back?'

'I'm not sure. Hopefully she won't be too long.'

'Bloody woman, she's always going out and leaving me on my own for hours.'

Simone didn't know him well enough to know if this querulousness was part of his stripped back zero-base personality, or simply his disease. She wanted to believe it was the latter, that he was not a man lacking in tender regard for his wife, but that his illness had taken him off on a side journey into cantankerous emotional absence. Otherwise it would be too easy not to like him.

'Who is going to make my dinner?'

'Well if she's not back, I expect I will.'

'But where has she gone?'

They continued to have more or less that conversation over and over. She found it sadly discouraging that he showed no concern for Clara at all. He never asked why she was at the medical centre.

Simone tried some variations in an attempt to distract him, but he didn't wish to discuss what she might make him for dinner, he didn't want to guess what kind of bird was chirping in a tree outside, and he didn't know who Inspector Clouseau was, let alone want to help her suppose what he might be up to. He just wanted to know where Clara was, when she'd be back, and who was going to make his dinner. Every time he spoke a small worry seemed to linger about his face that he may have said things that had come out all wrong.

This expression made Simone think of a concept Fraser had once come up with. He'd been trying to help the neighbour's kid learn some tricky new moves on a skateboard but the boy had thrown his board into the bushes in frustration and said he didn't want to do it any more. When Fraser asked him why, he said he didn't like looking like an idiot. Fraser sat him down and drew a room with a door on the left and a door on the right. He asked the boy to name two people he admired, and being ten he named an All Black and a hip-hop artist. Fraser told him the room was called the 'looking-like-an-idiot room'. He explained to him that All Blacks don't just wake up one morning and find out they're really good at rugby. Performers don't just fall out of bed and find they can freestyle. All people who are good at anything have spent some time in the room. It was in there they experimented with things that didn't work, so they could find out what did. They went in through one door, and came out the other having made a progression. Looking at Charlie's face, Simone thought he looked a bit like he was worried he'd accidentally wandered into the looking-like-an-idiot room and would never again be allowed out of either door.

And so, because she didn't want to take away any more dignity than that which had already been stolen, she sat beside him and tried to treat each question like it was a fresh and perfectly rational enquiry.

She heard Mrs Galloway call yoohoo from the kitchen and went to greet her. As she walked up the hallway, lined with bookshelves and photos of famous jazz musicians, she heard Charlie say in her wake, 'Who the bloody hell is that? Why isn't bloody Clara here?'

'I just popped back to relieve you dear. Clara's got her wrist in ice, waiting to get it strapped, just a bad sprain luckily. Toss is with her and the lovely practice nurse said she'd give them a ride back soon. How are things here?'

'Okay I think. He seems terribly confused.' Another woman would have handled this better, she thought. Another woman would have been able to comfort him more, would have found a way to lift the needle from the record.

Mrs Galloway said, 'I'm gasping so why don't you put the kettle on and I'll just pop along and pay him a visit.'

When the tea was ready she went to tell Mrs Galloway and found her sitting on the bed rubbing the back of Charlie's hand. 'So what do you feel like my darling?' she was saying, 'Some Round Wines with your tea? Or perhaps a chocolate treat if there are any.' He didn't respond and she said cheerfully, 'Well it'll have to be a lovely surprise then.' Back in the kitchen Mrs Galloway began checking inside Clara's pantry. 'Poor old sausage, he's bad today,' she said.

Later, over tea, she said, 'Call me Marjorie, dear.'

7

Nothing much. The handfuls around her hips that won't budge. A certain thickening where her neck meets her shoulders. A certain sagging in other places. An awareness of her bones in the morning. The short sharp pains that sometimes seem to signal a potentially disastrous malfunction. The occasional inability to grasp a floating word. Dark interior failings. Feeling dry. Nothing much. But to be alone with all that is to be a bit afraid of the future. Especially here, with all the end reality so present around her.

But if you were in a certain frame of mind, one look at a dog's idiot grin could almost convince you that you were getting all the company and care you could need. Just as television offers the illusion of companionship to those on their own, a dog provides something near a relationship. Clouseau's constant expression was one of adoration and collusion, and even as he slept he kept his ears tuned to her movements, jumping to his feet to stand staring by the bed the minute she stirred in the morning. He happily assumed things had been arranged so that everything she did was exclusively for his sake. If she put on her shoes he assumed it was to accompany him outside. If she opened the refrigerator door he assumed it was to find things for him to eat. And if she went into the toilet he waited only a moment before pushing open the door with his nose so she might have an opportunity to caress the top of his head while she was sitting down. Fall for it once, and it becomes the customary practice. Any outright demands, though, were always made with nudging affection, and in many ways this princely mixture of rightfulness and needfulness was quite familiar.

Simone had often come home from work to find Fraser waiting to take her by the hand and lead her down to his studio. She'd follow him into the basement room he'd appropriated, his private hovel, which she could only comfortably enter by invitation, and where she'd try not to notice the mould growing over forgotten cups of coffee in the corners. He'd be agitated, eager and impatient to show her his work at last, and the permeating odour of drying paint, and linseed oil, and fixative would linger in the air along with something more immediate – the suggestion of expended energy – the sweaty pungency of a man trapped in a lure, going too long without a break, obsessed with the detail of completion, the end in sight.

'What do you think?' he would ask, really wanting to know, a flash of insecurity flickering across his face. Before she looked she always experienced a tiny moment of fear that she might not like this one, and would have to say so. Mostly though, she liked it. Not just liked it, loved it. To look at his work was to see some inner working part of him, some conjurer's power to bring an idea alive from nothing. She would gaze down at the thing he had created and feel her brain shift sideways, lifted out of an everyday location in the world where dinner needed to be cooked, and cars needed to be filled with petrol, and press releases needed to be written about new television programmes. He made things she could marvel at. She'd never been able to separate loving his art from loving him. His work was special, which made him special, which made her make allowances for him. If he was flaky, if he was capricious, if he needed a certain messiness in his life to feed his art, to feed himself, he was entitled.

'What do you think?' he would ask, and that moment would make her feel truly seen. He trusted her to point out when it was too raw, too ugly, too stupid, too slapdash, too unfinished. Her honesty, he claimed, was important. 'Nobody understands me as well as you,' he would say. And he meant, also, that nobody understood his art, his whole body of work, as well as her. He wasn't creating safe little landscapes. His best works captured some kind of unprocessed longing or unfulfilment – which Simone's mother thought of as displays of hopeless immaturity, and his mother regarded as proof of a worrying unhappiness.

To get there he skidded around between dumb reflex and clever insight, between melancholy and a tipping state of euphoria.

To stay in that perilous spectrum he needed a believer, and she'd worked at it. In those times when inspiration deserted him she'd made it her job to bring him sparks and offerings. She went to the second-hand record store and came back with stacks of old vinyl. She woke him in the morning with funny stories she'd been saving for his ear. She made meals so exotic they took him to foreign countries. She rummaged in junk shops for cheap amusements, abandoned tools, and homeless toys. She taped quotes and riddles on the undersides of ordinary things. She read him lines from books. And he said nobody had ever done such things for him before.

Other times, when his fear that he wasn't truly talented or truly original or truly relevant made him pace and fidget, she put her arms around him and made him still. She made him tea from packets which promised to bring on calm and restfulness. She held his hand and made him walk in the dark night air with her. She read him lines from different books and made him face forward again. And he said nobody had ever understood him like that before.

But to think of that meant she was unable to avoid also thinking of the moment when he'd declared he'd given six years of his life to her and now he was going. As if it was that simple. As if she had given him nothing. As if having known him was gift enough.

It was impossible to live in a house filled with dolls. All those creepy eyes, so round, so blank, so sinister in their manufactured innocence. Simone gathered every single one into a box and carted it across the shocked, flattened garden to the little shed at the back of the house. She had to push hard against some encroaching vines to get the door open. Clouseau, who had been following her around, urged her on by leaning on her legs from behind. She'd envisaged the shed would be filled with unwanted pieces of furniture, piles of old magazines, broken lawnmowers, half-used tins of paint, and forgotten children's toys. And more of Alice's hoarding. But that wasn't what she found.

Apart from the dust and cobwebs and vines poking through the cracks, fingering their way in, it was tidy. A number of tools were hanging on a pegboard, with their shape outlined in felt pen. Each tool had an ownership-identifying stripe of blue paint that made them all look somehow like a gathering of unwilling supporters. And there were strange little cupboards and shelves everywhere, inexpertly but obsessively built.

On the workbench was a half-finished project, another cupboard. It was eerie. Whoever had been building this had just finished making a detail on the door. They had glued it, wound it into the vice to set, neatly put away their tools, and left the shed, never to return. It must have been Alice's husband. Perhaps he'd died and Alice had simply pulled the door to, leaving a spider-filled monument at the end of the garden.

She began opening doors and found that inside the cupboards were mostly just more cupboards. It seemed so eccentric. Perhaps they'd had an unhappy marriage. Perhaps he'd hated her undisciplined mess inside the house, and would escape out here to build cupboards inside his cupboards, thinking *that'll bloody show her.*

Pinned to the inside of one door was a calendar from a local hardware store featuring a half-naked blonde holding a screwdriver in her hands, 1978. It was the sort of thing her father had liked to hang in his own workshop, on the inside of the grubby toilet door – a place her mother was guaranteed not to visit. He would've laughed at this cupboard-inside-cupboard business. He would've thought it sissified and wasteful. He made solid things – gates and kennels and pump sheds and cattle trays for trucks – and he didn't particularly approve of pointless solitary endeavours. His shed was a place of manly pursuits, power tools, sweat, and rural concerns. A loitering spot for company-starved farmers who would amble in, offering up their dryly told tales – often about things as banal as their dog, or a rogue sheep, or what the missus was up to – which would later be retold, with a little embellishment, to the next man through the door.

And on quieter days it was a place where he'd put jigsaws, and routers, and other tools into her hands and teach her how to use them. In that shed there was only ever the slightest concession to the fact she wasn't a boy. He did force her to be much more careful with his machinery than he was himself. And if he happened to hurt himself in her presence he would let out a string of filthy expletives and then look over at her, remembering, and say, 'Well never mind . . . it'll be right by the time I'm a grandfather, eh.' Only he never got to be.

She ran her hand across the surface of the workbench, brushing away the dust and cobwebs. She liked the feel of grit on her hand. She liked the musty, mousey smell of stale grease and wood and glue. Here, at last, was something of a coming home, a place where all her senses could relax. She could make good use of all these tools, but if Alice recovered and found Simone had been in the shed would she be upset? Would she feel it was an intrusion? Then again she's not intending to take anything away – it's not as if it's stealing.

She had an idea for a project Alice might even approve of and took down the wheelbarrow from its place on the wall, smiling at the outline painted there. Whistling up the dog she headed to the beach, and when she passed Toss in his garden he said, 'I might be needing that wheelbarrow later to cart away all the veges that the blasted hoar frost ruined.'

'Be my guest,' she said, 'I'll pop it round later, when I'm through.'

'Nah,' he said, 'I was just having you on, girl. Collecting firewood?'

'Something like that,' she said.

At the edge of the tide a teenaged boy was trying to skim stones between the breaks. The dog bounded up to him, but the boy was scared and tried to run away. Clouseau thought it was a game and chased him. Simone abandoned the barrow and ran up to grab the dog's collar. 'I'm sorry,' she said. 'He really won't hurt you. He wanted to play.'

'Okay,' said the boy. He was clean faced, probably Indian, and looked like he'd dropped to earth and learnt to dress by watching music videos. He was ambitiously wearing gangsta-style clothes – heavy chains and long shorts which were in threat of falling right off his skinny hips – and with his meek, harmless face he looked too innocent and insubstantial for them. On his feet he was wearing only one flashy white trainer, and had a round knobby bandage on the big toe of his other foot.

'Come on you naughty dog,' she said to Clouseau, pulling on his collar so he was facing the other direction. She picked up her wheelbarrow and as she started down the beach the boy fell in beside her.

'Do you live here?' he asked.

'No, I'm just looking after somebody's house.'

'I'm not living here either. I'm with a different family in the city but they went on a holiday so I'm staying with their nana. They said I would like a little break here at the beach. It would be special, they said, but I think they're just wanting to solve the problem of not leaving me behind in their house when they're not there. She is a very old lady. A bit sad. Everything in her house is smelling like flowers. But not nice.'

He half-walked, half-hopped alongside her, and she could feel his unguarded intensity, his readiness to tell her anything.

'I am from India,' he offered. 'North India. And my name is Ravi.'

'And you are studying English here?'

'No, I am studying computers. At University. Also I am studying girls.' He laughed, showing his perfectly even teeth. She wondered what age he was, and as if he was reading her mind he asked first. 'How old are you?'

'Oh . . . I'm . . . er . . .' she hesitated, adding, 'you know, sometimes it's not so polite to just ask straight out like that.'

'You don't want to say?'

When she didn't reply he pointed to himself and said, 'Nineteen.'

He surprised her then, she'd thought much younger. He waited for her to ask another question, eagerly, as if hoping all day for a chance like this, and she had to search for something to say. 'Do you like it here?' she asked.

'Yes, there are many beautiful girls in this country.'

'Do you have a girlfriend?'

'No. Unfortunately not yet. My father says I will marry at twenty-four but I am wishing for New Zealand girlfriends, or maybe later I go to Aussie. They are funny girls. Also a bit naughty.' He grinned meaningfully at her as he bent to pick up a stone for skimming. When he threw it into the calm between the waves the dog looked on with interest and then decided against chasing it. They walked in silence for a while. He was probably thinking of all the naughty, funny girls he would find in Australia, and she was thinking of the inevitable hand wringing of his parents.

'How did you hurt your foot?' she asked.

'My friend ran over it with his new car. It was an accident. He is Muslim, and not a very good driver. It happened outside McDonald's.'

'Oh. Does it hurt much?'

'Yes much,' he said, and suddenly his limp seemed stronger. 'You know that family nana?'

'No, I don't know her.'

'She has a budgie in a cage. It can talk. Also a very bad cat.'

'You're staying with the lady called Zita?'

'Yes. You are familiar? Do you know what her budgie can say? Every time I come in it is shouting, "Bugger off, bugger off",' he told her, looking wounded.

Simone smiled. She half felt like saying something similar. There was something onerous about him. He helped her, though, finding the baby shells she needed, while she picked through the driftwood, collecting the likeliest pieces into her barrow.

*

Clouseau dozed underneath the bench while she worked in the shed, and she allowed her thoughts to drift towards Joey – the way he bent her over backwards to kiss her outside the bar, like a man who liked to live in the moment, who knew how to take what he wanted. She hadn't known much about that band they'd gone to together, some obscure Scandinavian punk outfit, but he had known their whole genealogy, like a real completist. He'd told her their song about Casper the ghost was a nod of respect to Daniel Johnston, an even more obscure American cult hero who had lived most of his life in institutions, creating songs on a Casio keyboard.

Later that night, sitting in the car outside his place, he'd told her about the time Daniel Johnston had been invited to play at a festival. His father flew him there in a twin-engine plane, and on the way back Daniel Johnston, high from the success of his performance, and also because he had stopped taking his meds a few days before, was reading a comic book and decided he and his father should fly like Casper. He leaned over and plucked the keys from the ignition, tossing them out the plane's window. They crashed, Joey told her, but they survived. He'd seen all that in a music documentary, he said, the kind of documentary he'd like to have made himself.

She knew he'd gone over to Australia to go to film school but he told her he'd dropped out because of all the wankery. Later on he'd got work making skateboards and snowboards and started hanging out taking photographs of the riders, which were sometimes published in underground magazines. It's all over now though, he told her, the scene's changed. It used to be antifashion, but now they've become so susceptible. Now it's all brand shit. He was sick of it all, he said, almost angrily, like a man who'd been unwittingly cast out of his own life.

She'd wanted to touch him then, reach up and touch the side of his face, put her fingers into that mass of curly brown hair with its beginning, telling flecks of grey. But she didn't. He wasn't easy to understand, and she was still too easily dejected to take any risks. He was unpredictable, a man of contradictions.

Heavily tattooed and yet gentle. Ambitious, but only about being unallied. Sharply intelligent, but willing to squander it. And sometimes he seemed to be so dangerously storming inside that if you came too close he might try and confound everything you ever trusted about yourself. She thought she recognised one important thing that night, though. His struggle, at its most basic, was the same as hers – how to go on now?

'Right I'm off,' he'd said, opening the door and leaping out. Scarpering.

Disappointed, she'd called out a casual goodbye and driven off, straight into the police roadblock where she'd been breathalysed, and later, relieved of her licence. 'Mea culpa,' she'd said to the cop when he showed her the positive test. And he'd replied, 'Who's that?'

Now in this isolated little shed she wondered what had been lost by not doing something. What would've happened if she had reached across? Brushed her hand over his arms, ran her fingers up those inked shadows? Maybe he would still have clung to that door. Said, *nah I don't fancy you.* Or maybe not. She'd like to have known his response if she had put her hand to the side of his face, his lovely strong profile, and touched him softly.

She wanted to think of it, to keep her thoughts on Joey, or the unlikely possibility of Joey, or at least the future possibility of something, because if she could keep her thoughts anchored there then there was a chance she could stay out of that much more dangerous undercurrent that was Fraser.

8

A person who decides their life, or perhaps just their head, is too full of noise might think peace and quiet is all they need. They might imagine walking alone on a windswept beach would be a clarifying, even romantic, escape. They might like the idea they could open the fridge and everything in it is theirs for the eating. They might think lying around in bed with a book would be a gratifying pleasure. And it is. But if that is all you have, it isn't. Simone was bored with the music on the radio. More bored with the talk in-between. Too bored to eat. Bored with reading. And bored with herself. Dangerously bored. She began to look forward to the night ahead.

Earlier that day Clara had stepped out from her garden. She was at a loose end, she told Simone. Charlie was down at the local community centre so could she join Simone and Clouseau on their walk? She was careful in the asking, anxious not to overstep. They'd walked together to the café, talking about books and literature and Clara had offered Simone the use of her own collection. Pop over any time, she'd said, she had shelves lining both sides of her hallway and there was bound to be a few things Simone hadn't yet read. At the café Clara had greeted the woman behind the counter by affectionately kissing her on the cheek and the usual brusqueness was dropped. 'Is there news Hanife?' Clara enquired.

She shook her head and Clara said, 'I've been hoping for you.'

Hanife said, 'Mother's back in Rotterdam. She likes seeing everybody but of course there is no news. It's been a long time now. Probably we never know.'

'Perhaps,' said Clara. 'That will be hard on your mother.'

After they left the café Clara explained that Hanife was from Kosovo. During the war her father had been taken in the middle of the night by Serb police. She and her mother escaped on a truck with fifteen other women to the Macedonian border, and later her mother resettled in the Netherlands where they had a cousin. Hanife met her New Zealand-born husband and came here with him, to this little seaside town. Every few years her mother returned to their village to see her old friends and neighbours and to keep alive the ever-fading hope of finally finding any clue about what happened to her husband. Thousands of uncovered bodies had now been identified through DNA testing, but still there had been no closure for Hanife's family.

When they got back to their street Clara asked another careful question. 'Would you like to come over later for a drink with the girls?'

The girls turned out to be Marjorie Galloway and the profoundly aged Zita. When Simone arrived they were sitting at the kitchen table with drinks in front of them. In the middle of the table was a bowl of nuts, a plate of blue cheese and crackers, and a pack of cards. Clara was standing behind the kitchen counter with her arm out of its sling but still bandaged, and Charlie came in from the adjacent sitting room, having heard the sound of the door, and greeted Simone warmly but in a general sort of way. He pulled out a chair for her between Marjorie and Zita and then sat down himself saying, 'Well, this *is* a nice surprise. How was the trip down?'

'Drink?' Clara asked, indicating the two choices – gin or Scotch. Marjorie and Zita both had straight Scotch. There were traces of the lipstick Marjorie was wearing on the rim of her glass, a dark red colour which toned exactly with the large ruby brooch she was wearing.

'Gin and tonic?' Simone suggested tentatively, at the same time that Charlie said, 'Oh go on then, twist my arm. Just the one because I've got to get to work later on.'

Three glasses were lined up and cubes of ice placed in each. Clara poured the slightest dash of whisky into one, topping it up with ginger ale. In the other two she tipped a generous slug of gin and about the equal amount of tonic. She passed the drinks over and came and stood beside Charlie's chair, her own glass in hand, as he sipped his weak whisky. His face showed faint dissatisfaction but there wasn't much commitment behind it. After a moment he slipped his free arm around Clara's thighs and pulled her ever so slightly closer to him, in a casual spousal gesture, and she rested her hip lightly against his shoulder. 'Darling, I think the Indy 500 is on soon if you want to watch it,' she said to him.

'Oh is it?' he said. 'Well if you ladies will excuse me I might just go and have a bit of a look.'

'You go right ahead, dear,' Marjorie said.

'I'll switch it on in the bedroom for you, if you like,' Clara said, and they both went off down the hall.

Marjorie began taking the cards out of their box, and Zita reached forward and picked up the bowl of nuts and offered them to Simone. 'Take a big handful why don't you,' she said. 'Can't have them myself. They get stuck in my dentures. Like it round here then, do you?' Simone assured her she did – very much. When Clara returned to the table it became clear the hope had been for a fourth hand at Bridge, and they made no attempt to hide their disappointment when Simone said she didn't play. We'll have to teach you, they all said, settling for Gin Rummy instead.

The sounds of motor racing came from down the hall. 'Is it on the television?' asked Zita, saying the word *television* with great affection.

'Well . . . not really. I sometimes tell him the Indy 500 is showing on the telly and then I put on this old video of his,' Clara told them. 'He never remembers it.'

For a few moments there was just the sound of ice tinkling in their glasses as drinks were sipped.

'Stanley always fancied himself a rally driver,' Marjorie offered. 'He'd go like a loon behind the wheel, always trying to take the corners at maximum speed. I'd say, Stanley slow down, I can feel the g-force. But he'd just ignore me.'

'And how is Stanley? Have you seen him lately?' asked Clara, so deadpan that Simone wondered if there was something mischievous about the enquiry.

Marjorie didn't reply, busying herself with the shuffling and the dealing. Zita began rummaging in the black handbag sitting on her lap. She put some of the contents onto the table so she could find whatever it was she was looking for. Clara picked up a small plastic pot of ground pepper and said, 'Good God, Zita, why are you carrying this around in there?'

'Oh I forgot I had that,' Zita said. She showed it to Simone. 'It's an old trick I learnt off my mother. If a fellow tries to attack you then you pull off the lid and toss it all in his face and make your getaway,' she explained.

'And have you ever had to try it out?' Clara asked.

'Oh no. But you never know. I like having it on me just in case.' She was a tiny woman, shrunk away to almost nothing by age, and the knuckles of her hands were twisted by arthritis. It was hard enough to imagine her getting the lid off in an emergency, let alone making a getaway. She found what she was looking for, a magnifying glass, and threw everything else back into her bag. 'Could you put that on the floor for me?' Zita asked Simone. 'It's a bit much of a bend for an old biddy like me.' She had a squinty smile and in this company she appeared to slightly enjoy playing up to her age, taking a minor personal entertainment in being at a frontier they had all yet to come to.

They picked up their hands and after a time of peering at her cards through her magnifying glass Zita said, 'I bid two clubs.'

'We're not playing Bridge remember, Zita, it's Rummy today,' Clara reminded her gently. 'Pity though, sounds like a super hand!'

Zita tried to fumble her cards into a different order and three fell face up onto the table. 'Oops-a-daisy,' she said.

Marjorie suggested rather unnecessarily, given how little was riding on any result, that they really ought to redeal the round. Her chair creaked as she shifted her weight around, stiff backed, gathering up the cards. Simone felt a long way from the city, her old life.

Zita shrugged and took a sip of her whisky. 'Once upon a time I wasn't too shabby at Bridge,' she said. 'Did I ever tell you about the time I nearly went to a tournament in the South Island?'

Clara and Marjorie shook their heads in such a way Simone suspected they may well have heard it before. Zita began to tell a long-winded story about how she and three others were going to represent their club but her husband had suddenly become sick. She had to stay behind to look after him and her three friends decided they couldn't go without her. 'There was a big ballyhoo over it. Dickie didn't really like me playing and I suspected he took ill on purpose. Anyway later on he reckoned he'd had a feeling in his water.'

'How do you mean?'

'Well, Cyclone Giselle struck. And guess what boat we were scheduled to come back from Lyttelton on?'

'Good Lord,' said Marjorie, as if on a cue, 'not the *Wahine*?'

Zita nodded. 'Imagine,' she said.

They concentrated on their cards for a while and then as if it was finally time to get down to the true activity of the evening, Marjorie turned to Simone and said, 'And tell us about yourself. You're not married?'

There was a brief period when Simone used to blurt it all out to the new people she met. 'Well I was with someone,' she used to say, 'but then I caught him with the next-door neighbour.' Sometimes she'd even add what she intended to be another painfully incriminating detail, 'And not that long after I'd had a miscarriage.' Quite often people would respond by saying she was probably better off without that bastard then, and she would find this momentarily helpful. Until the day she'd been having coffee with Ingrid and was introduced to a woman whose daughter went to the same school as the child of Fraser's lover. 'Do you know Caroline? Toby's mother?' Simone asked.

'Why yes, yes!' the woman replied. 'We often chat down at the school.'

'Well that's the slut who stole my partner,' Simone said, her voice sounding more grating and vicious than she'd expected.

She could see the woman was shocked. 'Well she always seemed like a lovely person to me,' she said, and quickly gathered up her daughter and left. Ingrid wouldn't meet her eye, and it was only then Simone realised that all along she hadn't really been getting the response she'd thought. That bastard, people had said, but they also must have been wondering why. Why had he done something like that? Was it all him, or was there something about her? Bitterness is repelling, but an unhealthy play for sympathy is ugly too.

It was obvious these three women could smell something there, could barely contain their appetite for a good telling of personal misfortune. If she gave them so much as a hint they'd be determined to get it all. And once she started who knows what would spill out of her, and a person like Marjorie might say *well what could you have expected when you chose a man like that in the first place?* 'No, I'm not with anyone,' she said.

'Never married?'

'No, never.'

'Don't have your eye on some nice young man somewhere?'

Would Joey qualify? Did one drunken kiss and some unrequited lust count? 'A girl could wish, I suppose,' she said.

'But how on earth did somebody like you come to be in that situation?'

Simone shrugged, 'Bad luck, I guess.'

'Well let's get our thinking caps on. Who do we know girls? Harold down at the panelbeaters? He's about your age and his wife just left him. And there's the new manager at the supermarket . . .'

Clara caught Simone's eye and smiled. 'You won't be

surprised Harold's wife left him when you meet him,' she said. 'He's as you would expect a man to be after many years of legally mandated solvent inhalation. And frankly Marjorie, that supermarket chap, he's a born bachelor if ever there was one. Would you really inflict that on – anybody?'

Zita said, 'These days a girl should just learn to how get on with things, I reckon. You can't rely on men. Like all my blinkin' taps leak but I can't even get my boys to come and fix them.'

'What about your boarder, couldn't he help?' Marjorie asked.

'Ravi? You've got to be kidding me. He's a good-for-nothing who has trouble lying straight in bed.'

'What about Toss, then? Could he do it?' suggested Clara.

'I can't ask Toss to lend a hand,' Zita said. 'Last time he came in my house he tried to connect the washing machine. The silly old coot attached the hot to the cold, and vice versa so now I never know where I am with the washing. It sends me round the bend. And I realised after it was because he was a bit – you know.'

Zita and Clara laughed, and Marjorie looked on with an expression of benign, sober forbearance. This was all done in such a tight, knowing way that for a moment Simone felt like the dutiful niece who was being discreetly excluded from a family secret.

They settled back to Zita's problem and Clara said rather wistfully, 'Well Charlie'd be no use, but then again he was always completely cack-handed at that kind of thing.'

'I don't know what the point is in having sons if they don't come and help out their mother,' Marjorie said.

'Yes, but what can you do?' Zita said.

'Threaten to cut them out of your will?' suggested Clara.

'And give them a good leathering while you're at it,' added Marjorie.

'Have you seen them lately? They're not exactly spring chickens, and they've both got big fat pukus a grizzly bear'd be pleased with,' Zita told them, not able to contain an element of pride.

'Couple of big oafs like that should be able to fix some taps then,' Marjorie muttered quietly.

After a pause Clara said mischievously, 'Well perhaps those darned elves will put in another appearance.'

Zita clapped her hands together, and said, 'Oh yes! Perhaps they will!' then teasingly poked a finger into Marjorie's arm, making her spill her drink.

When Marjorie had first discovered her new letter box – made out of sawn driftwood, with the number three spelt out in tiny shells – she'd announced it, in a surge of whimsy, the work of local bush elves. But also, as she repeated this among her neighbours, she couldn't resist saying it with a certain self-exalting vanity, as if it was fitting that any such creatures would single her out to be the deserving recipient of a good deed. Simone had even overheard her saying it to the contractor who came to mow her lawns. He had taken it in his stride, saying 'Oh yeah' as if she'd just mentioned she'd picked up the letter box down at the local service station. Simone hoped, then, he'd simply not been listening, and wouldn't go on to his next job saying *you'll never guess what that silly old biddy came out with*. She felt to blame as she had placed it there in the dead of night, and Marjorie clearly thought she was gaily entering into the spirit of gesture. It's not as if she didn't know the truth either, because the morning after a tacit thank you had been placed on Simone's doorstep in the form of a lush home-baked chocolate cake with a tiny note saying it was from 'the bush elves'.

Marjorie clearly didn't like to be at the butt-end of a joke though, because now she chose not to respond to the cackling tease of the other two.

Zita soon nodded off and was dozing in her chair like a little snuffling mouse. Marjorie gently nudged her awake and said, 'Come on Tiddlywinks, let's get you home.'

Simone stayed on to help Clara clean up. 'Sorry about the

game,' Clara said. 'We don't usually play Gin. Mostly it's Bridge and if we don't have a four, it's Spite and Malice.'

'What's that?'

'Cat and Mouse? It's sometimes called that too. I'll have to teach you, it's great fun and very unwholesome. It's one of those games where you have to be a bit sneaky, trying to get ahead, and all the while preventing the others from getting away on you.'

'I might be quite good at that,' Simone suggested.

'Oh you'd be surprised how good we are at it around here!' Clara replied with a jolly laugh.

Simone started rinsing the dirty glasses under the tap and Clara stood beside her trying to dry them. She was having difficulty managing, so Simone took the tea towel out of her good hand and passed her the dried glasses one by one so she could put them away. 'What happened to Stanley?' she asked.

'Well,' Clara began, 'Marjorie used to be different. Some people get all sort of bossy like that as a way of . . . you know.'

'He ran off with a younger woman?'

There was a brief hesitation, where Clara appeared to be torn for a moment between temptation and her sense of loyalty. 'I'm sure he might've liked to, but he has such a terrible mouthful of hoary old teeth. So no. And you'll never guess.'

'He's in jail?'

This startled a little laugh from Clara. 'How did you know?'

'I didn't. I was just suggesting the most unlikely thing that came into my head. Really? Jail?' Even just saying that word made her temperature rise a notch.

Clara nodded, 'Some sort of complicated fraud. Millions of dollars of government money. He'll be out soon. But don't tell Marjorie I told you. She'll think I'm such a dreadful old gossip.'

Earlier that day Simone had commented to Clara how she'd been to the café nearly every day, but she and Hanife had hardly even spoken to each other. She'd had no idea about her life.

'Oh, I see it as my job to find these things out,' Clara had said then.

That night Simone dreamt of driving. It had started off as pleasant, a coast road, a light breeze, no urgency of destination. But soon the road became winding, and there was cornering to do and she was unable to slow the car. Things were falling under the wheels and she didn't know what they were. Men in uniform kept stepping onto the road to try and stop her and she had to keep swerving to avoid them.

She woke in a sweat.

9

Further down the coast there's a bay which has a shallow reef out from the beach. The right conditions create a sweet left-hand break. But you've gotta watch it 'cos if you're not careful you can crack your nut coming off your board.

Simone learnt this from a surfer called Ollie. She'd gone to the café in the late afternoon, thinking she might try and chat to Hanife. But it was the weekend and the first fine day for a while so the café was busy with day trippers getting ice creams for the journey home. She sat down at the last free table with a coffee and soon Ollie plonked himself down beside her, eating crisps hungrily out of a bumper size pack.

She liked looking at him as he told her he'd caught some sick barrels before a grunty offshore breeze had turned the waves to pus. He had pale blue eyes that looked like they'd been leached from looking out to sea. His straggly salted hair framed a face that was speckled by sun. He was heading down country, he told her. Some mates had got him a seasonal job on the slopes. Just catching a few swells before he headed on in to the snow.

He was, she guessed, perhaps twenty-five at the most. Young enough never to have had anything snatched from him. Confident enough to flirt shamelessly with her. Old enough to go after what he wanted.

'Been sleeping in the back seat of my Holden,' he said. 'Gets cold real quick though. Never thought it would happen, but I'm starting to long for a real bed.'

'You could stay at my house, if you like,' she suggested.

'Sweet,' he said with a dirty grin. And it wasn't as if she didn't know exactly what kind of bargain she was really making. She was feeling dangerous.

He had a deep winter tan that ended at the top of his

buttocks. His legs were paler than his body. He said that was from sitting on his board with his wetsuit rolled down to his waist. He seemed to be filled to the skin with laughter. And he was generous too. He said he liked the curves of her body, they were womanly. He said he liked the whiteness of her skin, it looked nice against his. He said she was a good kisser. He said she had lovely tits. He said I just want you to lie there and enjoy this. He slid down her body. And then he said he wanted to make her sing. And he did too. Clouseau, who was locked in the laundry, howled at the sound of it.

She liked the way he slipped on the condom. It was fussless. Just slip it out of a pocket, tear the pack with the teeth, roll it on with one hand, and voilà, ready to go.

There was none of that fiddling and sighing and implied resentment. This wasn't a guy who'd grown up thinking a condom was some kind of imposition invented by women to ruin all the fun. The last man she'd tried to have sex with was forty-seven. He was not so easy. He'd insisted she put it on for him, like it was some kind of privilege, and then when his iffy erection subsided, he insinuated it was her fault. They had tried a couple more times but no matter what he couldn't keep it up. He said it had never happened before, in an accusing way. In the end, not liking him much, she'd given him a half-hearted hand job to finish him off. She'd been drunk when they started but by the time it was over she was painfully sober. She put her clothes on in silence and he pushed her out of the hotel room door without saying goodbye. It didn't help matters that he was her boss at the time.

It was much more fundamental with Ollie the surfer. He simply banged away at her, so that by the end she felt energetically and pleasantly fucked. It was base and real, and unreal at the same time. It was nothing more than simple human exchange. An invigorating, repairing moment. The salty, sweaty, seaweedy smell of him made her feel as though she was being swallowed by the ocean. He came with a grunt and a smile, threw off the filled condom, and collapsed into sleep with a look of wasted innocence on his face. Simone lay beside him but she couldn't sleep. They had done it in Alice's bed.

She went out and lay on the daybed, smiling. She'd never thought of herself as the one-night stand type. But he was good. He was nothing you'd ever have to regret.

The next morning she leaned against the kitchen bench drinking tea while he sat at the table eating the eggs she'd cooked for him. 'How long have you lived here?' he said, looking around at Alice's furnishings. She explained she was just looking after the place for somebody.

'Phew,' he said, 'for a minute I was thinking you must be a lot older than you look.'

'I am a bit older than you, but.'

'Yeah, well I figured that out,' he said.

She turned back to the bench, started scrubbing away at a pan.

'Still got a nice butt, but,' he offered belatedly, making her blush.

He finished his eggs and pushed his plate back, 'Wanna come sit on daddy bear's lap for a minute?'

She felt shy in the exposing morning light. She went to him and sat down and he twisted her around so she was facing the table. He started kissing the back of her neck. 'Like that bit,' he said.

He pulled up her T-shirt and started kissing the bones of her spine. 'This bit is nice too,' he said. She could feel him getting hard again. He pulled her T-shirt off her and licked her from the middle of her back all the way up to the lobe of her left ear and she couldn't help moaning. 'You really like doing it, don't you,' he laughed, and he started pulling off her underpants. She wriggled around on his lap to help him get them off. Now that she was naked he gently pushed her down under the table. He knelt down beside her, pulled out another condom, unzipped his fly and as his pants dropped he said, 'Take this young lady.' And she did. Gladly. Then afterwards they lay in each other's arms and laughed and laughed on the floor beneath the table. But in the midst of that laughter she felt the need to check herself, the back of her mind touching on the things she'd done, in the same way a person might feel around for a malignant growth under the skin just to get the horrible assurance it's still there.

He fell quiet for a moment and then he kissed her eyebrows, and her eyelids, and the tip of her nose, and her chin, and finally her mouth, and said, 'Surf's up. Gotta go.'

'I know,' she said, pulling the condom off him. 'It's been nice knowing you though.'

'Not as nice as knowing you.' He crawled out from under the table and found his pants. 'Have a good day,' he grinned, pulling up his zip. 'Know I will.' At the door he turned back for one last look and wolf-whistled before closing it behind him. She heard his car start up. It had a hole in the muffler, or maybe he meant it to sound like that. As he roared off up the street he kept his hand on the car horn, past Clara and Charlie's house, past Marjorie Galloway's house, past Toss's house, and past Zita's house too. At last he did a squealy turn into the main road. His final goodbye.

She still had the condom in her hand. She tied a knot in it and got out from under the table and went into the kitchen. She put her foot on the pedal of the rubbish bin and it gaped open. She stood there for a minute looking in to the waiting mouth, then took her foot off the pedal, and opened the freezer door instead.

10

There were three wrenches in the garden shed. A baby one. A medium one. And one big enough to kill a person with a single blow to the head. Simone took them all down.

The sun was shining and as she walked down the street she could still feel the secret thrill, the pinkish aftermath of a man's touch on her body. She felt warmed – jump-started.

Toss was in his garden and called out, 'Something's put a smile on your dial this morning.'

He knew. Of course he knew. That would mean they all knew.

She knocked on Zita's front door and Zita had to tug to get it open. 'I've been using the back door mostly,' she said half-apologetically and half-accusingly, as if Simone might've known better than to put her through this difficulty. Simone told her she'd come to fix the taps but Zita looked doubtful, perhaps thinking it wasn't possible a person like Simone could do such a thing properly. Simone showed her the three wrenches in her bag as some kind of proof of authenticity and Zita put her hand in, touched the big wrench, and let her in.

The sticky door. The dripping taps. These were not her only problems. In some places the wallpaper was curling away from the walls, some corners smelt of musty damp, parts of the carpet were wearing through, handles were missing from drawers, and in one place a draught was blowing in through a mouse hole. The bathroom tap was leaking so badly Zita had taped it up with a wide strip of Elastoplast and water was still spurting from the top. From somewhere inside Simone caught a faint whiff of marijuana and guessed Ravi had been having a quick, wicked toke, thinking Zita wouldn't know the difference. She didn't know where he might be but she could hear the budgie chirping away in the conservatory.

The dining room wall was covered with family photos. It only took one glance in their direction to set Zita off talking about them. She pointed out her two sons, Benjamin and Tony, who were captured in various stages of life, from fat little babies in photos so old and faded they almost looked Victorian, to knobbly kneed teenagers, to grooms, to young fathers, to fat-waisted middle-aged men. She pointed out their father, Dickie. A butcher, she told Simone. 'Worked hard all his life and then poor old soul had a heart attack three days after he finally sold up. That was, oooh, nearly thirty years ago now. My poor boys.' Then there were her grandchildren. Simone listened, like any good neighbour, as Zita told her about each one. This one had been the lead in a play once but unfortunately she didn't get to see it. They hoped she'd stick it out at university but she's decided she wanted to open a bathroom tile shop of all things. She's pregnant with her first now. This one was always good at maths and he does something with computers these days. He has two kiddies of his own but they live so far away she hasn't even met them yet. This one used to love going camping in the mountains and writes lovely letters, although the spelling is atrocious. When this one was a baby he had lovely thick head of hair but now he's shaved it all off and last time she saw him he had a painful looking earring in his lip. He said he was on the artist's wage, whatever that meant, but he was always good at drawing. They all had very busy lives. Their mothers worked. This one in real estate. This one doing the books for somebody. They worked so hard, both of them. She doesn't know how they did it. So busy. She doesn't get to see them all as much as she'd like.

'Well, shall we get started?' Simone asked. She didn't want Zita to wait any longer. She could see her life was now essentially about waiting. Not wanting to intrude. Not knowing how. She waits for phone calls. Waits for invitations. Waits for Christmas. 'Do you know where the water main is?'

'Oh dear. No,' replied Zita, in a worried voice, desperate not to disappoint.

72

'Never mind,' Simone said. 'Let's go for a walk around the garden and see if we can find it.'

Zita kept forgetting what they were looking for. She'd get distracted by a nest of snails in her lilies, or the roses which needed pruning before spring, and then she'd say, 'And what was it you wanted again, dear?' There was something endearing about her bumbling. Simone thought of her own mother, who has a slight horror of women like Zita. In her Gold Coast second life she has no time for the ones that 'let themselves go' and does everything humanly possible to deny the process of aging herself. She takes her vitamins religiously. She's become a zealot for healthy eating and has developed a scientific knowledge of the active ingredients in age-defying creams. She likes to 'keep up with the arts' and dresses in a timeless, expensive urbane style. And, despite the warnings, there is 'no way in hell' she's giving up her HRT. It's her miracle drug – she would rather increase her risk of heart disease than dry up like an old crone. 'And shoot me,' she says, 'if I go potty.'

The water main was under a floppy daisy bush and Simone began repairing the taps as best she could, starting in the kitchen and working round the rest of the house. All the while Zita hummed away in the kitchen, tinkering around inside her cupboards. Every now and then Simone would hear her turn on a tap and say, 'What the . . . ?' before remembering the water was turned off and she'd have to use what was in the kettle instead.

In the laundry Simone began fixing the washing machine, reconnecting the cold to the cold, and the hot to the hot. Feeling around the slippery interiors of the taps for scraps of washers she felt bold and brave. She felt a little revived. She liked this new self. There was something evolutionary about it.

Her very first encounter with a boy was in a Holden Kingswood much like Ollie's. The local bad boy. Around the time *Grease* came out because she could remember 'You're the one that I want' was playing on the car radio as he gave her a lift home from the local rugby club social. She'd sung along to it in what she hoped was a flirty way, watching him move his stick shift through the gears. He pulled up in her parents' driveway in just enough time for her 11pm curfew. They started kissing and he kept trying to get his hand inside her underpants, but when she said she couldn't and she had to go he pulled her hand towards him. Just touch it, he begged. She thought it might be okay to touch it once so she put her hand on it for about a second and when she went to get out of the car he grabbed her wrist and said in a pained voice, 'You can't leave me like this!' There was a much-whispered-about belief amongst her girlfriends at the time that if you teased a guy in the wrong kind of way, he could end up with a condition called blue balls, a painful swelling which could cripple for life. This was it then, she hadn't meant to but she'd done it – roused him to the point of harm. The deathly crippling part had obviously been spread about by the boys, but convincingly enough for her to do what he asked when he pulled her hand back towards him and urged her to 'just rub it'. She didn't know what was supposed to happen, didn't know what his grunts meant, and had no idea where all the wetness came from. How could she know? She was only fifteen. That was back in the days when she didn't even say hell, she said 'h–e–two legs'. It was different now. Girls were not bred so naïve, they seemed to know what was what from a much earlier age. But back then it was the boy's job to trick a girl into it, and the girl's job to try not to fall for it.

She could say hell now. She had done hellish things. She liked that she was no longer so trickless, not so easily fleeced. She had an edge, experience. She could be a hellcat, a hellslut if she wanted. A take-no-shit her. A sperm bandit even. All was possible.

Ravi came through the back door, slinking in like a barnyard cat.

'Hello,' he said. 'What are you doing here?'

'Fixing the taps.'

'Why are you doing that?'

'Why do you think?'

74

He shrugged. He stood watching her for a while and then said, 'Do you want to go somewhere later?'

She looked at him. 'Where?'

'A bar or somewhere. For a drink?' He blinked slowly, acting out cool. It made him seem childish and annoying.

'Is that even legal?' she said, knowing this would offend him.

'Yes. I am nineteen,' he said, his voice pitched a little high in his defensiveness. 'I told you so already.'

'No thanks,' she said.

He glanced at her tools. 'Is it because you are a lesbian?'

'No, don't be stupid. It's because I don't want to.'

'Okay then,' he said, and sauntered off down the hall.

She went out to the kitchen to explain to Zita that she would now be able to use the washing machine properly, and she responded as if it was a miracle that Simone was capable of doing what the men couldn't.

'I enjoyed it,' Simone told her.

Zita humbly picked up a cake tin and handed it to her. 'Just some treats. I know it's not much after you've sorted out all my whatyamacallits like that, but . . .'

On the lid was a portrait of Sir Edmund Hillary with a painted backdrop of Mt Everest. Zita tapped the top of the tin. 'You know I used to go to the same school as him for a while, at Tuakau Primary. He had something about him even back then. Some kind of tenacity. Although he was terribly, terribly shy. Me and a couple of cheeky girlfriends used to give him a bit of a ribbing. We'd threaten to kiss him and he'd run away from us. He'd do anything to get away. Climb up trees. Climb up telegraph poles. One time he even climbed up on the school roof. Reckon we gave him his start,' she said, with a throaty laugh.

Walking home Simone looked underneath Sir Edmund. Inside were two packets of biscuits, one of them was a brand that had been discontinued from the supermarket years ago.

11

The condom had frozen into a flat, solid lump. She poked at it. It was rock hard, and a bit disgusting. She had no real intention of defrosting it. She just liked the idea it was there.

Who's to say it would even work anyway? They probably had special equipment to snap freeze and defrost at fertility clinics. They probably didn't use your ordinary household fridge/freezer. And the truth was, and she had to face it, that even if it did work, it would be highly unlikely to work on her.

She was not a woman who could fall pregnant easily and was already too familiar with clinic procedures and all that accompanied them. She'd sat there, in a waiting room, with her fingers wrapped around a container, keeping it warm. Trying not to notice the clock on the opposite wall, ticking so loudly it was almost like someone wanted you to think only of the importance of time. Vaguely aware of others in the waiting room, but avoiding their faces because all you ever saw was desperation and anxiety and a sense of last resort. You never wanted to hear their stories, because yours was bad enough. There was something unwhole, unhuman about all of you. And you knew, too, that some of them were discreetly holding a container just like yours, but not the same.

The last time the doctor had turned up late with a newspaper tucked under his arm and a self-impressed expression on his face. He was never unkind exactly, rather a man pretending to be kind. He took the vial from her hands. Gave it a swirl right there in the waiting room and, in his version of good humour, said, 'Not a lot to work with is there?'

She'd wanted to cry then, but even overloaded with hormones as she was, no tears came, only a blindness at the edge of her vision, which the other people in the waiting room disappeared into. Until that happened she'd been wishing Fraser had found it in him to come with her, but now she had reason to be relieved he hadn't. Although he was not exactly unwilling, neither did he want to participate. There was a sense that if this was what they had to do then it was all wrong. It was just as well he wasn't here to be humiliated too.

Even when they first began trying for a baby they didn't really discuss it properly. She'd just asked him one day if she should go off the pill and he'd said yeah, okay. After a couple of years nothing happened so she began going to doctors, looking for answers. But she soon found that to speak too directly about it with Fraser was to invoke a look of fear and a desire to escape. Sometimes though, after they'd had particularly fantastic sex, he'd say, 'If that doesn't get you pregnant nothing will!' For him it was a simple matter of good chemistry, of virility. It was not a medical science. Not something to force, or face up to.

That morning she'd felt she had to lightly cajole him. She needed to get her container filled and the whole thing needed to be approached with delicacy. If she was too heavy-handed about it he might refuse, he might make an excuse, he might just run out the door. And that would be a month of injections wasted.

'How about it, big boy?' she'd said to him, picking her moment carefully. They were still in bed, but she'd made him coffee, brought him an almond croissant, told him a funny story she'd heard at work and had saved for three days.

'You're after the best part of me, aren't you!' he'd replied, and she knew he was going to play along after all. He'd probably known what she was up to the moment she'd appeared at the bedroom door with a pastry on a plate. If she didn't have her problem, or blockage, or whatever it was, then he'd simply fuck her and she'd get pregnant and then they'd both be in it together. But this way, it was like he was doing her some kind of favour, letting her do this. Some part of her resented it. She knew from the other couples she saw in the waiting rooms that not all men were like this.

She slipped her hand under the covers and started to stroke

77

his cock. 'Are you trying to turn me on, you little minx?' he'd said, settling back into the pillow, knowing this would be one morning when he wouldn't have to reciprocate in any way.

'Don't you know it, baby!' she'd replied.

Whenever he told the story of blowing up his grandmother's henhouse with the golden syrup tin, the highlight for him was always describing the way his grandfather had sat him down and had trouble disguising his own amusement as he'd rebuked him. 'Now son,' he'd said, 'that's no way to treat your granny's chickens.' They'd both had to suppress a giggle, while his grandmother sat in the living room, grim-faced and knitting, waiting for him to be told his pocket money would be stopped and his bike was to be confiscated for a month. But Simone always felt sorry for the poor granny, and even more for her poor chickens. It always made her feel he didn't have the right consideration for either. It was not the cruelty exactly, just the untroubled disregard. He never much liked to think about the consequences of things.

When the doctor nodded towards the room with the bed with the stirrups she followed him weakly. He was the recognised expert in his field. His name was often in the paper, defending the latest medical advance against those who believe in God's will. He seemed to think of himself as a new god. A modern god. Giving life, where there would otherwise be none. But she could tell he was tired of it all too. Weary of the constant procession of worried women, with their cycles out of whack and ovaries like shrivelled gooseberries. And their defective husbands.

He transferred the contents of the vial, her inadequate offering, into a syringe. She supposed he was probably thinking he could've done a better job of it himself. That in fact the world would be a better place if only he was permitted, what with his brains, his bone structure, his golf handicap.

'Try to relax,' he ordered from between her legs and she'd thought this is no way to make a baby.

12

The telephone in Alice's house sat on the bureau in the dining room. It was a novelty phone, a cream-coloured, pretend antique phone, with raised gold buttons. And it rang with a high-pitched, cheerful little chirrup, like it'd been programmed to always be the bearer of good news. Simone imagined Alice liked to arrange everything around her to best achieve this kind of manufactured optimism.

It was Lexie on the line. 'Just called up for a chat,' she said. They talked about Alice for a while; there had been no change. Lexie mentioned that Billy was off school with a cold. 'He's pretty funny though, I gave him some vitamin C and echinacea then he told his grandmother I was giving him euthanasia.'

Simone smiled. When Billy was younger he had a tendency to harden soft sounds like *ch* and *tr*. Instead of chippies he would say kippies. He liked *kees on kackers* and *gumping on the kampoline*, and his favourite movie was *gorge of the gungle*. Lexie and Anton fell into the habit of asking him questions which had these kinds of words as the answer, and in his sweet little way he would oblige by saying the words out loud with a beamingly complicit smile on his face, recognising it was a kind of party trick. He was cheerfully accepting and long after he'd managed to get his tongue around the sounds he would carry on with the mispronunciation if there was any likelihood of even slightly amusing a nearby adult.

'Other than that it's just the same old same old,' Lexie said. 'We went to a dinner party at Ingrid's the other night. You would've hated it. All they talked about was real estate and schools.'

'I know what that's like. What's become of her?'

'I know. You used to be able to rely on Ingrid for a laugh at least. Nowadays she gets you in a corner and bangs on about how you really should be putting your spare cash into an investment property,' Lexie said.

In a way this kind of focused intensity was typical of Ingrid. Simone had met her at university, and had later introduced her to Lexie, her flatmate. She'd always been a faddist, flinging herself wholeheartedly into everything. When she was about nineteen she decided – after inadvertently getting herself involved in a couple of marijuana-fuelled sexual threesomes – that she wasn't spiritual enough. She joined a church for a while, a charismatic congregation where she claimed she spoke in tongues. She tried to get everybody she knew to experience it too, and then one morning she said she just wasn't in the mood for any more clapping and singing. She followed that up with a fever for Jazzercise, when that was still a new craze . . . until the day an instructor suggested doing four classes in a row might not be so healthy. The endearing thing about her, though, was that once the fad had passed she could always see the funny side, and liked to parody herself, although she could never be tipped off at the time.

Eventually she found ways of focusing her energy in productively, and she started an event management business. Then when she had children she lost interest and concentrated instead on becoming an award-worthy mother. A kindy-volunteering, fundraising, carpooling, sideline-cheering, home-work-supervising, play-acting supermum. She hadn't had a particularly happy childhood herself. Although she rarely talked about it, Simone knew that her father – an Anglo-Italian with long eyelashes and a Mediterranean smile that was devastating enough even in a photograph – had left when she was seven and had started a new family in a neighbouring town. Her adult response was to keep a tight grip on certain things. Her children only ever ate organic, achieved at the top strata in all of their classes, did not watch too much television, had lovely manners – and would never have suspected their mother had once smoked a bong with two Australian rugby league players who then rooted her front and back. The kind of achievement

Ingrid preferred to boast about nowadays was more the time an iridologist had looked into the eyes of her children and pronounced them amongst the clearest he'd ever seen.

Not so long ago Simone had been invited to one of those dinner parties of Ingrid's, and had felt miserably left out as the rest of the table moved from a discussion about the nappy-free trend in toilet training to a heated conversation about the candidates for the board of the local primary. Ingrid's husband, who was seated next to her, said in an aside, 'This must be rather dull for you.' Then he just launched himself straight back into the fray. Mostly he liked to argue; he was a lawyer.

'Anyway, the real reason I was calling is Alice's son has arrived back from London,' Lexie said. 'He's spending some time with her but he might come and see the house at some stage, is that okay?'

'Of course,' Simone replied, instantly worried. What would he be like? Would he want to live here? Would he kick her out? Where would she go? Back?

'You're not getting too bored there?'

'Um no. I quite like not working. And there's not much to spend my money on so I'm lasting out okay.'

'Not missing the cut and thrust?'

'God no. I can't even imagine how I did that work. The biggest decision I make at the moment is what to have for dinner.'

'Oh yeah. And what are you having for dinner tonight?'

'Can't decide.'

Lexie laughed, and then there was a cautious pause. She cleared her throat. 'Um . . . listen . . . I saw Fraser . . .'

'Uh huh,' Simone said carefully.

'I told him you were on holiday.'

'Did you tell him where?'

'No. Did you want me to?'

There was some part of her that wanted to open the front door one day and find him there, begging her to forgive him, telling her that he now realised how wrong, how blind he'd been.

But another part of her didn't want to still be hoping for that. 'I don't know,' she said. 'I don't think so. How did he look?'

'Not that great.'

'Not unwell though?' Simone asked, thinking of the question she couldn't ask – *does he know I did it?*

'No. I don't think so,' Lexie said. 'He just looked sort of uncomfortable. It might've been bumping into me. He was always a bit lily-livered. Maybe he was scared I'd give him a bit of a seeing to.'

'Maybe you should've.'

'Maybe I was tempted.'

Lily-livered? She hadn't ever thought of him like that. Had she just chosen not to see him in that light? She'd always thought of him as somebody who acted freely on his impulses, and while that inevitably had its terrible consequences it was also what gave him his entitlement as an artist, and therefore his central being. It was the thing that, at the start, had impressed her the most about him. But maybe Lexie was seeing it for what it really was. Not impulsiveness, but elusiveness. Not reaching towards, but running away. Not taking a new lover, but fleeing an old one.

Lexie had been with her when she first she met him, so she had known him for at least as long, if not as intimately. Billy was still a toddler and Lexie had rung to say she had a leave pass for the night and wanted to make the most of it. Her former boyfriend's band was playing and she convinced Simone to go with her to see them. At the door Lexie tried to talk her way into the gig without paying on the basis she'd once dated the bass player. The guy on the door, who was Fraser, told her he knew the bloke well and in his opinion he was a bit of a dork so Lexie would have to pay after all. But her girlfriend could get in free, he said, because he liked that she had lipstick on her teeth. Lexie started to protest but he just laughed and waved them through, saying, 'It's your funeral, ladies!'

'That guy might be good-looking but he's too bloody cheeky for his own good,' Lexie muttered as they walked off.

The band was terrible. They were swinging their hair around so much they were having trouble keeping in time with each other, and at one stage the guitarist accidentally tripped on his mic lead, unplugging it. The drummer kept doing hundreds of show-off rolls, ruining any hope of rhythm. The audience was standing well back from the stage and nobody was dancing, or even tapping their feet. When they had to stop so the guitarist could retune, someone from out by the pool tables yelled, 'Get a day job ya useless fuckers.' Simone had last seen them seven years before when Lexie had briefly dated Jimmy, and couldn't get over the fact they'd been doing it for that long and were still so bad.

By the time they finished playing Lexie was deep in conversation with a girl who'd turned out to be Jimmy's current girlfriend. Simone couldn't hear what they were talking about, her ears were ringing from the din of the band, and she went off to buy another beer. It was crowded around the bar and Fraser squeezed in beside her. 'Shit weren't they,' he said. 'I feel so bad I was the one taking money off people.'

'Why did you then?' she asked.

'So I could let the pretty ones in for free,' he said, leaning on the bar and giving her a sly sideways grin.

'And who else did you let in?' she asked, feeling stupidly flattered, and looking around the bar trying to guess who else he might have thought was pretty.

'Oh her. And her. And her,' he said, straightening up and pointing vaguely across the room. 'And her. And her. And her. And her. And her. And her. And her. And her. And her. And the only one I really noticed was her,' he said finally, with his finger pointing directly at Simone.

He was tall, and she was unable to raise her eyes to look up at him, staring instead at the end of his finger. His nails looked like they'd been bitten off rather than cut. Her drink arrived and she pulled out her wallet to pay for it, but Fraser asked the barman to put it on the band's rider.

'Also I quite like the chaos,' he said. 'A couple of months

ago the lead singer went to do a stage dive and the crowd just parted so he did a complete gutser instead. Lucky he's so fat, he bounced. But he cracked a tooth and halfway through the next song it disintegrated, so he just spat it out and continued on. That's the kind of shit people pay to see.'

The barman pushed six handles towards Fraser and he gathered up three in each of his big hands. 'Going out the back for a spliff with the others,' he said. 'Wanna come?'

The band made a seat for her on top of an amp and she took a puff of a joint as it was passed around. The drummer pulled off his shirt and turned away from her to rub his body down with a towel. She leaned back against a carpeted wall which reeked of smoke and spirits, and watched. Fraser had introduced him as Scrotum. He had stringy, corded, drummer's muscles, and across the top of his shoulders he had a tattoo of an eagle which almost seemed to fly as he moved his arms. He swivelled back around on his stool once he had a fresh T-shirt on, and because she was having a little headrush she told him he was so energetic out there he reminded her of Animal. He looked pleased and said thanks, as if she'd just paid him a huge compliment. His response made her wonder if there was another famous drummer called Animal other than the one on the Muppets. And then it occurred to her that he was much younger than Fraser and the other two so maybe he didn't even know who Animal was. Was that possible? She looked over at Fraser and he was laughing, as if he knew what she was thinking.

They offered to sell her one of their T-shirts and it turned out Fraser had made the print. He'd also made their posters for them, they said, and as soon as it was mentioned she remembered that the posters had always been the coolest thing about this band. The posters and the T-shirts were in fact so cool they were probably the only reason they even had an audience at all. 'Yeah, Fraser's the Arturo Vega of this band,' the one called Kelvin said.

'Arturo Vega?'

84

'The guy who did the artwork for the Ramones.'

'And did the KKK take his baby away?' Simone asked.

A couple of them, including Fraser, raised their eyebrows in acknowledgement.

'Nah, I reckon he's more like Noel Crombie,' somebody else said.

'Noel Crombie?'

'That loon from Split Enz, who sewed up their nutty outfits and played the spoons and stuff.'

'Can you play the spoons?' she asked Fraser.

'If you come back to my place I'll show you what I can do,' he said. And because his long black fringe flopped into his eyes at exactly that moment, because she knew something exciting might happen, and because he gave her the kind of look that made a person feel like she was already known, she rose when he did.

He lived within walking distance from the bar, in a big rambling, half-rotting villa which he said he shared with six others. When they got to his place everybody else was either still out or already in bed. He took her into a kitchen, poured some vodka into a glass he wiped clean on the end of his T-shirt, and then said he had to do something. He went through one of the doors and she heard some noises, things being thrown around a room. She threw back the vodka in one gulp, trying not to let her lips touch the sides of the glass. It was too much, though, on top of the beer and the smoke, and it started to make her feel woozy. She should've eaten before she went out. She began to feel hot. She slipped off her jacket. She could feel beads of sweat forming on her top lip. And then she knew she was going to be sick. She started to panic as she had no idea where the bathroom was and she didn't know if she could hold it back long enough to ask Fraser, so she tugged the side window open and put her head out. The night air was instantly cooling but she still couldn't help heaving onto the porch roof below and when she turned around again, wiping her mouth, Fraser was standing watching from the kitchen door.

'I like a girl who knows how to express herself,' he said.

In the bright hard light of the kitchen she felt haggard and graceless. She grabbed open a cupboard door and hid her face behind it. 'I'm sorry,' she mumbled. 'I should go.'

'Yep. You could do that . . . or you could go and sit in my bed to keep warm, and I'll make you a cup of tea or something.'

When she didn't speak he stepped over and closed the cupboard door. He looked down at her with the same kind of smile you might reserve for a puppy you'd just found chewing your slippers, like he was trying not to laugh. The breeze from the window was making goosebumps form on her arms and he pulled her to him, wrapping her arms inside his jacket and briskly rubbed her back to warm her. The few straggly chest hairs sticking out of the top of his shirt tickled her cheek, and she breathed in the musky, steamy warmth of him.

'Okay then,' she said, because she didn't really want to go.

He led her into his room, where the bed was made, but only just. Everything was low-lit by a yellow bulb set into the crown of a pair of deer antlers on the floor in the corner. He pulled back the edge of the duvet and she climbed into the bed and then he went back out to the kitchen. It probably wasn't a room which could stand up to any kind of close inspection. Even in the dim light she could see a dark mould was colonising one corner of the ceiling, spreading out like a map of the underworld. And on the wooden floor she could still see some telltale outlines of dust where things had been hastily removed and somehow disposed of. In some way she was touched he'd made this hurried, rudimentary effort for her. Ineffective as it was, it did indicate he wanted to make a reasonably good impression, or at least lessen a potentially bad one.

Of his art there were a few canvases stacked against the walls, facing in, but hung nearby was a collage, pasted onto a broken wooden ski. It was constructed mostly of old ski passes, and postcards of Mt Ruapehu, with one displayed writing side out. She slipped out of the bed to read it – in big loopy uneven letters it said:

Dear Mum, Had a great trip down to the lodge.
Stopped for gas at Tokoroa but the Rogers gang went
passed and tooted. Dad reckened he was laughing at
us so no time for icecreams and he drove like a bat out
of hell. We soon got in front and Dad rigguled all over
the road so Mr Rogers couldn't pass again. Me and
Tils hung out the back windows shaking our fists. It
was hillarious. Love from Fraser.

Fraser came up behind her and said, 'That's the postcard which famously got me and my Dad into big, big trouble.' He handed her one of two mugs he was carrying, keeping the more chipped one for himself, and they climbed into either side of the bed with their clothes on.

After she'd taken a few sips of the hot, sweet tea he said, 'Better?'

'Yes, except . . . a bit weirded out. I still feel so embarrassed I can hardly look at you.'

'Shall I tell you about one of my most embarrassing moments then? Will that even us up?'

'Go on then,' she said, nestling further down under the duvet.

'All right,' he said. 'Let me think.' He leaned his head back against the wall and closed his eyes for such a long time she was beginning to think he might've fallen asleep. Eventually he said, 'Okay this is a real good one. Are you ready?'

'As I'll ever be,' she said.

'Okay. I was about thirteen, or maybe twelve, and my older sister Tilly had this girlfriend called Mona right, who I liked 'cos she had quite big knockers for her age. Anyway Mona was staying over and this day I went into the bathroom just after her. It smelled real good in there, all soft and flowery and little speckles of talcum on the floor. So I started to undress to have a shower and then I noticed this pair of underwear in the corner. This like little pair of black panties, all sort of lacy around the edges. And I guessed she must've dropped them on her way out.

87

By this time I'm naked anyway so I figure I might just as well try them on. So I'm standing in front of the mirror, looking at myself in this girl Mona's knickers and I start to feel real horny. Just when I'm thinking I'll have to do something about it the door flies open and Tils's standing there with her mouth open. She's looking at me, with this big boner poking out the top of these skimpy girly undies, and she says, "Fraser Lee Curtis you little creep, get my pants off this minute!"'

'They were hers?'

He nodded slowly. 'Yep. My own sister's.'

'Fraser Lee Curtis, that's a pretty pervy story to tell a girl you hardly know.'

'Oh, I think I know you,' he said.

At that moment the double doors on his wardrobe squeaked open and an avalanche of junk slid out into the room – unopened bills and scrunched up clothes, dirty leather boots and beer bottles, greasy plates and bread crusts, half-finished canvases and jam jars coated on the inside with dried paint. 'They like to be free,' he said, laughing once more.

He leaned over and took the mug out of her hands and put it on the wooden crate that served as his side table. Then he settled her down in the bed, and lay behind her with his arms around her and his knees pressing the back of hers. She could hardly sleep, she liked the feel and the smell of him so much. It wasn't until the morning that they took off their clothes and had the kind of sex that made her never want to be with anybody else. He undid her completely.

Gorgeous, Fraser used to call her. Hi Gorgeous, bye Gorgeous. Give us a kiss Gorgeous. Sometimes just Gorg. And she used to call him Spunkypants. Dreamboy. Hunkbucket. And in bed. You're so gorgeous, no you are, no you are, no you are, no you are.

It turned out he was quite a lot of things. Impetuous. Flirty. Irresistible. Chaotic. Irresponsible. And disloyal. Lily-livered too.

A few years later, when they were living together, he hit a

dry patch with his work. By that stage he had begun to build a reputation and his art was largely considered collectable but his exhibitions could still be hit and miss. There were periods when he didn't have enough incomings and she would have to support him for a while. Ingrid had said, 'Do you think you'd let him get away with so much if he wasn't so handsome?' Ingrid's own husband was not ugly, but he wasn't handsome. Before she'd first brought him over to meet Simone and Lexie she had rung ahead to say they had to act normally and pretend not to notice he had a very small head. He earned well though, and now they had their children, and she seemed to be thinking that by comparison her life had gone to some kind of model plan. 'The trouble with handsome,' she'd said, 'is opportunity comes its way.' At the time Simone had laughed it off, because that was before.

Now, though, after everything, it occurred to her that maybe it was just the kind of natural lesson Ingrid had learned much earlier than everybody else.

13

'So you fixed Zita's taps then,' Clara commented as she peered down into a promising-looking rock pool. She and Simone were out collecting paua shells. Clara claimed the poachers shuck them just offshore, and the shells often wash up after a southerly storm. They were down at the opposite end of the beach to the café and had left Charlie sitting in the sun on an old log while they clambered over the rocks with Clouseau.

'Yes, as best I could anyway.'

'That was nice of you. Do you know how old she is?'

'Not a clue.'

'Eighty-nine. She'll be ninety soon.'

'God. I had no idea.'

'I know. Around here we don't like talk of getting old or elderly, we like to say seasoned. And of all of us Zita is the most well seasoned.' Clara pointed downwards. 'Look there!'

Simone shifted her eyes to where she was indicating and saw the bluish-green iridescence gleaming up from within a deep pool. Clara passed her the stick which she normally used for hooking open the louvre window above her back door. Simone knelt down, pushed up her sleeve, and guided the end of the stick down towards the shell, trying to get the hook in under the curve. Clouseau crouched beside her, peering into the pool, and in his demented eagerness to see what she was reaching for, slipped into the water. He seemed to try and pretend he meant to go for a swim all along and paddled around a bit before getting out again.

'It's amazing to think about all that time, isn't it,' said Clara, holding on to the back of Simone's shirt while she leaned out over the water. 'She was born right in the middle of World War One, I suppose. I must ask her one time.'

Simone floated the shell up to the surface. 'That's a beauty,'

Clara exclaimed. 'So big!' They weren't collecting them for any particular reason. Only because they were pretty. Cheap treasures. Good ashtrays. Garden decorations. This one could almost be a serving dish.

'You keep it,' Simone said.

'No, that one's yours,' Clara insisted. 'You fished for it.'

It was a truly beautiful thing. Crusty on the outside, but lustrous inside. Its colouring better than anything you could paint. Its shape more lovely than anything you could invent.

They carried it up to show Charlie. He fingered it admiringly and said, 'What a lovely . . . um. I'll look after it for you.' He took it in two shaky hands and laid it carefully on the log beside him, as if it was a delicate porcelain plate.

Clara poured him a cup of tea from a Thermos and kissed him on the cheek as she handed it over. He seemed quite happy, sitting there with the sun on his face. When they'd first arrived at the beach he had taken the time to explain that the shoreline had once been much further up but the government had sucked out the water to reclaim more land for farming. Simone thought, from the look on Clara's face, that this was probably not true.

As they walked back towards the rocks Clara said, 'That's always the first sign, did you know? Forgetting words. Or getting them mixed up a bit. It can be quite . . . funny . . . sort of, sometimes. One time early on he came back from the beach and said he'd seen a rotary hoe up in the sky. I worked out later he meant a helicopter.'

'That's quite strange, isn't it. It's so nearly right it's almost clever.'

'I know. I always think it's a bit like they sent in an apprentice electrician to do the repairs, but he's so inept he connected the hall light to the shaving socket and the bedroom lamp to the kitchen whiz,' said Clara, glancing back towards Charlie. 'He often gets a bit worse as the day goes on. You know they say you have a one in five chance of getting it at his age, but once you're over eighty-five it's one in three. Zita's quite lucky. She might be a bit doddery but she's pretty good really.'

91

Zita's daily struggle was definitely more with her mobility than her mind. She was nervous on her feet and manoeuvred her way around feeling with her hands for the nearest wall or piece of furniture as she went. Simone hardly ever saw her outside, and knew Marjorie did her shopping. While she liked to play up to her age, she also tried to deny any particular difficulty as much as possible, and according to Clara, when Marjorie had recently suggested she might try a walker she'd replied indignantly, 'I'm not that far gone!' Clara mentioned how she'd once tripped on a rug and knocked herself unconscious on the edge of the table. When she came to she found she'd bruised her face nastily but her main concern was that people might think that after such a silly accident she was past coping. She phoned Marjorie and told her she was calling from her son's and he'd unexpectedly come to pick her up for a short stay. She planned to hide indoors until the bruise faded, not turning on the lights in case they noticed. She might have got away with it too, except that Toss decided to stack some firewood on the back porch and glimpsed her through the window. Later she told them that when she came to she found she'd only missed the news but not Coronation Street, as if that was proof of hardiness. After that they'd all agreed, everybody on the street, to keep in touch every day.

Simone didn't know Clara's age, somewhere in her seventies probably, years younger than Zita anyway. Although in her own way, she too was trying to defy everything expected of her simply because of her age. Unlike Marjorie, who seemed to think that with age came indubitable good sense, and who quite liked to tell people what they ought to do, Clara was much less likely to assume any tiers or constraints. She often dressed not exactly fashionably but quite flamboyantly, and was not at all cautious in what she said. And there was a likeable vigour about her which suggested she was able to move more easily than most from one juncture to the next. Did she ever feel burdened by Charlie? Simone wondered. Did she ever want to run away? It must be horribly depressing to witness a stealthy, insidious rot taking the mind of someone you once depended on.

'Zita showed me her photos,' Simone said.

'Did she? You saw her sons? Couple of big ugly lumps aren't they. Did you see the awful wives? I'm sure those money-grubbers would love to get their hands on her property.'

'They looked like a couple of cows.'

'Have you been to Marjorie's shop yet?'

'No, haven't quite got around all the local attractions yet.'

'It's quite something,' Clara said. 'You should go and see it.'

It was a bright, warm day, with sun shimmering on the surface of the rock pools. Out to sea a red fishing boat was heading towards the horizon with a band of squawking seagulls trailing after it, like a bunch of neighbourhood brats chasing a Mr Whippy van.

These early hints of summer were having a curiously uplifting effect on the day. A couple of hours ago Simone had arrived next door to borrow some books and found Charlie sitting on the front steps with all the windows open and the sound of Elvis Presley's voice blasting out of the house. She sat down beside him and could already tell from his body language and the look in his eye that he was in one of his more present moments, temporarily unyoked. 'So ... "Mystery Train"?' she'd said.

'It's been a long time since I heard this,' Charlie commented. 'Back in the day it was pretty important which way you swung. Into Elvis or not – you had to take a position and it said a lot about who you were.'

'And which way were you?' Simone asked.

Charlie leaned away from her, put his hand on his hip and rearranged his face into a playful delinquent's sneer. 'Elvis is a pussy,' he quipped, rolling his eyes.

It'd made Simone smile. It made her wish she'd known him back then. For an instant it was possible to see what he might've been like. It'd made her wish also that it was possible to know him better now. That small glimpse of the real him, like a crack of light showing through a part open door, had the effect of

93

prevailing over everything else, dismissing any fractiousness he might've displayed on that day of the frost.

Now Simone skipped across a narrow crevice and as she leaned back to help Clara over she asked, 'Do you have children?' The sound of this question coming from her own mouth made her cringe a little. She didn't really like it when people asked her the same thing. It was odd, she noticed, how often people asked it of her now. People she hardly knew. Always women. Strangers, often, who wouldn't dare to suddenly ask a different kind of personal question. It was like they were asking if she was a member of their particular club – a club which had an unquestioned sense of natural order as its esprit de corps. There would always be an awkward moment or two, after she'd said no, when she could see them trying to decide which category she might fit into – selfish career woman, sufferer of imperfect biology, or cannot get a man. Simone wasn't surprised when Clara said no. There was that slight detachment, or perhaps carelessness, which suggested she'd never really been inclined to set an example for others.

'Charlie had two young children when I met him. He didn't really want any more. I never really thought about it much. It wasn't an issue for me at the time. Charlie and me, it seemed like enough. We liked going out, being at the centre of things. At one time we were very sociable. But now I'm losing him I've had times when I wish we had had children.'

'Do you see his?'

'Well that's always been complicated. His wife was very bitter and didn't want me anywhere near them. So Charlie could only see them at her place, and she'd always be horrible to him, or crying and begging. He tried to be a good father but of course the kids . . . they used to call me "the Strumpet". And we were in London for quite some while for Charlie's career. It took a terribly long time for them to accept me in his life.'

'But they do now?'

'Oh I suppose so. We don't see them much. Now that Charlie's sick it's hard for them. Sometimes he doesn't remember who they are and that cuts deep. And even when he does it only lasts a little while and then he often starts talking about things that never happened, or things that did but not with his children. I suppose it makes it easier for them to justify not coming to see him.'

They rounded a corner where a big pohutukawa tree overhung a small clearing of sand and pebbles. A tangle of seaweed had trawled up some driftwood and several paua shells, and also a single orange rubber glove with all the fingers cut off.

'This has always been the spot. For some reason the sea always throws them up here,' said Clara. 'And what about you? No children?'

'No. I wanted to. It didn't work out,' Simone replied, aiming to sound robust and reconciled.

'Maybe you still can?'

'No, I think . . . no.'

'I'm sorry,' Clara said. She'd collected so many shells now that she'd pulled up the edge of her jersey and was stacking them into the pouch it made. 'You had trouble?'

'I did,' Simone said, not completely sure she wanted to talk about it, feeling her shoulders tighten.

'And you're having a bad time about it?'

'No. I was a bit messed up for a while, but I'm fine now. Only I don't like shopping centres.'

'Shopping centres?'

'There's something about those women with pushchairs. Somehow they always look quite smug when they're shopping. I can't help looking in their faces and wondering how they came to have a baby at all with an attitude like that.' That wasn't even quite the truth. What she really used to think was *You're ugly, but somebody still fucked you.* It was mad, she knew. Mad. Sad. Unkind. Unhealthy. And so base she didn't know where it came from.

'Smug?' Clara said. 'I always see women out struggling with some little horror having a tantrum and I think poor them.'

95

They sat down on two low humps of a pohutukawa branch which dived in and out of the sand like a fat petrified serpent. 'I do sometimes think that when I see those stories in women's magazines about children with terrible illnesses,' Simone said. 'I think poor them, and I think at least I won't have to go through anything as heartbreaking as that.' She had other things on her 'at least I won't have to' list too. At least she didn't have to get out of bed and make a school lunch every day, at least she wouldn't have to spend her Saturdays on the side of a windy sports field, at least she'd never have to peg out bumper-sized washing loads every morning or keep her floors clean enough to eat a dinner off, at least she didn't have to find babysitting money every time she escaped the house, and at least she'd never have to say things like *you're not going out of this house wearing that get-up*. It was a bit sad, her 'at least' list. And if she thought about it too hard it would start to collapse into the inverse, the things she was missing out on, the extra reasons to get out of bed every day, the simple sense of achievement as the sun shines down on all those cute little clothes, experiencing close at hand the passionate wide-eyed obsessions with things like peanut butter beats marmite, your chest bursting when your child scores their first goal, those kittenish goodnight cuddles, the love.

Clara tipped her shells onto the sand in front of them. She reached over and lifted the shells out of Simone's hands and added them to the pile. 'Let's have a smoke,' she said, pulling a rolled cigarette and a lighter out of her side pocket. It wasn't until she'd lit it, taken a long hard draw and then exhaled that Simone smelled the sweetness. Clara passed it to her. 'Good for arthritis and whatever else ails you,' she said.

Simone smirked to cover her surprise, and Clara laughed. Simone accepted the joint saying, 'You're much more wicked than you look, aren't you.'

'Aren't I,' Clara said.

They passed it between them for a while and then Clara said, 'I sort of know what you mean. About finding reasons to be grateful.'

14

Life is full of demarcation lines, Simone thought later. Eighty-five is the cut-off age when the risk of losing your mind suddenly narrows from one in five to one in three. Funded IVF is cut off at forty, the age of improbability. Experts are fond of saying that after forty a woman's fertility drops to blah blah percent. As if a 39-year-old woman wanting a baby and a 40-year-old woman wanting a baby are very different things. If time is running out for the 39-year-old, then the 40-year-old better bloody wake up to herself.

There was an old bottle of Baileys at the back of one of Alice's kitchen cupboards. Simone had only meant to take one shot. But once she let the first glassful slide down her throat it was impossible to restrain herself from taking more. She lay down on the couch with a book she'd found on Alice's shelves. Having forgotten to bring home a book from Clara's earlier she was reduced to choosing from Alice's selection, which generally implied she was more of a doer than a thinker. They were mostly instructional books. Flower arranging. Baking, of the jelly mould and sponge cake kind. Picture books on cats. Making dyes from plants. A ten-volume set on knitting and crochet (1972). One whole shelf was devoted to the Encyclopaedia Britannica. Volume six and volume eleven were missing, Simone noted. She picked out a book called *The Garbo of the Skies*, about the life of the aviatrix Jean Batten. She sipped more of the warming, almost-musty liquor as she read, and just as she was beginning to succumb to a sleepy undertow the dog made her jump, barking at the door.

'Who's there?' she called out, momentarily frightened. It was dark outside and the door wasn't locked.

'Sorry. Sorry. It is only me. Ravi.'

She got to her feet, accidentally knocking over a little side table, surprised by how unsteady she was, and opened the door.

'Sorry. I was wanting to talk,' he said.

'It's late.'

'Did you have somewhere to be?' he asked with a smile.

'You have a point,' she said.

They stood there awkwardly for a moment. She didn't really want to invite him inside, he had the look of an earnest salesman and she had the feeling she was about to be talked into something she didn't want.

'I'm going back to the city tomorrow,' he said. 'On the bus.'

'We'll miss you,' she said automatically.

'Really?' He looked grateful, and then slightly flattened when he read on her face she hadn't really meant it.

'A bit,' she said. And in trying to make herself less mean, waved him in.

She offered him some of the Baileys, but when she picked up the bottle she saw there was barely a glassful left. He said he didn't drink stuff like that. He didn't sit down right away, but moved around the room, touching the tops of things, picking up ornaments and placing them back down again. She didn't know what it was about him she didn't quite trust. He had a certain unworldly innocence and yet was he too intent? Too eager? She wasn't sure.

'I have a problem,' Ravi said at last. 'A girl problem. I am wanting to ask your advice.'

'Okay.' The alcohol she'd consumed made her feel thickly half-absent.

She sank into an armchair, and instead of taking the other chair he sat down on the arm of hers. He started talking in the tone of voice you might use when starting a long-rehearsed parable, looking down at her as he spoke. She tugged at the top of her T-shirt to make sure he wasn't looking into her cleavage.

'Well. One night I went out with my friends,' he said. 'To the city and we met some girls. I was talking to this one girl. She was being very friendly. She said I was nice looking.' He paused and smiled creamily. 'We started kissing. I never kissed such a girl before. I think she was a good kisser. It's okay? I tell you this?'

Simone nodded. He seemed to be leaning into her so she adjusted her body weight a little, bending away from him.

'Well, she had a tattoo on her neck. A rose. And I said she had a nice tattoo. So she said I could kiss it if I liked. So I did. It was very nice. I liked it. And then she said did I want to go somewhere. I said yes. And we walked, holding hands you know. Then we got to an old church and we were around the back and she said did I want to feel her titties.' He paused a moment, daring Simone to stop him. She knew she probably should but some part of her was intrigued enough, in a faulty kind of way, to see how far he'd go with this.

'So she lifted up her top and I put my hands on her titties. That was very nice. And she put her hand on my trousers and I was getting a very hard thing.' Simone could feel his eyes on her, trying to gauge her reaction. She didn't look at him, but kept her head down, staring instead at a rusty-coloured stain on the carpet. 'Then she said, "Do you want to fuck me?"'

The stain on the carpet almost seemed to be moving. Was this a bad thing to do? To let this boy say these things to her? She knew he wanted her to react in some way. To comment. To laugh. To tell him that was enough. She had an inclination to do all of these things, but it was almost as if the Baileys she had consumed before had now dulled her response mechanisms. It was like being trapped in the room with a mosquito and instead of swatting and slapping at it, her lazy curiosity allowed her to do nothing but dice with being bitten. 'But I had to say no,' he continued. 'I ran away. Because I have never done that, you see. I need someone to teach me.'

She could feel him looking at her. Imploringly now. With his eager brown eyes. And smiling. With his too-wide smile.

His smile that had just the edge of fear at its corners. He said nothing more, waiting for her response.

'It's not going to be me,' she spluttered, hoping her voice contained a sufficient tone of deterring outrage.

'But you are my friend, my only lady friend.'

'No.'

'I knew a guy and he had an older lady who taught him the right way and I thought maybe . . .'

'No.' But she let herself contemplate it for a moment. She could. There was something wickedly possible about it. I'm going to teach you how to please a woman, she could say. You must do everything I say. And she might in fact feel the satisfaction of the good coach – but it was more likely she'd feel like the disgraceful corrupter. Those skinny legs. Those narrow hips. There was too much of the barely matured boy about him, and here he was in a place foreign to his upbringing, acting with desperation made bold. 'You have to go home now,' she said.

'But maybe I could make you happy. I'd try hard.'

'No.' But very briefly her mind passed over her night with Ollie.

'But if not you, then who?'

'Go home.'

'What are you scared of? You should do it.'

He would try hard, she knew. But in the morning he would get on the bus and travel back to the city, having rid himself of his virginity. He would be newly open to all sorts of terrible possibilities – with no more need to flee that opportunistic sex behind public buildings. And for her? She would wake up and wonder how did it come to this? They get so young I must teach them what to do? I resort to going to bed with young boys who beg me for it, choosing me, they say, because there is nobody else?

'No. Go,' she urged.

'Okay. Sorry. I go.' He stood and went to the door, his shoulders drooping with exaggerated dejection. He turned and made one last silent, wounded plea. It was a look very similar to the one Clouseau sometimes gave her when he thought she might be going out without him. She shook her head. No. He let the door slam lightly behind him.

She felt like laughing then.

In the morning she wondered what it was that made Ravi think he could proposition her like that. Did he know about Ollie? Did he think she was ripe then, up for any ride? Or was it just that he was horny and she was the only woman in the neighbourhood under seventy? Perhaps her encounter with Ollie had triggered something that made her reek of pheromones and had brought him to her door like a dirty dog.

There was some part of her that was pleased he thought she might have been a suitable contender. Perhaps she should've just done it. Perhaps the idea should be to take every presented opportunity while you still have some remaining appeal, some bargaining chips on your side. Because for a while she'd had difficulty imagining anybody wanting her. Fraser's leaving had made her feel distinctly unsexy, a drudge, a bane, a dry old bird kicked from the nest. But look at her now! The local youth are knocking down her door. And those boys, Ollie and Ravi, their wanting was so refreshingly basic and transparent. The transactions were simple. Yes to one, no to the other. No complications.

At a certain point getting older seems to become a perpetual process of learning to maintain resilience against certain inevitabilities. Back when she was thirty she'd given no more thought to her internals than she did to the quality of the skin on her throat, but she did carry concerns about her looks, hair, her proportion. And now at forty she can look back at that and think relatively, it was a waste of time, she should've celebrated what she was back then. And probably at fifty she'll be completely susceptible to the promises of French skincare companies that offer the hope of looking at least as externally supple as she is right now. And maybe too she'll even wonder why she let a little thing like failing to have a baby make her feel so wholly and completely inadequate.

Perhaps she shouldn't have said no. Instead just go for a few moments of complete abandon, while you still can. While you're not yet preoccupied with major inconveniences like post-menopausal dryness, breakable bones, and the fear of wetting the bed when you laugh.

15

Somebody had sprayed graffiti on the post holding up the No Exit sign at the end of the street. In vertical lettering it said *God plays everyone*. Simone couldn't decide what the person who wrote it had meant. Some days she walked past and imagined their god as a great doll-master playing all creations off against each other, placing them in compromising situations for his amusement. Sometimes with kindness, sometimes with a kind of bored vengeance.

Other days she thought they might have meant their god could inhabit anyone you could meet. She imagined this god might play someone she knew, like Toss, or Marjorie, or even Charlie. On those days she looked into faces expecting at any moment a good or great thing to be said or done. Somehow just the simple expectation illuminated everything a little.

Hanife's café was getting busier now with the improving weather. Her awareness of Simone seemed to be more acute, but whenever Simone began to think there might be a chance for friendship she encountered an impenetrable expression. Hanife did all the serving, and although she operated the great steaming coffee machine with deft efficiency there had been times, especially on the weekends, when Simone looked at the queues and thought the wait wouldn't be worth it. She always felt disappointed on those days. She liked the ritual of walking the dog to the café and having an espresso. She'd got into the habit of spending her mornings reading the paper, and there were always plenty of magazines lying around which she gratefully absorbed, satisfying a habitual need to stay informed which a former journalist, even one as rusty as her, probably never lost. This all made her feel connected in the least of ways, a small part of the operating world still.

A drizzly Monday meant the café was quieter than it had

been for a while. 'Why don't you join me?' Simone suggested as she ordered her coffee. She wasn't sure why it was now so important to befriend Hanife but she almost felt relief when Hanife reached for a second cup.

They sat down at a table near the window and Simone said, 'Do you like it here?'

'You Kiwis always ask that,' Hanife replied.

Hoping she hadn't already disappointed her, Simone said vaguely, 'Do we? I wonder why that is.' She often felt a confused admiration for the blunt way Hanife handled everyday conversation. She had a certain in-house persona. She was always efficient, but also indifferent about politeness. The day trippers were often taken aback by her apparent rudeness, but the regulars came to anticipate it. Somehow it made her popular locally. Risking an insult as you ordered your coffee quickened the blood. It's true, of course, what she said. Kiwis are always desperate to know that others in the world like them. It's something in their nature. Perhaps it's a small-country thing. Simone wondered if people from Iceland, or Luxembourg, or Singapore were as eager for affirmation.

'I think it should be possible to be happy here,' Hanife offered, looking out the window at the drizzling rain and the choppy waves.

'Are you?' Simone asked.

'You have no history in this country,' Hanife said, obstinately flicking her long plait over her shoulder.

'But we do!' Simone heard the slight note of defensiveness in her own voice. 'Just not in that European style of old buildings and kings and queens and centuries of feuds and things.'

'Yes, that is part of what I mean. Also no culture.'

Was she trying to antagonise her? Or is confrontation just a conversational form to her? 'Are you homesick?' Simone asked.

Hanife seemed to give this some serious consideration. 'You know I am from Kosovo?'

Simone nodded.

'Well I come from a small village. When the war came the people who were neighbours suddenly become enemies. All because of some pieces of history. Some difference in religion. They burn houses. They force us to leave. My father he was a policeman and these men who were his colleagues take him to the police station where he work beside them and torture him. When they come we recognised their voices under the balaclavas. I never see him again. Then after the war some people move back. But how can you do that? How can you look at such faces of your neighbours again? With their black hearts and their guilt. Turns out not so much, because then the Serbs go. I have no home there now. So. That is my story.' She looked up for a moment with a fierce expression on her face that made Simone think of ancient grievances, generations of anger, but almost instantly it was relinquished. 'And you?' she asked. 'Some days you look sad. You are sick for something?'

'It's nothing. Just a broken heart, is all.' Simone blushed. A broken heart suddenly seemed like such a frivolous thing to have.

'Me too,' Hanife said, 'Is what we two have.'

Neither of them spoke for a moment and then Hanife reached forward and took up two sugar sachets. She held them together, ripped the tops of them both and poured the contents into her cup. 'If you do two like this then you can pretend it was accident and you didn't mean to take so much sugar.'

Simone took up two sachets and did the same.

'It's my bad drug,' Hanife said. 'Sugar, and coffee. And sweets too. Look!' She put her hand into her pocket and pulled out a handful of chocolates. 'I come here for peace. It's pretty. And safe. Except for some crazy druggies on P. Is all you ever read about in the papers. You know in some Europe countries people are starting to get angry about migrants. They say they make crime and they elect governments to stop people bringing their relatives. But in this country people are nice. They are kind. Mostly.'

'Well it's peaceful around here anyway.'

'Too peaceful for you?'

'No. I needed to . . . sort myself out.'

'You know I didn't come here as refugee. I came here as wife of New Zealand man. I met my husband in camps in Macedonia. He was relief worker.'

'Is his family from round here?'

'No, we choose here to be by sea. And work. And be with peace. But it turn out we have different ideas. I like here because it was gentle but it is too much for him. He liked to be big man saving people. When he comes here to quiet he looks around for people to save.'

'And did he find them?'

'Oh yes. He save a lot of married woman when their husbands at work,' she laughed bleakly. 'I kick him out. No good slutty man. He's gone. I get the café for payout.'

'And that's okay?'

'Yes. Of course. It's a good deal. What is your work?'

Simone hesitated. 'My last job was sponsorship manager at a television network.'

'What does that do?'

'Negotiating naming rights for TV programmes mostly.'

'A big job,' Hanife said in a tone which wasn't admiring. 'Nothing like that round here.'

'Yeah. Well. Thank goodness, in a way.'

Hanife leaned back in her chair and looked at Simone like she was appraising her in some way. For an instant Simone had the feeling she was deciding if she liked her enough to bother about being friends, but then she said, 'You want to help me make coffees? Just at busy time. Few hours a day, perhaps?'

'Okay. But I don't know how long I'll be here.'

'That's okay. I can't pay much.'

'That's okay.'

16

Long black, short black, flat white, cappuccino or latte. That was all. If you tried to order anything fancier you risked a withering glance from Hanife and directions to the nearest Starbucks, one hundred and seventy-nine kilometres away.

Simone liked the simplicity of the transaction. They came. They ordered. They paid. And she delivered what they wanted as soon as possible. If they made conversation at all it was about the shine of the sun, or the beauty of the beach, or the roll of the waves. There was none of the loaded, slippery talk of her last job. Nobody came to the counter and said things like 'we'd like to push the envelope this time' which, in her old world usually meant something borderline in terms of taste and/or morality.

The advertising executives and the brand managers who used to come and sit opposite her would mostly ask for too much. They had something to promote and it was their job to get whatever it was noticed. They'd actually have it in the shows if she let them – would have the actors drinking their brand, the newsreaders recommending their product, the game show contestants wearing their logo. They'd have their name included in, and bigger than, the title of the show. They'd flash a product image in the middle of a scene, if she let them. They inherently believed that if they pitched enough money then everything had its price. They liked fighting talk. They liked 'dominance', 'tactics', 'ambush', 'going for the jugular', and 'killing the competition'. Her role was basically to find the line between their desire for intrusiveness, and the network's appetite for their money. Another person might have liked the combative game of it, but she felt she was assisting the world down into a callow, unconscionable pit.

Somehow she'd strayed off her intended career path and

found herself an alien being in that jarring domain. She'd started out in journalism with as much idealism as any other fresh graduate – had put in her time on provincial papers, and the rest. When she first started living with Fraser she was still writing, making a reasonable, if irregular living as a freelancer. But Fraser, she soon discovered, was hopeless with money and recklessly capable of not worrying about how they'd pay their bills. At first she tried to journey with it, living for the moment, enjoying the irresponsibility. But one day she'd found herself searching down the back of the sofa for enough cash to buy bread at the dairy, and not long after she'd applied for a job at a TV network's publicity department – the first uncomfortable detour from the serious features and the prominent bylines she'd imagined she was heading towards. But she felt back then that while she had skills Fraser was gifted with an unworldly talent, a kind of emanating life force – and she found it a necessity of existence that they should both somehow remain within its glow. Her job was more a means of keeping them both afloat than anything else, and she was able to convince herself of the temporary practicality. Only in the deepest recesses of her mind did she worry about the lowering of her own aspirations – where would that ultimately leave her in the balance sheet of respect? But she had an overarching belief, which on reflection might always have been a fantasy, that she was part of a team and a time would come when he would look after her.

The real slide downwards, though, began with her miscarriage. Almost instantly she'd become too joyless and flattened to come up with enough gush for the copy. A general unhappiness inflicted itself upon her so that she wore it like chronically stubborn mange. Fraser took her off on holiday to a lovely island in Fiji to try to shake it. She used up all of her leave but came back unchanged. After a time her low output was starting to be noticed and she was spooked into applying for a job in Sponsorship. It seemed more plainly specific, was much better paid, and how hard could it be? She'd had an innate ability for publicity and on the basis of some solid past achievements she'd received what was seen, in essence, as an internal promotion. Reality hit almost immediately. She discovered she didn't have much natural instinct for resolving conflict and it required strenuous effort on her part to stand up to their reaching demands. It wasn't something she could ever have enjoyed, even under the best of circumstances.

She hesitated to leave at first because she couldn't think what else to do. *And then Fraser left her.* These momentous events of her life were irrelevant to the internal workings of a corporation. Within sight of her tears they reluctantly agreed to a further week's unpaid leave and she flew off again, this time to the resort in Vanuatu. If she'd been hoping for some miraculous tropical cure for her heart, it was mere folly. When she came back she could still hardly think at all, had slightly ruptured something inside her head. A spell of lethargy, as bad as any virus, ground her down into a moribund uselessness. She knew she was letting them win too much. She was developing a reputation for being an easy touch.

She kept it together only long enough to be invited to an advertising awards ceremony down south. She was to accompany her boss, who was presenting one of the awards. She bought a new dress. A new black dress with a low slit down the cleavage that promised a kind of flagrant sexuality she didn't feel inside. She put it on in her hotel room. She carefully applied more make-up than she'd ever worn before. She piled her hair up into a style she hoped passed for messy chic.

Young women stood at the entrance to the hotel ballroom dressed as naughty nurses, and as everybody passed by they told them to take their medicine and handed them jelly shots in little paper pill cups. People were taking two or three at a time and throwing them back as they entered, so Simone did the same, hoping for an anaesthetising effect if nothing else. By the time people had entered the room the tone had already been lowered, and as Simone tried to find the table with her place-setting she overheard a giggling woman say to the man beside her, 'Listen mutt-head how many times do I have to tell you to get your hand off my arse?' To which the man replied, 'Sorry, it's just I heard that was the way to Brazil.'

The wine flowed freely and she drank. She smiled and she drank as awards were given out. They congratulated each other effusively, these men and women around her. They were powerful communicators, they believed they could convince you of anything. That fruit drinks consisting mostly of sugar are healthy for children. That it's cool to buy big gas-gobbling SUVs and go crashing through native bush and pristine rivers. That gratuitous cleavage shots are now an ironically amusing challenge to political correctness. She smiled and she drank as people whooped and high-fived around her.

Soon the atmosphere began to erupt. The flowing alcohol brought forth the war words and the room was beginning to feel like some kind of fierce and gloating hell. Her boss leaned in and whispered in her ear, 'Anything is possible if you have honesty and sincerity faked.'

It was enough for her to look at him afresh. She'd never seen much beyond his tailored suit. His expensive shoes. His company-man exterior. All their conversations had previously been restricted to revenue targets and projected budgets. She'd assumed he bought in to all of this behaviour. To find he shared, to some extent, her disaffection was revealing. Now that she looked at him he did have a nice, crinkled smile. Clever eyes. Earlier in the evening she'd caught a hint of discreet cologne. She remembered thinking he had nice hands as he reached for a bread roll. He had a kind of innate superiority that made you want to behave. Or not.

He brought her a chocolate éclair from the buffet table and snorted into his napkin when she bit into it and cream inevitably spurted out. Before he turned in he whispered the words 'Room 517' in her ear. A deep vein of self-destructiveness flamed by three jelly shots and too much red wine led her to his hotel room door. He ushered her in with a knowing smile and asked her if she was wearing stockings or tights under that dress. She wouldn't have lifted up her hem to reveal the lacy tops of her stockings if she'd known what would happen in his bed.

Back at the network his discomfort had transformed into a seething hatred that he struggled to disguise. Everything she did at work immediately came under his coloured scrutiny. Her lack of effectiveness and extended work absences were noted. She was given a warning. Her lack of initiative and failure to broaden her goals was noted. She was given a warning.

Through sheer lack of any plan of her own she willed him to get rid of her.

She was called to a formal meeting in his office. Sitting alongside him was a woman from the human resources department who was wearing a smile of artificial geniality and a dark blue two-piece suitable for delivering a deathblow. Her boss spoke carefully. 'This is an initial meeting where we would like to discuss some proposed changes to your role.'

'Are you making me redundant?' she asked.

He glanced over at the Human Resources Manager who nodded encouragement. They were following a pre-arranged script. 'Well, it's a likely outcome but at this stage we would like to outline the proposal. Then we'll set up another appointment where you may bring a representative. Do you understand?' He spoke with weatherproof authority.

She nodded. She was relieved they were going for redundancy instead of just sacking her. She understood why. Sacking was a legal minefield these days, and this network hated negative publicity. Now this moment was here, the moment she'd both desired and feared, she felt a blurry serenity. She was ready to coolly push up her sleeves and allow them to chop off her hands.

He began reading from the proposal. 'We've decided to review the option of integrating the Sponsorship Manager's role into the existing Sales and Marketing function. There have been a number of incidents which have led to this review and these are . . .'

'Oh why don't you just make me your offer?'

'It's important we go through the correct procedures,' he replied in a clipped voice. He'd been planning this, carefully wording it. He wanted an opportunity to outline her weaknesses out loud.

'Not really that important. What is your offer?'

He looked directly at her for the first time in weeks and she stared unsteadily back at him. She could see he was suddenly torn between continuing on with the planned torture or just getting rid of her once and for all. After a brutal pause he said, 'Six weeks notice, which you will not be required to work out, plus three months further compensation as per the terms of your contract.'

'Okay. I accept your offer but I want an additional one-off payment, let's say $20,000.' She was surprised at herself, surprised at what she was about to do. She felt like she'd just come to in the middle of an underwater dive.

The HR representative leaned forward, pleased to have a chance to demonstrate her professional experience in these matters. 'I'm sorry but you have no grounds. Under clause 5.4 of your contract, we have a copy here if you'd like to see it, we've offered you the legal requirement.'

'Grounds? Well of course I would have to consult a lawyer but off the top of my head I might have a case for constructive dismissal. Or even perhaps sexual harassment. Would you say it's wrong for a senior manager to get his subordinate drunk and try to shag her in his hotel room?'

'That was private,' he hissed, losing the thin veneer of composure.

It was hardly fair, she knew, after all she'd got herself drunk. And she'd gone to his room. This was never the outcome she'd intended. But ever since that night he'd treated her like she had *dirty little slapper* tattooed on her forehead.

The representative looked at him and blanched and then said, 'Would you excuse us for a moment.' Simone went out into the hallway. Her chest was tight with anxiety and she resisted the urge to peer into his office though the slats of the venetian blind. She imagined the representative giving him a ticking off. Or perhaps he was trying to explain the circumstances without making himself look bad. *But I didn't come*, he could say.

When they called her back in again the representative had been on the phone to the executive floor upstairs. 'Terms as discussed plus I've been authorised to offer a one-off $10,000 payment. But you'll have to agree right now and sign a non-disclosure contract.'

Her boss was leaning back in his chair with his arms folded, staring fixedly at a painting on his wall, like a child refusing to play. 'Okay,' she said, shrugging, pretending indifference.

'Okay then,' the woman said, sounding relieved. 'A legal contract will be couriered to your home this afternoon. Once that's signed the payment will be processed.' She reached for the phone. 'In the meantime a security guard will escort you off the premises.'

People stared as she walked out of the building with the security guard. She knew she'd leave lots of rumours rippling around behind her but she didn't care. Or so she told herself. She'd got what she wanted, she told herself, she'd got out with some money in her pocket. But it didn't feel good. When she got home she couldn't think what to do. She climbed into bed and a couple of hours later got out again to answer her ringing cellphone. It was a guy from one of the sound studios, who obviously wasn't in any kind of gossip loop, wanting to query the pronunciation of a product name for a voice-over script. She didn't even hang up, just went over to the kitchen sink and dropped the phone into the wastemaster. The hungry silver teeth crunched down as his distant voice said, 'Hello, are you still . . .'

17

Tea, not coffee, used to be her mother's thing. China cups. Milk first. There was always the point on an outing where she would declare she 'couldn't take another step' and off they would go to the nearest café. Her mother loved the civility of it. Places which gave you teabags instead of leaf were never visited again. Her first sip would be an indication of how the rest of the afternoon would go. If there was a sigh of satisfaction, all would be well. But if the tea was lukewarm, the milk a little soured, then a mood of disappointment would linger.

This preference for tea was unusual in that she mostly liked to think of herself as somebody who did things *the French way*. That is she liked croissants with jam in the morning, liked to tie jaunty little scarves around her neck, liked to dab Chanel No5 on her wrists, and once insisted her husband buy her a Citroën.

She'd never actually been to France but had studied the language at boarding school and later, because the local school was small and desperate, and because she'd almost completed her teacher college training before she'd married, she managed to get a job three mornings a week as a French tutor. As far as Simone could tell the part of her teaching day she enjoyed the most was the moment where she turned the key in her Citroën DS, preparing to leave, and crowds of schoolboys craned their necks to see the car rise up on its haunches.

This was not the life she'd expected to lead, she was fond of telling Simone. She'd always envisaged she would have many, many children of her own to keep her busy. But she was not as *blessed* as she would have wished. And not for want of trying either, she would sometimes add with a rueful smile which always made Simone cringe and stare at the ground. Her mother lived under the illusion that had she been more blessed she would have sailed more serenely through all the domesticity involved, although that was difficult for Simone to imagine.

As the years went by, she earned herself a reputation for crabbiness. She would often end up teaching whole families of children, and she particularly seemed to pick on the siblings of ones who had come before. 'Ton grand frère lui aussi était un ignare, mais tu es encore pire,' she would spit out. Few of the children who had earned this insult had the skills to translate those words into their English meaning: *Your older brother was an ignoramus too, but now you have managed to exceed him.*

At home they noticed the worst of the crabbiness came in cycles of about four to five weeks. A poisonous rage would come over her, like a gathering of black clouds, and suddenly there would be no pleasing her. Her favourite grievance, at these times, was that there were not more in the family to love and appreciate her.

'I get only one daughter,' she would say as she slammed plates of food down on the table, 'and she has to take after her father. Not a scrap of me in her!' Simone would've done something as innocent as skip out to the shed to tell her father dinner was nearly ready, and take too long to bring him back to the table. 'Not a scrap of me,' she would screech, like that was a bad thing.

At these times many of her provocations toward Simone's father would start with the expression, 'If you were a real man . . .' As in 'If you were a real man we could afford to live somewhere better than this tinpot house.' Or 'If you were a real man we would have a better social life, instead of this boring night after night sitting in at home.' Both Simone and her father recognised these were manufactured complaints because at other times she had pride enough in her home and her husband. She never actually managed to say the one sentence she was so obviously skirting . . . 'If you were a real man we would've had more babies and I would've been happy.' This though could not be said, because even with her loosened grip on materiality, she knew this accusation to be too unjust.

Most of the hurtful slurs that came flying out of her mouth like fiery spitballs were ill thought out, designed only to shift some of the burden of her pressing discontent onto whoever was closest. And while Simone couldn't help but take on board that she amounted to a disappointing yield for her mother, her father was a whistling-hearted man who would deal with the situation by melting out to the shed and finding an important absorbing project to do until the kinder, calmer woman he regarded as his real wife would re-emerge. Sometime in the seventies he would take to whistling a song off the radio . . . *riders on the storm . . . riders on the storm . . .*

After he died so suddenly, and before her sights were reset towards remarriage and rescue in Australia, Simone's mother cultivated a belief that if life hadn't seen fit to give her what her heart desired, then at the very least she deserved to make some material demands. Among other things, she developed a habit of always making a fuss in restaurants.

'This table is in a draught,' she would tell the waiter, insisting on being moved. 'A pity we're now missing the lovely view,' she might say wistfully after they'd been reseated. Simone would sit opposite her, stomach knotted, waiting for the food to come to give her mother something else to find fault with.

Her mother would've met her match in Hanife though, Simone thought. Nobody dared make a complaint at Hanife's. There were other cafés down at the shopping centre, where people who didn't care about their coffee could go, but Hanife roasted her own beans so there was a unique quality to her brew. Regulars would come into the café with the look of addicts seeking a hit. There was no price list posted anywhere and after a few days Simone realised Hanife had a system of charging that was based on how worthy she thought the customer was.

The day trippers were charged the most. They'd enter the café tousled and giddy from their encounter with the elements and arrive at the till expecting at least a three-star conversation about the weather. In that they'd be greatly disappointed, and sometimes even visibly shocked by Hanife's rude lack of interest. As they went off to their tables they often seemed to be muttering that Hanife should be reported to some kind of tourism authority.

The morning-tea mothers were also on maximum. A chatty group would wheel in their pushchairs and begin noisily shoving tables together and rearranging chairs. They wouldn't blink as Hanife charged them her bullish prices. Some raw recruit with a newborn might say, 'Gosh I could get it cheaper down the road,' but the others would quickly shush her. Simone thought it fair to overcharge them, as they would sit at the tables for hours, spreading out their clutter of tommee tippees and plastic rattles and bowls of mush. And as they shovelled things into their toddlers' mouths, or clamped them to their breasts, they would talk loudly of feeding times, and small milestones, and sleep deprivation, and discipline, and, more often than not, poos.

The prices were considerably scaled down for those more vulnerable. Certain people Hanife accepted as somehow kindred. Like the petite goth girl who dragged in a pushchair every day containing a small boy with ears a little too low on his face. Hanife would ask kindly how she was and would even lean over the counter and pass a sweet to the boy, who would accept it solemnly, but never show any interest in sucking it. The girl, Ange, would sit with her coffee at one of the tables as far as possible from the morning-tea mothers, where she'd look across at them with both dark scorn and involuntary longing on her face. Whenever Hanife wasn't too busy she'd go over, lift the expressionless boy onto her knees, and distract Ange with quiet conversation.

The plumber was one of hers too. Every morning he'd bring his van to a noisy gassy stop in the rear car park and enter the café with a freshly lit cigarette between his lips. By the time he got to the counter he'd removed the cigarette from his mouth and had been known to park it, still burning, somewhere in his tangled beard, the better to accept his coffee and talk to Hanife. He wore a cap pulled low on his head and would squint out from beneath the peak as he passed her a book in a brown paper bag. 'A good one,' he might say in low voice. Or once, 'Thought the guy was a bit of a bed-wetter.' As Hanife took his order she'd pass him back another brown paper bag from under the counter and he'd take it stealthily, as if accepting a packet of cocaine. Hanife sometimes gave Simone a sideways look as he scrambled to the nearest table to wait for his coffee, retrieve his cigarette, and sneak a quick peak inside the bag. He wouldn't dare open it fully in a public place.

Hanife didn't allow anybody else to smoke indoors, but she quite liked that the day trippers and the mothers would glare at her plumber. Every time he came in Simone found herself willing somebody to complain so she could hear, once again, Hanife explain, as if she was talking perfect sense, that he'd filled out a form in triplicate and posted it to the Prime Minister in order to earn the right to smoke in her café.

One afternoon, when it was quiet and they were both restless, Hanife showed Simone the cheap romance novel inside the brown bag. He was too shy to buy them for himself so Hanife collected them and doled them out one by one. 'Sometime I slip in a book of literature in between. "Went on a bit," was all he said when he brought *Anna Karenina* back,' she laughed. 'Sometime he get so thrilled by the story he come knock on my door at night and say he wanna talk about it. He bring whisky too so it's okay.' She shrugged in an offhand way.

Simone liked that she didn't know what to expect from Hanife. She had none of that outspoken and mercurial nature, but admired it and liked to be around it. She wanted to be scared and amused by it, and looked forward to going to work every day. She suspected too, that Hanife enjoyed having an audience. It seemed her behaviour was becoming more and more fantastic.

Simone supposed herself to be the sort of person others somehow made their accessory. As a child her father had a way of enlisting her. Whenever they got in the car together, just the two of them, he'd always swerve off course somewhere along the way. One day he pulled into a driveway after seeing a cardboard sign and bought the goat that became infamous later for eating her mother's roses. Another time he stopped to visit an old friend and they came away with a boat attached to the tow bar. Once he had driven for miles and miles along a hill road, making her miss the first round in her away-game netball tournament, just because he wanted to find out what was at the top, which turned out to be nothing but a nice view. He never did these kinds of things when her mother was in the car.

And then there was Fraser. He'd often bring people home for dinner unannounced. Some malnourished ex-colleague from art school who was failing to make a living. Or a street performer he'd got talking to outside a shop. Maybe a homeless man needing a bath who he'd found sleeping on a park bench. Or a bewildered and homesick German backpacker. One time he came home with the effeminate Samoan boy who'd packed the groceries she'd sent him out for.

He'd pick them up like stray kittens and occasionally they were the sort of people she might not have felt comfortable with if she was on her own, but somehow Fraser made it okay. He had a knack for making them feel they were his friend. He drew them out, went in all their crazy directions, and talked to them on a level that made them feel respected. But it made him feel good too. He liked to think that he alone had seen their inner worth. But he needed her to be his witness.

He liked to appear generous, although it was her that stood in the kitchen dishing up bowls of hot food. She knew they often looked at her and thought he was lucky to have somebody like her to come home to. If it wasn't for her he might just appear like some eccentric guy with suspect motives. Mostly she admired him for doing it, liked to be forced outside her own limits, liked to be caught up in his acts of generosity. Without it she was afraid she'd end up living like her mother in Australia, spending all her time making sure every surface was immaculate, how she'd planned it, without mess, without personal exposure, rigorously plugging up all the places from which her buried regrets could leak out.

She wondered if Fraser still brought those people home to his new partner. She liked the possibility of that woman's discomfort.

A man and two children noisily entered the café, and the children immediately began squabbling over which ice cream they were going to have, because apparently they couldn't have the same one. 'Howdy,' said the father at the counter. Hanife didn't reply but waited for him to state his order. Taken aback, but trying not to show it, he asked for 'a good strong coffee' in an American accent and told his children to hurry up and make up their minds because in another second they wouldn't get any. When they moved off to a table Hanife leaned in to Simone, 'Sometimes I do my pelvic floor exercises while I serve people,' she whispered. 'You should try it.'

After the lunch rush was over, Hanife began wiping the bench down, working her way towards the coffee machine and Simone. 'This broken heart you have,' she enquired, 'it was a man?'

Simone nodded, 'He left me for another woman.'

'And you want him back?'

She shrugged and began grinding some beans. When Hanife had first shown Simone what to do she'd told her that making coffee wasn't an ordinary skill. The most important part, she said, was the roasting of the beans, and this she still did herself because it was a matter of instinct. Hanife preferred the customers to order a short black. For these customers, she said, we will make a true coffee to vibrate the bones. It wasn't often Simone was tempted to make one for herself, just breathing it in was stimulant enough to dry her eyeballs, and by the end of the day caffeine seemed to have penetrated the layers of her skin.

Once she'd mastered the procedures she began to amuse herself privately by striving for flair with each minute movement. The way she tamped down the coffee, the way she clicked the lever into place, placement of the cup beneath, frothing of the milk. She tried to do it all with a certain musicality but with Hanife watching her so closely her timing stumbled a little.

'You want him back even when he show he has this perishing kind of love?' Hanife asked, standing so close Simone could smell the spiciness of her skin over the coffee.

'It was complicated,' she replied, not wanting to appear weak, but also not wishing to be less than truthful.

'Well, you know what they say. Plenty more fishes,' Hanife said, pointing vaguely out the window. 'No need to obsess on him. You think you let him go now?'

Simone distractedly followed the line of Hanife's finger, thinking about how a few days before she'd overheard Toss complaining he couldn't catch any decent snapper off the beach any more because of the commercial trawlers. And lately actual statistics showing the shortage of men compared to available women were frequently offered up in the media, sometimes with the seemingly gleeful intent to make single women feel hopeless.

'You know what made it so hard? I couldn't see what it was he saw in that woman he went off with. She always seemed sort of . . . limited, to me. I mean, if he had to go off with somebody else then I wish it was somebody I could've been more impressed by.'

Hanife nodded. 'Like my husband too. That's what men do. Some women make them feel like bigger man. Men don't think like us. Much lower down.' They smirked at each other for a moment, knowing this to be too easy, but Simone was in the mood to accept a primitive explanation. She finished making the coffees and took them to the tables. When she came back she asked Hanife if she missed her husband.

'I tell you a story,' Hanife said. 'When I first meet my husband he was doing something very kind. I think I tell myself he's a good man, the kind of man to marry, but I don't think I love him. It just happen he found me at a certain time, and in a way I was lucky. He help me escape from a bad life.'

'But you're not sorry he's gone?'

'When we get here I think he saw in my eye I don't care about him the way he care about me. So that's when all the other women start. Now I can go acting all the time like I was the one who got wronged, but truth is I hurted him too. Still, it make a better story, eh, to be the innocent one.' She gave Simone a long look, as if she knew this truth to be universal.

18

Clara's front window was thrown open as Simone was passing. 'Drink?' Clara called, clinking the ice around in her glass. By the time Simone was through the front door a gin and tonic had been mixed for her. Marjorie was already moored within the soft cushions of the sofa, glass in hand. A John Coltrane recording was playing so softly on the stereo that only the peaks could really be heard.

'I was just telling Marjorie about my terrible day,' Clara said, explaining Charlie had gone missing. She'd raced up and down the road trying to find him, and just as she was beginning to panic a bus had pulled up with Charlie on board. He'd been walking along the main road and the kindly local driver picked him up, going off his route to drop him home. 'I couldn't help turning into a bit of an angry old shrew and I sent him packing off to bed,' Clara told her, laughing in a tight, sad way. 'Honestly! I don't know.'

Marjorie said, 'I was just saying to Clara, there'll come a time . . .'

Briskly Clara interrupted, 'And I was just saying to Marjorie, I don't want to hear it. I just wish there was something I could do about the wandering, that's all, to keep him safe.'

Without really thinking what she was saying Simone began to tell a story about a dog belonging to the friend of a friend. It used to run away all the time and the owner would spend hours driving around the streets looking for it and when he got it back home he'd give it a telling off and it would run away again the next day. Her friend figured out that the dog always got the scolding once it was back inside the house so it'd begun to associate the disciplining with coming home. So he suggested to his mate he should scold the puppy where he found him and then give it a treat when it got back to the house.

'And?' said Marjorie. 'Did it work?'

'Well it seemed it did, more or less.'

'Right. So you two think its okay to associate Charlie's behaviour with a dog do you?' Clara asked quite forcefully.

'No, no. I'm sorry,' Simone exclaimed, reddening a little. 'I didn't mean . . .'

'It's okay,' Clara said. 'You might be right. I probably should give him a kiss and a piece of bloody cake or something when he gets back to the house.' She sighed, sounded exhausted. 'It's just I can't help getting upset about it all. I know I shouldn't but I can't help taking his running away as a personal thing, like he's trying to escape from me or something.'

'Where is he going?' Simone asked. 'Does he ever say?'

'Well if I ask him he always says there was something he had to do, but he's vague about it,' Clara told her. 'It's difficult to make sense of but it's like he leaves the house in search of something, but as soon as he's out the door he forgets what it is and thinks if he keeps on walking he'll find it. Or something like that. Or maybe nothing like that. I really don't know.'

'That's the trouble with it,' Marjorie said. 'There isn't any logic.'

'Anyway, let's change the subject. I've had enough for today,' Clara said, holding her drink up in the air. 'Cheers, girls. Here's to something else.'

'But don't you think it's starting to get a bit much now?' Marjorie persisted. 'You're not going to be able to manage for much longer. Perhaps it's time to start investigating . . .' She trailed off, unwilling to say it exactly.

The last of the day's light slanted lengthways in through the windows and Clara got out of her chair to switch on the art deco lamp which sat on her sideboard. She was silent for a little while and then said, 'Let me tell you about how I met Charlie.' There was now a slightly stubborn note in her voice. She told them she'd grown up on a big sheep station in Hawkes Bay. Her mother, a strong-minded woman, had badly wanted Clara to marry somebody with the prospect of land, as she herself had done. She made sure that by the time her daughter was of marriageable age she knew all about weekly menus, and preserves, and keeping laying chickens, and managing household staff, and all the other skills that might be useful in her future. But what Clara really loved to do was sew. She was allowed to subscribe to a monthly magazine from London. They had to come by sea in those days and it was always months old by the time it got there, but as soon as it arrived the local book store owner would ring to say the order was in and she would beg and nag for somebody to run her into town to collect it. Her next stop would always be the local haberdashers for fabric and then she'd spend all her time behind the sewing machine recreating the fashions within the pages. Her parents treated this obsession as an adolescent amusement she'd grow out of soon enough, but the reason she liked making those clothes was that they made her feel she belonged to some wider world, at least for a little while. Her mother soon began to hint that what she really ought to be concentrating on was her own wedding dress and by the time Clara was nineteen she'd obediently become engaged to a boy called Royston whose father owned a holding just down the road. She'd gone to school with him, their mothers were close friends, their fathers helped each other out with stock, and their whole lives they had gone to practically all the same social events. They already knew everything there was to know about each other and he was kind and good and regular.

'And then one day this dance band turned up in town.' In those days, Clara commented to Simone, a Saturday night dance was the highlight of their week and the better known dance bands used to tour the country.

'Yes, I remember those dances,' Marjorie said. 'It's what we did before the days of television. Matinees and dances.'

This band, Clara said, was billeted in their town for a couple of days and everybody noticed. They hung around the milk bar with their slicked back hair, and their leather ex-RAF jackets looking like big-city trouble, and all the parents were worried.

'Those were the types they used to call the Milk Bar

Cowboys back then,' Marjorie interjected in a tone of voice which implied she'd had the good sense to steer well clear of those *types* herself.

'Yes, well they were just a bunch of silly posing young men, I suppose, but they liked whistling at the girls as they went past so of course we went past, and we went past,' Clara laughed. She told them that at first, on Saturday night, she hadn't particularly noticed Charlie behind his big double bass. But then in one instant he picked her out and smiled down at her from the stage and he didn't take his eyes away from her and she began to feel like she'd been shot through the stomach.

'Later I went to the ladies' room and he was slouching near the edge of the hall, having a smoke, and when I came out he was waiting for me. "Like your clothes," he said. "I've noticed you about," he said. And then he took a long cool draw on his cigarette and added, "and I reckon this town is too small for a girl like you." And you know at that moment I felt like something inside me just went ping, as if I'd been waiting my whole life for somebody to notice that much about me.'

'So you broke off the engagement?' Marjorie asked.

'Well technically Royston broke it off when he found us snogging in the back of one of those big old Fords.' After that she moved to the city and Charlie, who knew all sorts of interesting people, helped her get a job at a hairdressers. 'All day we girls used to pore over fashion books,' she said. 'And at night I'd sew up these way-out clothes and on the weekends go out dancing wherever Charlie was playing. People used to queue around corners to get in to see their band back then. He was already married, of course, had married very young after getting his girlfriend pregnant at seventeen, but I never thought about it much. I was smitten, and he said it had been a big mistake. It just felt like the two of us were living by different rules than everybody else. And then a couple of years later he decided to go to London because he could play more over there. He took me with him and left his wife and kids behind.'

She paused and looked directly at Marjorie. 'So you see

126

hardly a day has passed by when I haven't felt grateful to him for saving me from a different kind of life. So why would I not make a few sacrifices now for him, in his hour of need?'

Marjorie wasn't quite able to limit the reproof in her voice as she asked, 'And the wife?'

'Well yes. I didn't really care at the time, but sometimes I look back on it now and think how hard it must've been for her.'

'But you don't really think you can cope with it all on your own, do you?' Marjorie said. 'It's progressive, of course. With Stanley's mother it just got worse and worse and . . .'

'I know how it goes Marjorie. It's amazing how people always tell me stories about how bad it gets. About cranky old men who spray all over the toilet walls just because they feel like it. About the poor souls who unzip their flies and fiddle with themselves. And the ones that spit their food at you and tell you you're trying to poison them. But right now that's not what we're going through, and mostly we're okay and I'm a bit sick of hearing it.'

'Well far be it for me to be like that . . . I was just trying to be practical, dear,' Marjorie remarked. She shot Simone a quick look that implied she expected some support, but Simone didn't think this was the way to help. For Clara life was offering up a view of the future that was like looking through the wrong end of a telescope, with everything she valued becoming smaller, and less dependable, and right now, today, Clara clearly didn't want to be forced to look.

'Marjorie, he's not so bad,' Clara said irritably, her face becoming just a little flushed. 'Every day there are still times when the confusion clears a little and for however long he's my funny Charlie again. Why should I think ahead? I'm happy to live for those moments.'

'But the confusion, as you call it, will eventually . . .'

'What do you sell in the shop, Marjorie?' Simone interrupted. Marjorie had, for a moment, reminded her of the way her mother liked to battle onwards, blind to certain important signals. Travelling through France once, Simone had discovered the school pronunciation her mother had taught was completely unrecognisable to the French. She'd been awed then by the knowledge her mother had ploughed on through so many generations of children, operating a syllabus in a practical way but steadfastly oblivious to the finer context. Marjorie had some of her stoic determination, and this afternoon her pursuit of an efficiently pragmatic solution was all the more uncomfortable because she didn't seem quite willing to acknowledge the lovely, rare kind of love at the root of the problem.

Marjorie took a vague sip of her drink before saying, 'Well we just sell a few local bits and pieces. It's a collective. I work there part-time, a couple of days a week.'

'I think I'll just go find us a nibble or two,' Clara said, getting up from her chair, and moving out of the room.

'And you? Do you make something?' Simone asked, thinking of the glimpses she sometimes caught, while out walking Clouseau at night, of Marjorie sitting down at her dinner table with her single plate in front of her, and a long, lone night stretching ahead of her.

'I just sell my silly old photos,' Marjorie said.

'Photos?'

'Yes. They're aeons old now. But they seem to have come into fashion somehow.' Marjorie explained her husband had been a diplomat and during the seventies they lived in a number of foreign countries for a while. She wasn't allowed to work, and they had staff to do everything for them, so to keep busy she spent her days teaching herself photography, taking instruction from imported books.

How cruelly Marjorie had been robbed by her husband's incarceration, Simone thought. It must have been on those diplomatic postings where she'd acquired that air of highbred authority. Now she'd been left behind to reclaim whatever weight she could in a domain so small it was almost a void. 'What kind of things?' Simone asked.

'Oh just people going about their day. The markets. We

lived in Russia during the cold war and the people there were suspicious of Westerners with cameras. One had to keep it casual, snapping things here and there during the day, like a tourist,' she explained. 'Everything was so erratic that whenever you went to the market and saw something useful you had to buy as much as possible. So I have one photo of women trudging home in the snow with enormous bundles of toilet paper tied up with string. That's the sort of thing. Poor blighters, even then it was the texture of sandpaper. We had ours imported from Helsinki, of course.'

'They sound interesting,' Simone said.

Clara reappeared at the doorway with a small bowl of cashew nuts just as Simone was casually asking if Stanley was still a diplomat.

'Oh no, he gave all that up,' Marjorie said without blinking.

'More, anyone?' Clara asked, impassive. She refilled their glasses and offered around the salted nuts. 'Did you pass Toss in his tux?' she asked Simone.

'Toss?'

'On the way to the point?'

'Oh yes, I think I did see him,' Simone said, thinking back to her walk home from the café. There'd been an atmosphere of closing up for the night on the beach. The low late sun had dipped behind the dunes, leaving long shadows and the chill air which chased out the last, lingering day trippers. And off in the far distance, Simone remembered now, she'd seen the lonely figure of a man heading out towards the point. 'But what was he doing in a tux?'

'He does it every year,' Clara said.

'On the anniversary of his wife's death,' Marjorie added.

'He takes his clarinet and plays a tune on the spot where his wife's ashes were scattered at sundown.'

'Gosh I never would've taken him for the sentimental type.'

'You'd be surprised,' Clara said, explaining he could only

129

actually play one song. He'd bought the clarinet and taken some secret lessons so he could play it for his wife as a surprise on their forty-fifth wedding anniversary, four years ago.

'But by the time the day came around she was in the hospice,' Marjorie said.

'So did he get to play it?'

'Oh yes! He was determined. All the nurses crowded into the room, and when he got to the end of the song there wasn't a dry eye in the house.'

'Were you there too?'

'Oh yes. The lot of us were. She was very, very sick by then, had hardly spoken for days but the smile on her face was priceless.'

'What was the song?'

'"The Glory of Love".'

'Sweet.'

'Yes. It's strange to say this but sometimes I think she was the luckiest of all of us in a way,' Marjorie said. 'Totally adored right up until the very minute she died.'

19

Simone had begun spending her evenings in the shed experimenting with making little lidded wooden boxes. It'd started when she found some weathered fence posts on the beach and cut into them. She had been surprised by their rich red core, still alive despite their fossilised appearance. Before she commenced any piece she'd always hold the wood in her hands, feeling for its individuality.

Sometimes the wood was warped and knotted and the shape of the box would be dictated by the deformities. She'd tried different methods for abutting the edges, at first nailing and gluing, and after a few failures, perfecting a rudimentary dovetailing technique. Some she decorated with insets or mosaics, using odd things she picked up on her walks – twisted shells and salt-bleached bird bones, and sea glass, and strange fragments of creatures from the deep, and sometimes other more human leavings like crushed bottle tops, scraps of pages, and unrecognisable plastic things. The more lopsided and imperfect and characterful the better.

She wasn't making them for any particular reason. She didn't really know exactly what it was about the patterning of these pieces that was so appealing, only that the basic anatomy of making something from scratch was a fundamental and constructive thing to do. She felt like the finished objects provided some irrefutable evidence against the passing notion that she didn't really exist any more, and was merely wandering around as a self-deceiving ghost. It had become a compulsion.

She'd begun to paint patterns on the interiors too, and then one night she put some of Alice's dolls inside. At first she'd just liked how macabre their prone little bodies looked when you opened the lid, but soon she was looking around for other things to go inside the boxes along with the dolls.

In the cutlery drawer, where the teaspoons were meant to go, she'd found some tiny pieces of a doll's tea set, and these inspired her, this evening, to begin fashioning two little chairs and a small table. As she worked she found herself humming Toss's song. She could just picture him getting ready. Brushing down his tux. Taking out a fresh pair of those big white underpants she sees scaring the sparrows from his washing line. Standing in front of the mirror to check himself out, perhaps sucking in his stomach a little as he realises the tuxedo doesn't quite fit the way it used to. He probably would've buffed up his shoes too. On his way out he may have picked one of those flirty red roses from the bush near his front porch.

'The Glory of Love' was the kind of song that could be played two ways. Slowly it could be the saddest song in the world. Or, like Bette Midler, you could belt it out with a hearty skipping joy.

You've got to give a little, take a little . . .

Simone decided Toss, the jolly-joker of the neighbourhood, probably played it a little bit upbeat, rushing over . . . *and let your poor heart break a little.*

But why had he picked that particular song? They were married for forty-five years, perhaps there was a moment when he and his wife were young. Perhaps the day they met. Maybe they were at a dance together and he was in his tux and as he held her close she put her mouth to his ear and hummed along with the band:

You've got to laugh a little, cry a little
Until the clouds roll by a little . . .

That's the kind of thing that would've intrigued Fraser. He was always attached to the idea that something beautiful only ever came from a certain type of melancholia. He would seek it out in the music he listened to while he was working – searching for the perfect moment of rawness, of beautiful–terrible, of exquisite pain. That was his inspiration. For weeks, sometimes months, he wouldn't be able to work without the accompanying backdrop of whichever performer was occupying him, or rather, he was trying to occupy. He'd buy every recording he could of a particular artist, and from there work his way back through the influences until he'd peeled everything back to its core, in the hope of excavating some truth. He'd listen to those lyrics endlessly, obsessively, repetitively – without the fear of crossover taint, of unintentional influence, that his musician friends had.

If he'd had the talent he probably would've preferred to be a musician, but instead he found some consolation in the way he approached his work. He listened as if he was trying to climb into the hearts of all the damaged, lost boys whose music he liked. From them he drew artistic energy, their motifs began to subtly slip into his pieces. And from them he accepted that love was not love unless it was heightened, aching, passionate, and more or less doomed. Love, as Gram Parsons sang so angelically, hurts.

What chance, then, did the mundane reality of everyday life ever have? He'd emerge from his studio mid-obsession, half-crazed, burning with impassioned ideals, intoxicated with romantic dysfunction. And he'd find her doing something necessary and ordinary, like washing the dishes, or sorting the laundry. She'd always be disappointed to be caught like that, amid chores. She'd have preferred to be thought of as a more interesting muse.

'Listen to this,' he said one day, emerging from his studio carrying a record in his hands, an enthusiastic, self-gratified grin on his face. 'Listen.' He put a recording of Alex Chilton singing the song that began . . . *there was a boy* . . . on the stereo. 'Did you hear it?' he asked. Simone had listened carefully, not knowing exactly what she was supposed to find. He turned it up and played it again.

'There, that moment. That soft little clunk in the background. What do you think that is?' He hardly waited for her reply, he was bursting to share the one small moment he now owned because he was the one who'd found it. 'I reckon it's the music falling on the piano,' he said. 'And listen to his voice. See? It sounds like he might be suppressing a laugh. Just for an instant.

I love that they kept that take, with its tiny flaw. I love that the whole performance mattered more.'

And he went on to show her the moment he loved above all others on the same record, where somebody bangs on a cowbell for no particularly good reason. A moment of accidental genius, his favourite kind.

Simone took the tiny teapot and two tiny cups and glued them to the table. She seated a small doll in each of the chairs and attached a dot of glue to the bottom of the chair legs and the four table legs. She placed the table and chairs inside the box and turned the dolls heads so they were looking upwards. Then she closed the lid. After a few moments she opened the lid again and the two little dolls looked up at her as if she was rudely interrupting their private conversation.

The next time she saw Toss he was out digging in the garden with a very strangely dressed man. As she approached Toss called out, 'We've got some lovely big carrots today.'

She scrutinised his face to see if he was being suggestive, perhaps making some inference about Ollie's visit, but it didn't seem so. He came over to the fence proudly holding up some big, bright, almost-radioactive looking carrots by their foliage. The other man came up behind him and Simone noticed the resemblance. He was muttering, and it seemed to be about her.

'Average height,' he said. 'Approximately thirty-five years of age. Shoulder-length, darkish hair. Tight jeans, sweatshirt the colour of our garden hose, and two-toned sneakers with worn bits. Coffee-coloured stain lower centre front of shirt.' The man was somehow able to achieve this unflattering appraisal without even looking directly at her.

Toss chuckled and introduced his son, Hughie. 'That's his thing. Gonna be the Chief of Police some day, aren't you son.' He moved to playfully punch him on the shoulder but his son wriggled away from his touch.

'Approximately forty,' Simone thought, 'but perhaps somewhat younger developmentally. Dark home-cut hair, dumpy around the waist, dressed in blue overalls with a silver cape, impossible to tell the colour of his eyes because of evasive nature of eye contact.'

'Hello Hughie,' she said.

Hughie walked away, back to the garden. There was something not quite right about his movement. 'Say hello to Simone, son,' Toss urged, but Hughie didn't respond. 'Bit shy,' Toss explained. 'He's spending the day with his old Dad and I told him we'd be putting in some tomatoes. Now he's on a roll he's keen to get on with it, aren't you, son.'

Hughie shrugged grumpily and Toss laughed but there was also the briefest flash of exasperation in his face. Simone imagined Toss might feel the loss of his wife most keenly through this relationship with his son. He was an old man left with the lonely difficulty of loving this boy, whose affection seemed hard earned. They looked incomplete and uncomfortable together, like there was a big gap between them, a gap that used to be filled by someone softer, more embracing, more tender. Simone wondered where he lived normally. A sheltered home perhaps.

'Well, can't hold off the horses any longer,' Toss said. 'Best get on. I'll pop these beauties on your doorstep later, eh lass.'

As Simone walked on to the café she couldn't help smiling over the small vanity that Toss's son had underestimated her age by five years. Although she also liked to believe her just-tumbled-out-of-bed look had a kind of louche, understated sexiness, but his description stole some confidence from that thought.

She'd occasionally seen Toss get into a car with another elderly man, perhaps he was being driven off to visit his son. The other man would draw up outside Toss's house and toot and Toss would come out, usually with an offering from his garden in hand, and climb into the car. They'd drive off and for some reason Simone always found the glimpse of two old men companionably going off on some sort of day trip strangely touching. She'd often found herself wondering what they talked about. Did they discuss their history? What they missed? The

135

great imaginative leaps they'd had that week? Did they begin sentences with things like, 'I read in the latest *Scientific Weekly* . . .'? Or was it all just the plain old stuff of daily living – the weather? the price of petrol? Toss's cabbages?

They often made her think of the friendship her father had once had with Taffy, whom he had known from the local RSA, although Taffy was the only one of them who had actually served during a war. Later on Taffy retired from his job at the Post Office, his wife died, and he began to hang around her father's workshop. He'd listen to the talk, make cups of tea, sweep away the sawdust, deliver the orders in the truck. He wouldn't accept any money because he said it would mess with his pension. They had a kind of gentlemen's agreement where every Friday her father would tell Taffy he had an errand he needed to run and would ask to borrow his car. Taffy would shrug and hand him the keys and her father would return an hour later, having filled the car with petrol and loaded the back seat with enough groceries and booze to keep Taffy going for another week.

She once witnessed one of their stickier moments, when her father had a hangover and was trying to do something tricky on the lathe and Taffy stood beside him going on and on about the old widow who lived next door and had trimmed her box hedge practically to the ground. Her father suddenly threw down the chair leg he was working on and said, 'Christ, Taffy, sometimes you are enough to drive a man to drink. I'll give you fifty bucks right now if you'll just belt up and go home for the day!'

Poor Taffy's face collapsed. There was a pained silence for a few moments and then he said, 'No, I won't do that. But I will go out the back and start making up that order of gates.' He went out through the side door, pulling it shut behind him so gently it made as big a statement as if he had slammed it.

Her father went over to the bench and made himself an instant coffee. He took his mug to the window and looked out at Taffy for a few moments before going back to his lathe. He didn't turn it on straight away, but sat scratching the back of his head, and then without looking up, muttered guiltily, 'Well a man's friendship ought to be able to take a bit of straight talking now and again, surely.'

Down on the beach, past the cockle bed where a gang of sandpipers do their best work, past the old dinghy skeleton that Clouseau likes to greet with a lifted back leg, it occurred to Simone that when you've been parted from somebody you've loved it's like having rubber bands attached to your backs while you head off in opposite directions. The smallest intimacies are the ones that snap first and are forgotten. Common, banal things like knowing their preferences for coffee over tea, or a shared liking for a particular television programme. Other things stretch further, take much longer to break, leaving their painful welts. Those particular turns of phrase. The transferred affection in a smile. The intimacy of knowing their most interesting singular obsessions. Shared hopes.

The hardest thing not to miss about Fraser was his grand confidence of living, the feeling that fortune was smiling brightly when he was around. It was Fraser's friend who had the runaway dog and Fraser often liked to tell that story as a demonstration of his own superior intuition. It was amazing how easy it was to accept. But actually, as far as dogs were concerned anyway, it was pretty simple psychology. There were two things that always made it seem remarkable. The first was that the friend, who owned the dog, hadn't figured it out for himself. And the second was the way Fraser told it. Somehow his own unswerving confidence that this anecdote was further evidence he had some kind of exceptional endowment always made others believe it too. It was a bit like that when they first discovered they were the same age. 'That was a very good year,' he announced, but said it in such a way that for him it was a bold fact of birthright, and for her an accident of lucky association.

20

'I've found you at last. Surprise! An old lady told me I'd find you here.'

Simone looked up from her work to find Ingrid at the counter. She walked around and hugged her friend, breathing in the warm, familiar smell of her – the mingling perfumes of her scent, her hair gel, the lemony smell of her clothes, and the faintly sweetsour trace a toddler manages to leave on his mother's skin. 'My God. What on earth are you doing here?' she asked.

'Can't a girl just spring a visit on her mate?' Ingrid replied. 'Or is that not allowed in your hideout?'

'Hideout? You make it sound like I'm a crim on the run. Wasn't I just doing Lexie's family a favour?'

'Of course you are,' Ingrid said, smiling to show she hadn't meant to imply anything else, at least not expressly. 'God that coffee smells great. Can I have one right now?'

As Simone turned to make the coffee, she was glad for a brief, gathering diversion. A couple of minutes ago she'd been quietly doing her job, a day like any other day, operating within the slow predictable rhythm of this life she'd taken on. And now, suddenly, here was Ingrid – alive and just a bit hyper – sweeping in the uncertain residue of the city in her wake. For the briefest of moments she wondered if she would've dived under the counter if she'd seen Ingrid first.

Hanife came back from the car park where she'd been talking to the woman who delivers the cake selection, and Simone introduced them. Ingrid leaned on the counter, waiting for her coffee, and chatted to Hanife about the long drive and the lovely spring sunshine. She was so effusive there was no need for Hanife to say anything back, so sparkling and cheerful she made everybody else feel uneasy.

They carried their coffees out to the beach, sitting down in a flat sunny dip between two dunes. 'Staying the night?' Simone enquired.

'No, I can't. The kids,' Ingrid said, stretching her legs out in front of her and smiling apologetically. 'Just wanted to get out of the house for a bit. So, what have you been up to?'

'A three-and-a-half-hour trip! It's lovely to see you but that's quite an afternoon drive.'

'I know. One minute I was driving Isobel to school and then I just decided to drop Todd off at Mum's and hit the road.' After a pause she added, 'And I wanted to see you, of course.'

'Any special reason?'

Ingrid didn't reply immediately but slung her free arm across Simone's shoulders. It was the kind of gesture which would've been absolutely fine if they were drunk, or drinking, or at least having a laugh together, but sitting in the sand balancing hot coffees it was a little unnatural. 'Bastard, isn't he,' she said. 'Driving you out of town like this.'

Simone realised Ingrid was saying this as something of an opener, but the pointedness of it, and the chummy arm across her shoulder, provoked her into replying as obliquely as possible. 'But it's nice here,' she said. 'Besides I didn't come here because of him.'

Ingrid set her coffee down in the sand, rummaged around in her bag and brought out a packet of cigarettes.

'You're smoking now?' Simone said.

'A mummy's gotta have her secret vice,' Ingrid replied drolly. 'Want one?' Simone took the offered cigarette. Ingrid was making her nervous.

'Actually you probably did the right thing getting out of town,' Ingrid conceded. 'If my husband ever had an affair I'd like to think I'd do something dramatic. Kick his arse anyway. Kick his arse, slam the door, and forget him.'

Ingrid had said this kind of thing before. She'd never been all that interested in the intricacies of what had happened with Fraser in the end. The fact he'd started an affair was evidence enough he was at fault, irredeemable and hardly worth a backward look. As Simone drew smoke into her lungs she thought saying you were going to slam the door and forget him was too easy, too simply reductive. Just as sitting on the sand and agreeing Fraser's a bastard would do nothing more than reduce everything they'd ever been to one act at the very end. The whole of it is not broken so easily. It might be a matter of record that Fraser *behaved* like a bastard, but even in doing something so intractable and unforgivable he hadn't essentially changed his character. Somebody, she couldn't remember who, had once described him as guileless and she had thought that perfectly apt. He was like a charming but thoughtless child, who never intentionally set out to hurt other people, but it was his lack of the right kind of effort that was the most wounding of all. In Simone's mind, to be able to slam the door and instantly forget was not to have loved much in the first place.

Ingrid lay back, using her handbag as a pillow to keep the sand from her hair. Looking up at the clouds she said, 'You know sometimes I dream of being free enough to run off somewhere.'

'Like here?'

'God no. It's too cold to even swim here. I mean overseas. If you wanted to you could just get on a plane to New York tomorrow. How fab would that be? Or Paris. Or anywhere.'

Right now Simone could only picture herself gazing up at the top of tall buildings in New York and feeling too insubstantial to cope. 'You know I don't really want to at the moment, but maybe if you see Fraser you could just tell him that as far as you know I'm in Europe somewhere.'

'Can do,' Ingrid giggled. 'But I'd be off around the world if I was you. In a way I'm quite envious of your freedom. I'm so rooted down in friggin' school lunches and bedtime stories and buying vegetables at the organic greengrocers.'

'I thought you loved all that.'

'Nah. Wanna swap?'

'You don't mean that.'

'No. Probably not.'

Simone lay back beside Ingrid. 'What would I want with all that noise and trouble anyway?'

Ingrid nodded her head up and down, as if this made perfect sense to her. 'You know this morning I was driving away from the school with little Todd strapped in the back. Anyway this guy pulls out in front of me and I slam my hand on the horn, and then Todd said in a sweet little voice, "Was that a wanker, Mummy?" And I realised he thought that was the definitive word for a bad driver. I'm so angry all the time I'm driving around swearing at people in front of my kid, who's only three, and I don't even know I'm doing it.'

'Why are you angry all the time? I thought you were sort of . . .'

Ingrid shrugged. 'Happy? Who's happy? I thought you and Fraser were happy.'

'Well, yeah.'

Ingrid rolled onto her side, and supporting her head with one arm, looked at Simone with deadeye intensity. 'Do you still think . . . you know . . . about the baby thing?'

Simone sat up. 'Not really,' she said. She flicked a sandhopper off her knee and then added, more conclusively, 'I'm over all that now.'

There was a pause before Ingrid said, 'Well that's good then.' They had known each other for a long time. Simone knew Ingrid so well she knew that when she'd conceived her first child she'd waited for her husband to leave the room and had done a handstand against the wardrobe door. She knew her children didn't ever get earwax but sometimes she'd wished they did just so she'd have the satisfaction of putting a cotton bud in their ears and coming out with something. And she also knew that once when her husband was fucking her from behind he'd offered to pay to have the long black hairs on the back of her legs permanently removed. And Ingrid knew her well enough to at least allow her a bit of faked equanimity.

'Sometimes I think there's a kind of terrible conspiracy to

get women to have babies,' Ingrid said, flopping lazily onto her back. 'You meet these women with their first baby and they bang on about how great it is, how there's nothing else like it, how they've found the meaning of life and you ought to do it too. And as soon as you do it all changes and they start talking about how hard it is, and how invisible they feel, and how they're tired all the time and how they grieve for their lost life. And then they have a second one and they start going on about how much better two is than one, and you should have another one too. Then as soon as you're in that club they start on about how much more time everything takes, and how their life is destroyed, and how they wish they'd stuck with one.'

'Do you?'

'What?'

'Wish you'd stuck with one?'

Ingrid didn't answer immediately. 'Sometimes I wish I'd stuck with none . . . but . . . well when you already have them you can't possibly wish them away.'

For a little while neither of them spoke. They both turned their gaze towards the tide's edge where three small children were playing a game of chicken with the oncoming waves. They were standing ankle deep in the water, and at the very last minute running away squealing. One little smart-alecky boy left it too late and got bowled by a huge, thrashing wave. Simone instinctively jumped to her feet but the boy's two little girlfriends picked him up off the sand as the wave receded and he ran up the beach, screaming for his mother. When Simone looked back Ingrid was busy lighting a fresh cigarette off the end of her last one. 'Do you think it's possible to stay with someone when you've seen a hole in their moral fibre?' she asked.

'What? What are you talking about?'

'You know how you are just trucking along and then one day you have a great moment of clarity and everything from the back of your head falls into place, and suddenly you can't help seeing somebody differently.'

'Well yes, but enlighten me.'

142

'Okay,' Ingrid shrugged, 'I was at a children's party last week and this woman I know came up to me, she's sort of a friend of a friend, but we've been to dinner parties together. One of her kids is at school with Isobel. Anyway she comes up to me and says she doesn't know how my husband can sit with her at a dinner one night and then the next thing you know he's representing the bastard who assaulted her sister. She went on and on, yelling into my face, and I was in shock.'

They stopped talking for a moment as the mother of the wet boy came stomping past them, holding him sniffling in her arms inside a towel. 'Well it's your fault,' she was telling him, 'you'll just have to stay in the damn towel all the way home now.'

'A day at the beach always ends in tears,' Ingrid whispered. Simone smiled and looked over her shoulder at the woman and saw Clouseau lying on the deck of the café with a deflated beach ball in his mouth.

'You know I didn't even know her sister had been assaulted,' Ingrid continued. 'And I didn't know Robert had taken the case. Anyway I left in tears. Later on I asked Robert about it. He reckoned it was his duty to take it on. He trotted out the old "everybody deserves a defence" argument. So now I can never face that woman again.'

'And that makes you struggle with your marriage?' Simone asked. She realised how tightly she'd been holding herself in anticipation, wondering what had really made Ingrid come all this way. Now she figured it must be for this reason – to sound out her doubts.

Ingrid sighed hard. 'But it isn't just that. He had another case, the son of this dubious rich bastard, the kid was accused of participating in some kind of credit card scam. He did it, but Robert got him off on a technicality. And that night he came home with a magnum of champagne. And I started really thinking about what it was he did for a living. Representing bastards mostly.'

'Surely not always?'

'It's all about winning with him. Winning, winning, at

whatever cost. Suddenly everything in our lives feels filthy. Our new couch. The swimming pool we had put in last year. The ballet lessons for our daughter. Filthy. Scum money.'

'But aren't lawyers sort of obliged to take cases on?'

'Oh who cares,' Ingrid said, not of any mind to allow concessions.

'What are you going to do?' Simone asked.

'Probably nothing,' Ingrid said. 'Drive back to town, sit on our sofa, watch our daughter dance, and try to get over it, I suppose.'

They stood and shook sand from their clothes. The tide had receded a long way down the beach, but was not yet on the turn. More people than usual were scattered across the sand on this bright, fine spring day. Simone picked out Toss, taking a stroll with his son across the wet tidemark. Every now and then Hughie would bend to examine something on the ground, but instead of crouching down, as most people would, he bent himself over from the hips until he was nearly folded in half, like a staple. He looked awkward and unnatural and while he was in this position Toss would kick at the sand, or gaze out to sea, avoiding eye contact with other people. Simone imagined that if his wife was still alive they might've glanced sideways at each other over the top of their son's gloriously conspicuous bottom. They might even have allowed themselves a knowing, indulgent smile. But without her Toss is just there alone, struggling manfully with his son's socially oblivious manner. He looked weighed down and weary, like he was trailing many tattered ends.

Ingrid bent to pick up her handbag, and then rummaged around inside for her car keys. She looked hesitant and mildly distracted, as if there was more she'd wanted to say but she was having trouble finding the words. As they began to walk back towards the café she said, 'Do you think it'd be okay to stay the night?'

'Of course.'

'Good,' she said, pulling a cellphone from her bag. 'I'll just make a call and then let's go get drunk and talk a lot of shit.'

*

'But what have you been eating?' Ingrid exclaimed when she looked inside Simone's fridge.

'Mostly stuff from the café,' Simone mumbled. 'Hanife gives me leftovers every day. And I have a sort of tab there for anything else.'

'And what have you been doing with yourself?' she asked, looking around at Alice's furnishings.

'I don't know. Sometimes I borrow books from the neighbours. And I work at the café every day, and other stuff.'

'What stuff?'

'Well, there's the dog. He likes to go on a lot of walks.' It sounded pathetic. She could've told her about the work in the shed but she was afraid that if she opened that door the one thing that gave her so much solitary pleasure might all start to look a little insular and disturbed, even to her. She'd been able to ignore, until that moment, how confined her circuit had become. But when Ingrid picked up her car keys and suggested a visit to the supermarket down the road Simone found herself making an excuse to stay behind and sort the beds out – as if there was something undesirable about stepping outside the perimeter line she'd drawn around herself, as if it might invite some awful waiting fate to befall her.

Ingrid came back with a monstrous amount of supplies, and filled the door of the fridge with bottles of wine. After they'd eaten Ingrid picked up her glass and moved from the dining table to the couch.

'I should've seen the signs really,' she said, stretching her legs out in front of her and continuing on her theme, which was basically an endless cataloguing of her husband's failings. During the meal she'd revelled in the treachery of describing his new gym shorts, which were white, too short, had splits up the sides, and revealed not the well-muscled thigh he imagined in his own head but rather an unsightly quiver of blue-white flesh. 'The first time he said he loved me it was during sex and he said, "I love you-er feet." Fucking lawyers. He couldn't even manage to say it outright, just a sort of quasi declaration. There had to

145

be something irrefutable about it. And you want to know what was really so weird?' she asked, kicking off her shoes. 'Well just look at them! They're nothing special, my feet. I've got fat toes. What the fuck?'

Simone, who was sitting on the floor with her back propped against the couch, was now forced to examine the feet which were being waved around in the air near her head, and which, as far as she could judge, were neither lovely nor horrible.

'At least he said it, or tried to say it . . . at least.'

'Didn't Fraser?'

'Well of course, at the beginning he did, yes. A lot. But then after that he couldn't quite say it at the right time, and when he tried he could only ever manage it with a slight stutter.' Instantly Simone felt the need to explain further, to try and disentangle herself from what might've sounded like an unwitting revelation that Fraser hadn't loved her for a long time, which she didn't think was true at all. 'I mean we're talking about the man who could barely commit his work into any solid form, who would've burnt his art as soon as it was created if somebody didn't stop him. He had a bit of a spaz out at an opening once. It was at this gallery which didn't normally carry his work and there were red dots everywhere and he couldn't bear the idea that the people there, standing around, gulping back the wine, would be allowed to keep his work forever. He didn't like anything irrefutable either.'

'Fucking artists,' Ingrid said, swigging back more wine.

For a few seconds they both stared into the flickering flame of the big, yellow church candle Simone had found in a kitchen drawer. It lent the room a moony, transcendent quality and Simone began to tell Ingrid about a fantasy she'd had lately where she and Fraser would meet in the street and he'd pull her to him and kiss her passionately and when he stopped she'd say, *nah I didn't feel anything,* and turn around and walk away. She was going to go on and joke blackly that in reality if it happened she'd probably weaken and fail to pull it off, but Ingrid was quick to say, 'Good!' Adding, 'He's a bastard.'

'Do you really think so? A hundred per cent? Irrefutably?'

Ingrid opened her mouth to say something, a disclosure of some kind, and then appeared to think better of it. 'Oh. He's a bastard, all right,' she said instead.

Simone shrugged and decided to light another cigarette, even though they'd smoked so many she was beginning to feel sick. Perhaps Ingrid had been about to admit she used to secretly admire him. The first time Simone had introduced them was at Ingrid's engagement party. She and Fraser had only been dating a short while and they arrived late, missing the first hour of the party where Ingrid had been mixing up big jugs of some potent cocktail made with vodka, schnapps and spoonfuls of lemon and lime sorbet. As they entered Ingrid happened to be standing on the dining table singing. This was well before she'd first become pregnant and had ascended much nearer to a sense of responsibility. They were barely through the door when Ingrid leapt from the table onto Fraser, causing him to stagger backwards. By the time they'd hit the carpet Ingrid had managed to cover his face with red lipstick, and she stood up, adjusted her bra strap, and said, 'Mmmm, tasty, we'll keep him.' She left him on the floor, as she meandered off towards the blender, and Simone put out a hand to help Fraser to his feet. She could see on his face that this crazy introduction had enhanced her own relatively untested standing with him. He liked it, back then, that her friends were a little bit mental.

'Did you ever get so mad . . . about . . . that you felt like doing something to him?' Ingrid asked.

'Er, yes,' Simone said, not meeting Ingrid's eye. She had a cigarette in her mouth and was reaching for the lighter.

'Me too,' Ingrid said.

Simone thought she was referring to her own husband, that she sometimes felt such fury at him. But then, just as she flicked the lighter, Ingrid blurted out what she'd been saving all day.

'I've got something to show you!' She pulled a magazine out of the handbag she'd been keeping near her all night, as if she'd been waiting for just the right moment, as if this had now arrived. 'I wasn't sure if I should, but . . .'

Ingrid flipped the magazine open at an earmarked page and as soon as Simone saw the picture her hands began to shake. She put it on her knee so she could finish lighting the cigarette but she couldn't quite get the flame near the end and Ingrid leaned forward and put her fingers around Simone's wrist to steady it.

'It's about a themed group show they're having in the City Gallery, called "Guerrilla Love". They interviewed some of the artists in this sycophantic kind of way and . . .'

There was a large central photograph of Fraser's installation piece. It was like nothing he had ever done before – a series of scratch drawings created on blackened, slightly irregular squares. Each panel had a depiction of two tigers tussling, though they were wearing skirts and bras so perhaps they were tigresses. They were not comic though, the knottiness of the detail and the power of the struggle lent them a strangely compelling veracity. As the series progressed the clothes became completely ripped to shreds, pieces of the skirts falling to the ground in tatty rags. The series, according to the article, was called 'Love Lies Bleeding'.

> These stunning works were created on tin squares the artist cut from his own car, after it had been stolen and later found burnt-out behind an abandoned factory. When unusual things also occurred inside his house, most symbolically his girlfriend's clothes were tampered with, he realised an estranged ex was responsible. His stalker has since moved away but the artist admitted the episode was affecting: 'Some weird part of me was quite interested in that feistiness but I was relieved when a mutual friend convinced her to leave town. My girlfriend's pregnant and her clothes falling apart really freaked her out.'

'Did you . . . ?' Ingrid asked.

'She's pregnant?' Simone whispered, and then found she couldn't speak at all.

21

They had taken their last holiday together in Fiji, although she didn't know then it would be their last. At the time it seemed like a good place for forgetting. The Yasawa Islands. A week in a bure set amongst coconut palms, at the edge of the white sand. The simplicity of the place – no electricity, concrete floors, candles inside jars for lighting – it should have been romantic. The bed swathed in mosquito nets. But the bareness of it all just seemed to heighten the things they were unable to speak about. They'd tried to be amorous but it felt like they were actors simulating the motions. She was distracted by her unsightly ghoul, and he had a faraway look in his eyes. In the mornings, while he slept, she'd reach for her bathing suit. In the doorway of their bure she'd quietly pull on her flippers, adjust her mask and goggles. From there it was only a few careful backward steps to the sea and submergence. Even the rustling coconut palms would be stilled at daybreak, but under the water's surface life swarmed and shifted. She would drift there, in that blood-warm sea, amid the scattering flit of fish, and think about the words the obstetrician had used – *failed to thrive*.

The nurses try to be kind but they always say the same thing when you've had a medical miscarriage like that – an evacuation, they sometimes call it. It's nature's way. It wasn't meant to happen. It's probably for the best. You'll try again. Only there were details they weren't aware of. They didn't know it had taken her years to get pregnant in the first place. They couldn't know she'd looked in a book only the week before and found out the baby's ears were in place, its lips were formed, its fingerprints were beginning to emerge. They weren't there when the specialist mentioned, quite casually, that someone of her age and *factors* now had a much higher risk of further failures.

By mid-morning the sun would begin to burn and blister

her back but she didn't care. She had no respect for her body any more. When she came ashore she'd find Fraser sitting under some palm trees in a circle of Fijian men. She'd recently given him a guitar as a sort of consolation present and he asked them to teach him the farewell song they sang whenever a boat left their shores. They demonstrated it for him on their tinny little ukuleles, and took turns showing the likely chord progressions on his guitar. He picked up the melody quickly, and they teased and flattered him. He noticed one of the men had a festering sore on his foot and he took off his Converse sneakers and gave them to him.

At night they'd drink beer in the restaurant made of sticks poked into the sand and a thatched roof, glad of the conversation with the others staying at the resort. One night they sat with a man who said he was half Fijian and half Australian. He'd been studying at university in Melbourne. He'd spent his day at the village over the hill, where the locals lived. He told them about the villagers' lives, how they had few possessions and yet everyday they helped cater for holidaymakers who lay about under their coconut trees, on their white beaches, using up their water supplies, treating their village homes like a tourist attraction, and threatening their fishing with the sewage that was created. They were the serfs at the resorts and not the owners, he said. They'd given away fifty-year leases for practically nothing. He'd talked about empowerment but they didn't listen carefully enough. Too lazy, he accused. It seemed significant he was staying at the resort, and not in the village where there was diabetes and tuberculosis and ulcers that didn't heal. And their root-bound sense of society.

The morning after the sneakers had been handed over the men came early. They were singing their songs quietly outside the bure. Fraser went outside and sat with them, once again, but not before banning her from more sun. She lay on the bed reading, finding comfort in the stinging pain on her skin.

The woman who swept the sand from the bure every day, Maria, came bursting through the door. She pointed out through the glassless window at one of the men and shouted, 'Why did your man give that to him? He's a bad man.' Outside one man had received Fraser's watch, another, the one Maria had pointed to, his Leatherman. A low bird call whistled through the trees and the men dissolved away.

The Australian resort manager appeared in the distance, heading towards the little hut where he collected money and allocated rooms. 'Enjoying your stay?' he called out, without requiring an answer.

She hadn't got a good look at the man who had acquired the Leatherman but she worried about what kind of *bad man* he was. She imagined him going around his village at night looking for girls, with the blade of the Leatherman extended. She suggested to Fraser that perhaps giving it away like that wasn't such a great idea. He told her harshly not to be so uptight. Like sometimes he couldn't be bothered being gentle any more.

When Maria came again later that day she asked why she said he was a bad man. Maria laughed and said, 'He's okay, he's my cousin.' She offered her the set of five nail polishes that had been bought at the duty-free shop. Maria quickly tucked it into her apron, eyeing their bottle of duty-free vodka hopefully.

At first, when they were told the baby was no longer viable, when the doctor had said, shockingly, that it had begun to disintegrate and its arm had already floated away from the body, at first Fraser said all the right things. He held her hand in the hospital. He said no matter we'll try again. Whatever it took. It would work out okay. They had each other. But before long he seemed to become disconnected. One day she went downstairs to his studio to take him a cup of coffee and he was working on a pencil sketch. He covered it over, quickly, guiltily. She asked what it was and he said it was nothing, crap, a doodle. Later, when he went out, she went down and found it. It was what he said, not proper work, more of an idle doodle, a cartoon, of a cartoon man, a superhuman, that looked like him, bursting out through the roof of a house and heading into space, a wide expanse of whiteness. She put it back where she found it. It was around this time she happened to open her eyes in the middle of a kiss and noticed Fraser seemed to be looking around the room. The next time he kissed her she did the same, to see what it felt like, to have wandering eyes while your lips were kissing. It felt like a flight from intimacy.

The day they were to board the boat he held all the other passengers up. So many people had come from the village to wish him farewell. They played their song, and then he played it back to them. They laughed with childlike glee to hear him muddle up words that were strange to his tongue. They sang some more as they carried him out to the boat, many hands holding him above their heads, like a hero, and at the last second he gave them the guitar. They waved and waved, and he waved, until the boat rounded the point and they were out of sight.

As the boat increased speed he leaned back on his seat, laughing, and said, 'One day I'd like to bring my kids back here.'

The first thing she noticed was that he'd said *kids* and she'd thought, 'Don't you realise that at this stage we'd probably only ever manage one, if we're lucky.' And as the wake plumed behind them she began to think about how he'd said *my kids*.

22

A few months after they had returned from Fiji they'd been invited next door to watch the Oscars with their neighbour and her son. Apart from the occasional over-the-fence conversation they hadn't had much to do with the single mother living next door for the past few years, Simone thought, but once they were settled in her living room she was surprised by the easy familiarity between Fraser and Caroline. A small feast had been laid out on the coffee table and when the ceremony began, the four of them – Simone, Fraser, Caroline and her son Toby – decided to make a competition of trying to guess the winners. Toby kept score on a piece of paper and as the evening wore on Caroline showed a particular aptitude for guessing correctly. As the last Oscar was handed out, and Caroline had once again predicted the winners, Fraser leaned over and gave her an affectionate horse-bite on her knee by way of congratulation. Just before his hand actually landed on her flesh there was a moment of hesitation, and Simone saw in that instant he'd been waiting for the right opportunity, had wanted to touch her skin all night. Even then Simone, foolishly in retrospect, had not really considered Caroline a serious threat.

What troubled her later, what still troubled her now, was that she could understand how Fraser could have lusty thoughts about a pair of slender legs, but not how he could actually leave her for someone like Caroline. Not long after she'd first moved in next door, Simone happened to meet her in the backyard as they were both hanging out washing. It was summer time, a couple of weeks after the big tsunami disaster, and Simone had just returned from Lexie's where Billy had come running in from a friend's excited by his new joke. He'd asked them if they'd heard about the shock win at the Hawaii Surf Championships: 'It had been won in a surprise move by a Sri Lankan who'd come in through the surf on top of a wooden wardrobe'. In the wake of the disaster there were a lot of those kind of jokes going around, a sort of antidote to the underlying shock, and Billy was too young to fully understand it. She and Lexie had stifled their response, and when he left the room, they looked at each other and giggled. It's not like she didn't know it was a terrible joke when she repeated it over the fence to her new neighbour, but Caroline's response was to give her a morally superior look and say, 'That's awful,' in a cold, half-reprimanding way. 'Those poor survivors.'

Simone felt piqued, and a slight moment of defiance caused her to riff a little, 'And what do you think he said at the award ceremony . . . has anyone seen my wife?'

After that, whenever they did have occasion to talk, Caroline was inclined to say self-defining things like 'I'm the sort of person who can't sleep unless my living room is tidy', or 'I'm the sort of person who's happy in my own company'. Simone thought she probably wasn't the sort of person who was happy in her own company if she had to say it, and was stunned into silence by such remarks, wondering why Caroline thought other people might find a statement like that interesting. She told Simone she worked part-time running an after-school programme for children of working parents, and for some reason Simone always imagined her presenting that same expression of moral authority when any of the parents arrived a little late to collect their child. But the main reason Simone never thought she'd be of significant interest to Fraser is that she could often be seen trimming the edge of her lawn with scissors and once mentioned she didn't really have much time for reading, or other things like art.

But she did have perfectly even features, and immaculately straightened hair, and those lean, toned legs she liked to display. And early on they both came to understand the talent for loving nurture in their neighbour. You could hear it in her voice as she called her son in for dinner. You could see it in the manner in which she instigated happy backyard cricket games with the neighbourhood kids. And it was never more obvious than those times when she appeared open-armed on her doorstep to welcome her son home from his weekly visit to his father. From a distance these sightings exuded a kind of earthy, sunny-natured, pie-on-the-windowsill ideal, and perhaps Simone should have paid more attention to their power.

After that Oscar night Simone had sometimes seen Fraser looking over at those playing children in their neighbouring backyard with an expression close to yearning, and soon enough he was down there among them, bat in hand. At the time she'd somehow completely misunderstood the appeal. She thought it was all about seeking a close-at-hand diversion. He'd been seriously brooding about his approaching birthday and had come to a complete halt in his studio. As an artist who'd built his reputation on a sort of shambolic, almost accidental series of improvisations, he'd always attracted descriptive labels such as 'young', 'inventive' and 'promising'. The oncoming of such a symbolic birthday was messing with his idea of himself and making him acutely aware of a whole new wave of artists rearing up from behind – with angrier ideas, and rawer approaches, whose work was capturing attention just because it was fresh and new and properly youthful. He was stalled and trying not to be envious of the generation that still had the freedom of nothing to maintain. Continuing to come up with something new was starting to be a struggle, and sooner or later, he knew, that struggle would start to look like failure.

Simone thought Fraser's forays into the next-door back garden were all about him trying to recapture something in himself by joining in with the league of wide-eyed boys. She thought it was nothing significant, only a slightly misguided effort on his part to prove to himself he was still capable of playfulness and youthful impetuosity. That was why, on all those occasions when Caroline had called him indoors for lunch along with the rest of the gang, Simone had stupidly failed to realise it wasn't the promise of jam sandwiches that made Fraser enter the house so eagerly.

One morning, on her way to work, she'd had a car accident around the corner from the house. Three wide-boys in a black sports car banged into the back of her at an intersection, shunting her car across the road and into a power pole. She got out and said she wasn't personally hurt but they should give her their contact details to which they replied, 'Whadya mean give you our details? You should be apologising to us. You stopped so suddenly we thought what the hell is she doing? We thought you were going around the turn and then you stopped. You're the one to blame.' They were all wearing tight T-shirts and black leather jackets and stood over her in such an aggressive way she was intimidated. 'Just look at our car,' they said, pointing to a dent on the front fender. 'Look at all the damage you caused.'

Not quite knowing what to do Simone made a note of their number plate and pulled out her cellphone to contact Fraser. She needed him, he'd know how to deal with these idiots. He didn't answer the phone and as she'd only left the house a few minutes before, she thought he might be in the shower or something. Simone tried to point out to the men, in a reasonable voice, that as they had rear-ended her they were the ones at fault. One of the men replied by saying, 'Are you calling me a liar? We are saying you are the one who is to blame. Just look at me. I'm an on-to-it guy. I know what I'm talking about. You, lady, are the bad driver here.'

Realising they were prepared to argue all day long, that this would never end, Simone decided to walk back home. The men got into their car and crept along the curb beside her, yelling out badgering remarks through their open windows. 'Just look at how you walk,' they said. 'You think you know everything, don't you. You can't walk away like that. You're only doing that 'cos you know you're in the wrong! And look how ugly you walk. You should take lessons on how to walk like a proper girl.'

One of the men took a call on his cellphone and when he hung up they all started arguing among themselves in another language, and suddenly the car did a u-turn and screeched off down the road. When Simone reached the house she called out to Fraser but he wasn't there, although the back door was wide open. He wasn't in the garden, and he wasn't in his studio either. Shaky from the encounter, she put the kettle on and made herself tea. Half an hour later she was still sitting in the window seat when she saw him vault over the back fence. She watched him cross the lawn, whistling happily, scratching his crotch. When he came inside the house and saw her seated there, he immediately rearranged his expression into one of guilty denial. At last she understood.

In the heated conversation that followed they said a lot of things they may not have really meant, but he blurted out something so dismal that in the instant it had been said they both knew it would reverberate forever – 'The only thing I remember feeling after you lost the baby was relief.'

23

On the radio there was a news story about an old woman who had died and left a fortune to charity. Simone heard it repeated several times, as she lay on the daybed, and they always left it until the end to report that she had no children and had lived alone with her two cats. It made Simone wonder what was to become of the cats, but more than that, she wondered why they'd felt it necessary to report her pets. It was because, she supposed, they were trying to amp up the pathos – the two cats were tidily emblematic of a lonely spinsterhood, and that in itself had all the implications of sad regret, silly misjudgement and twittering repression. The inevitable lot of women who let themselves be alone for too long.

Ingrid was on her way back to the city now, probably wondering if she'd done the right thing. Before she left they'd sat down together over a pot of tea, their voices croaky, their lungs tarred and trashed, and their complexions a little paler than the night before. Ingrid, having spent most of yesterday trying to clamber onto her subject through various side avenues, now had no further time for deflections. She wanted straight-talking details and in the face of her expectations Simone tried to provide an explanation for the actions Fraser had so neatly labelled.

It wasn't exactly malice, she told her, more that she had no place to put her feelings. For the first couple of months, in the shock of his leaving, it was like falling into the slipstream with no energy to act, she'd just floated along letting the flow take her. Letting tears fall all over her face in Vanuatu, lifting her skirt for the wrong person, losing her job, toying with pills. Only sooner or later a person realises the only way out is to swim, and by then it doesn't matter what kind of footing you head for. It's the bid itself that's saving.

And so . . . she'd followed him, she'd stolen his car, she'd lit a fire. There was no particular reasoning involved, at least not that she could articulate now. And what she ended up with was a set of keys. A useless car key, and one small, silver, inviting front door key. Who, in her position, would not have at least thought of trying it out? It had taken her many days to pluck up the courage to enter their house, the new house they'd set up together. She'd sat outside for hours, in the restaurant car park across the road, disguised in her cap and big fly glasses. She stayed there until she knew their routine, until she'd seen Caroline kiss him on the doorstep so many times it no longer made the neurons in her head go into a blinding derangement. She didn't even know if the key would work. Would they have changed the locks? In the beginning the most she could bring herself to do was steal their mail. But, back then, she had plenty of time. There was no job suddenly, nowhere else she had to be.

And then another Friday rolled around. The day Caroline always went off to a resource meeting for her stupid job, her son Toby went to school, and Fraser went down to the community centre where he always spent a few hours every week helping a group of young adults with disabilities make puppets. As soon as they were out of sight she slipped across the road and quickly let herself in. Practically the only thing she noticed, that first time, was the matching set of cushions. And that on a shelf in the kitchen were mugs with the same pattern as the cushion fabric. These had presumably been purchased because they complemented the colours in his painting hanging over the sofa. As if they were living some kind of superficially exemplary life. As if symmetry and order were some sort of abiding principle. How could Fraser's spirit survive in this place where the volume was turned so low? What could a woman who shopped at designer stores where cushions matched coffee mugs tell him about his art? His chaotic, charged, brilliant art? She left without touching anything, that first time. A torpor, like a falling sky, came over her.

But by the next Friday she'd gathered up some rage and a plan that seemed absolutely logical at the time. She thought she was beginning to see what there might be between the two of them. Like all chaotic people, Fraser sometimes longed for order and structure to free him from his own disorderly impulses. He used to have occasional fantasies of being sent to jail, where all the liberties and choices of daily management were removed from him, believing that in this he would find true artistic licence. But even though he occasionally craved structure as a way of escaping himself, it was a fleeting novelty and it wasn't in his nature to settle for it for too long. She wanted to speed up the tension, in subtle, secret ways. She had no intention of doing anything they could pin directly on her. She didn't want to be caught there because then it would be easy for them to dismiss her, to say she was simply mad. And Fraser might begin to congratulate himself for leaving her. She wanted to do only enough to put an initial tremor in their sense of order, shake Caroline's foundations, unravel her composure.

So . . . she opened the wardrobe door and started snipping. Every single button of every one of Caroline's shirts and jackets. Not all the threads. Just a few. Just enough for the buttons to work themselves loose. So everywhere she'd go they'd start popping off. So she wouldn't be so neat any more. It was difficult to resist the urge to just start slashing everything in sight, to rip Caroline's horrible clothes to pieces, leaving her nothing. She snipped a couple of stitches on every hem of every skirt and every pair of trousers. Caroline would begin to come undone. She'd wonder what was happening to her.

In the kitchen a carton of milk had been left on the bench. Probably by Fraser, the last to leave the house. She tipped it over and watched as the milk pooled on the bench and fell to the floor, creeping slowly across the lino towards the carpet, as if it was an obliging co-conspirator finding the best place to haul up and fester. Before she left the house she adjusted all the clocks and timers she could find, so they would begin to think even their appliances were against them.

On her next visit she opened the door to the sunny back bedroom and found where he was working – newspaper on the floor, the usual tubes of paint and canvases and soaking brushes, and all the familiar, ritualised tools lined up and ready – his mother's old spatula, the set of damaging-looking doctors' instruments he'd found in a second-hand store, the fine-bristle brush he'd had since he was seven, the old-fashioned perfume bottle he liked to use as a spritzer. But the whole room looked dry and uninspired. In his old studio he'd pinned things to nearly every centimetre of wall but it looked like he wasn't allowed to here. She located his diary and noted down all the appointments he had in the coming weeks. Later on she'd ring every single one, saying she was Caroline, and make some excuse to shift the appointment time. He'd arrive an hour late for tennis, two days early at a dealer's gallery, a few hours late to discuss a new commission, and an hour and a half early at the doctors. This last had made her particularly uncomfortable, as it had both their names by it, and at the time she'd thought Caroline was trying to exert her control not just in his studio but over his most personal matters too. But now, looking back with all the facts, it's obvious it was something else, something which concerned them both.

She tried to explain to Ingrid that while she was ashamed of herself even as she was doing these things, there was also a kind of addictively rewarding sense of dignity in being able to wield that secret power where she would otherwise have had none. But there came a moment so lacking even in any kind of confused virtue that she knew to go any further forward would be life defining. She found herself hovering over a bottle of bleach wondering if she'd have the nerve to actually try and kill Caroline if she knew she could get away with it. She'd gone to the house intending to use the bleach to ruin the cushions, perhaps a few of Fraser's paintings, but she knew at that moment that even that was way too far.

'Thank God you didn't do it,' Ingrid said. 'Thank God you came here and got well away from all that.'

But that wasn't quite what had made her stop.

She'd stood in their living room thinking it was only a matter of days before she'd turn forty. She was becoming far too old to allow herself to be enslaved to the outer edges of a spurned relationship. This was no way to live. Suddenly she knew she had to change.

She left the house and drove around to Lexie's, and found her in the kitchen, in the midst of a baking frenzy. Simone stood at the bench beside her, offering to help, feeling like she'd just tunnelled her way out of a pit and was slightly dazzled by the well-lit normality she'd found.

'I was just thinking about Joey,' Lexie said, sifting flour into a bowl. 'He just rang to say he's coming over this afternoon and I was thinking about how he's been living overseas for so long I don't feel like I know him that well. He and Dad had a big fight when he dropped out of film school, and I don't think either of them ever really got over it. I don't know how he feels about it now and he doesn't really talk about stuff like that. I sort of wish he would. I feel like there's something I'm supposed to do.'

At that point Simone had seen Joey only once since he'd come back, at the funeral, and there, seeing him amidst all the mourners, she'd been amazed how he'd changed over the years. So different from the skinny, smirking younger brother of her friend who left on a plane, certain fame and fortune was just a few well-constructed lengths of celluloid away.

'A weird thing happens when your parent dies,' Simone offered. 'No matter what your relationship. For a little while you feel as if they're looking down on you. And you feel like you ought to live a better life.'

'Oh,' Lexie said. 'I keep forgetting about your father. Do you still feel like that? After all this time?'

'No. I suppose it passes after a while,' Simone said, not wanting to imagine her father watching her. Those things she'd been doing were too freshly shameful even to share with Lexie. Certainly they weren't the kind of things you liked to think your dead father was observing through the celestial mist.

Lexie sighed and said she wanted to talk about it, but then she didn't as well, and began instead to talk about Simone's imminent birthday.

'Come on, if you can't celebrate big birthdays what can you celebrate? And we all need a good excuse for a party,' she'd said, adding, 'It's not as if it's all about you, you know.' The weird materiality of that statement had made Simone concede, agreeing to a bar, just a few people, and nobody mentioning the number.

'Okay,' Lexie said. 'That's my birthday promise to you.'

Billy, just home from school, came into the kitchen and opened the refrigerator door. 'The best thing about birthdays,' he said, 'is you get presents.'

He was just starting to gel his hair. His pants were hanging low on his hips, a tentative new look for him. 'Cool. And what are you going to get me?' Simone asked.

'Nada,' he said, completely comfortable with the existing convention that when it came to the adults in his life there was only one natural flow for presents, or any kind of attention for that matter. 'Dad says he needs a beer,' he said, reaching in and tucking one under his arm. When he reached for a second one Lexie leaned over and took it off him, replacing it with a can of coke.

He went back out the door and Lexie said, 'Honestly, he's only nine and he's already such a trier. Imagine what he's gonna be like at fourteen.'

'Where is Anton? I haven't seen him for ages.'

'You don't want to see him today. He's out in the shed being all righteous with his spanners and stuff.'

'How come?'

'He left his lawnmower in the driveway this morning and I accidentally ran over it.'

'Oops.'

'Yep. He's been in a sulk ever since.'

163

'Well he shouldn't have left it there then.'

'Exactly what I said,' Lexie replied, giggling.

Simone was greasing a cake tin for the batter Lexie was mixing, when Joey walked in. 'Hey, big momma,' he said to Lexie. 'The workers tell me they're giving out beers in here.' When he saw Simone he added, 'Sorry, what I should've said is hey, big mommas.'

'Yeah there's beer,' Lexie replied, 'but it's only for the grown-ups.'

'Hey I'm a grown-up,' he said. 'I buy my own shorts and I'm even over the minor crush I used to have on Bonnie from *Knight Rider*.'

'Oh all right then, I s'pose that proves it,' Lexie said, holding open the fridge door for him.

Earlier, as Simone had driven away from Fraser's house with the bottle of bleach on the seat beside her, she'd begun to wonder how she'd feel if she got what she thought she wanted – if Fraser tired of Caroline, as he inevitably would, and came back to her. She'd have to find some way to forgive him, because without that there'd be no way forward. But where would the line be drawn then? What was that saying to him? I will do anything. I will accept anything. I am worth nothing. And once he had accepted her forgiveness would he begin to feel he could rely on it in the future? The next time an attractive woman moved in next door? And lies would furnish their lives like a set of tripwires. She'd have to remember never to mention the things she'd seen, the car, the inside of the house. She'd have to forget the words he said. Everything they had once been was so irrevocably spoiled that perhaps it was better to look to an alternative.

And here, right in front of her, was an interesting face, Joey's face, a curious possibility, all grown up but still with such dirty, preposterous freckles you just wanted to lick the corner of your hankie and dab them right off his skin. She knew it wasn't that easy, you didn't just make a simple switch like that, but there was a point where you had to start trying.

Lexie squeezed some lemons, and then crushed ice into the juice, topping it up with vodka. She put a glass in front of Simone and took the other out into the garden to pick some herbs for a terrine she wanted to make. Simone sat at the table with Joey and they began to chat about music. Sipping her drink she felt like she was shedding a skin, a rough and sour one, a dislikeable her, and assuming another. And just as if she wasn't the kind of woman that, less than an hour ago, had a red-hot compulsion for revenge worming within her, Simone mentioned cheerfully and very casually, that she was thinking of going to see a touring Scandinavian band later that night but she didn't have anyone to go with . . .

24

Hanife, returning to the counter with some cups that needed rinsing, noticed her face and said, 'You look tired. That talky one give you some bad news from the city or something?'

Simone found she had to flee to the bathroom. Inside the cubicle she leaned her forehead into the cool brick wall, feeling like the blood in her veins had slowed below the rate that oxygenated the brain. The knowledge of that coming baby was weighing heavily on her, an awful new presence that felt like a familiar old pain. And more than that she was struggling with the way Fraser had depicted her. As if she was some little-known acquaintance from his past, a person of no consequence who'd taken to making a nuisance of herself. She felt, even more than before, mutinously abandoned – like he'd pushed her out of a moving car with his foot and driven off without glancing back, leaving her bruised and alone at the roadside. She inhaled the claustrophobic plastic smell of lavender air-freshener. This is stupid, she thought. Elsewhere in the world there are people dying in wars. Whole countries dying of starvation. People being consumed by cancer. She opened the door and washed her hands, and then her face, looking into the mirror. Just above the hand-dryer somebody had written:

Kylie & Josh
lovers 4eva
like you neva
had.

She didn't want to surrender to any tears. She felt like the dam-gates were only just holding, and now was the time to stay staunch. Get over it, Simone, she told herself. Just get over it. Hanife's family has been decimated. Charlie is losing all his thoughts. Sorrow over some stupid guy? So damn what. Happens to millions every day. Go make coffee.

The morning-tea mothers had arrived while she was in the bathroom. They were the only ones in this morning, and were being a little louder than usual. Normally they seemed to enjoy communicating to each other how well they were coping, in an almost competitive way, but today their discussion was lively and ripe with grievance. There had been a story in the paper that morning about a seventy-one per cent decline in the love life of new mothers, and that had set them off:

'It astounds me how he manages to sleep while our baby screams its lungs out in the next room.'

'I'm still getting up three times a night, and he gets up maybe once a week. And then he expects me to treat him like a bloody hero just for that!'

'We have this deal that I cook the meals and he does the dishes and every single night I have to remind him to do it. It's like he's doing me a big fat favour and I hate his attitude so much that sometimes I just do it myself to save the aggro.'

'I told him if he wants sex he's just going to have to look after himself for a while – I just can't be bothered!'

Hanife whispered to Simone, 'Listen to them! Make you glad you don't have a husband?'

'Or a baby, for that matter,' Simone muttered.

One of the younger women said, 'This morning he made me a cup of tea and when he came back to bed he put his cock right in my face. As if! I wanted to bat the thing away.' When she finished speaking there was a slightly shocked silence at the table and somebody tactfully changed the subject.

Later Hanife went out to pick up some supplies and while she was gone Simone went over to the magazine racks and tipped the three magazines with the article about Fraser's exhibition into her bag, spreading out the rest to cover the gap. One of the mothers came over and said she was just about to buy one of those.

'Sorry, you can't,' Simone said.

'Why not?' she asked, slightly insistent.

'There's been a recall.'

167

'I've never heard of that before!'

'Happens all the time,' Simone said, and began grinding some beans.

After work she walked to the point with Clouseau, and stood at the edge of the sea ripping the magazines into pieces and throwing them into the water. Fuck Guerrilla Love. Fuck Fraser. Fuck the fish. Fuck the sea.

She was about to rip up the last one when she stopped herself. She sat down and leaned back against a bony rock and read it from cover to cover. It was one of those hip urban magazines, obsessed mostly with the underculture of movies, music, fashion, and design. The only part of the magazine she didn't read were the pages about the exhibition.

Near the back page was a furniture advertisement. There was a photograph of a man sitting on a brown leather sofa holding aloft a big buttery baby. Exactly the kind of baby she'd once imagined she might have. She made herself look at it. Aversion therapy, she told herself. Stare at the big buttery baby until you can say you don't want it. You don't want it. You shall never have it. Fuck the big buttery baby. And fuck the man in the picture too. Somebody's idea of a perfect husband. He looked like he'd just arrived home from work. He was wearing a black polo with a suit jacket. He had success written all over him. He was too tight. He wasn't somebody who had a free imagination. That could invent a game out of nothing but a piece of belly-button fluff and a used matchstick. That could make amazing puppets and do all the crazy voices. That knew all about the looking-like-an-idiot room.

She ripped that last magazine up and threw it into the sea too, reminding herself that if she'd managed to have a baby with Fraser she would've ended up sitting around moaning just like those women in the café. He'd have been a shirker, for sure. Not only that but he wasn't a particularly good provider either, too much of a dreamer. She probably would've ended up exhausted and shitty – having to find ways to pay the mortgage and look after the baby. Might as well not have had him around at all.

But how could he say that? That he felt nothing but relief? And take himself armed and dangerous right next door.

That evening Simone sat down on Alice's front stoop to breathe some fresh air into her lungs. She didn't habitually smoke, had spent all day recovering from nicotine overload, and tonight she promised herself she never would again. It was a beautiful clear night and she leant back against the door frame and looked up at the stars, trying to pick out the planets, and thinking about poor wretched Pluto, kicked off the executive – duping everybody for years, presenting itself as something proud and fine and true, when all along it was just a puny dilettante, nothing but mist and gas.

Earlier she'd taken her tools over to Zita's, thinking the performance of a small kindness would make her feel better. She'd thought perhaps she'd make a start on fixing that front door. Maybe block up the mouse hole. But after knocking at the back door she saw a curtain twitch and a few moments later she heard Zita say in a frightened voice, 'Nothing today, thank you.'

'Zita, it's me, Simone.'

'Yes that's right.'

'Zita, did you hear me? I've come to see if I can fix your front door for you.'

The door opened a crack, 'I'm all right today thank you.' There was a smell of simmering soup from within the house. Simone told her again why she was there.

'Yes, I see,' Zita said. She seemed to contemplate letting Simone in for a moment then her face hardened with some kind of resolve and she said, 'There's no need.'

'But . . . have I come at a bad time?'

'Yes that's right,' Zita said firmly. 'It's not convenient right now. My son will do it for me later.' And she shut the door.

Clouseau sat companionably on the lawn in front of her, in his lord-of-the-kingdom pose, his nose twitching about, taking in the smellscape all around. The phrase 'dog of splendour' came to her from nowhere, but there was an odd familiarity about it. Suddenly she remembered – her and Fraser lying wasted and entangled one afternoon after sex and she had whispered into his ear, 'You are the god of splendour.' He had whispered something equally as fanciful back to her. She didn't want to recall this. With all that had happened since, it came to her as a savage, negative pain, like a dead thing rising up to the surface of a swamp. Nothing good could be remembered any more with innocent indulgence. If she could she'd annihilate all memory of him, but the only real possibility she had available was to rid herself of every last physical remainder. A sort of ceremony. There was so little left now, just a few remnants to be gathered up.

That last photo of them together. Him standing with his arm around her, in front of a coconut palm. The sun shining, the sand white, the sea blue, smiles – but if you looked carefully into the faces you could see they weren't happy.

An enamelled necklace that she'd always loved, but could not wear without thinking of him. He'd given it to her for a birthday, but had bought it with her credit card.

And the white handkerchief, always kept zipped up in one of the inside pockets of her handbag. One of their first few dates when he'd taken her to an abandoned railway tunnel to see the glow-worms. They'd had to fight their way in through a tangle of blackberry vines, which he stomped down for her, very manfully. And as he stood gazing up at the sprinkle of lights she'd sneaked a look across at him, in her smitten way, and noticed a scratch on his neck had begun to bleed. She'd lent him her handkerchief and afterwards had taken it back and secreted it in her bag to carry around with her for the entire duration of their relationship – her private, useless charm.

She took these three things out to the shed and placed them inside one of her boxes. Clouseau looked at her curiously when she took the spade down from its place on the wall. On the way out her eye caught on something which had always bothered

170

her. In the cardboard box of dolls there was one in particular with a missing arm. She seemed to snag herself on it every time she searched through the collection, and somehow it always worked its way to the top of the pile. She plucked it out and placed that inside the box as well.

It was a quiet, calm night, brightly lit by a plump and watchful moon. As Simone dug a hole in Alice's lawn under the apple tree, Clouseau crowded near, sniffing at every fresh shovelful of dirt with eager expectancy. When the hole was big enough she crouched and placed the box inside. The dog stuck his nose in to see and then looked back at her with loyal acceptance.

She scraped the dirt back over the hole and was just compacting it down with her boot when Clouseau's ears pricked up and he began to growl softly. Suddenly she felt vulnerable out in the garden at night. She squinted into the distance to try and see what had him on guard. The beam of some torches came around the side of the house and she quickly tried to hide behind the tree. Clouseau began to bark aggressively from her side – working himself up into something fearsome. The torches went directly to Clouseau and then onto the parts of her which were not hidden by the trunk of the tree.

'Police!' one of the strangers shouted. 'Get your dog under control!'

'How do I know you are the police?' she shouted back, in a voice too high-pitched to achieve the desirable assertiveness.

The torchlight was moved away from her face. 'Step forward, Wayne,' she heard one of the men say, and a uniformed policeman came forward, although keeping well back from Clouseau who continued to growl, spiny-backed.

She tried to quieten Clouseau, but he was too excited, so with her heart thumping, she had to pull him by the collar towards the shed and shut him in. Back in the garden, the three men, two in plain clothes and one in uniform, were standing looking at the spade and the fresh dirt covering her hole. 'Burying a cat?' the tallest one said.

'No. Um. Well something like that,' she mumbled, with a horrible sense of failing.

'Mind if we take a look then?'

'Can you do that? Just come onto someone's property like that?'

'We can if we have a warrant,' he said smoothly, patting his upper pocket.

He had a warrant? After all this time had passed? Not knowing what else to do she looked helplessly down at the ground and tried to think if the things in the box could be somehow incriminating in their eyes.

The tall one gave a curt nod and the uniformed constable took up the spade and began digging. The man who seemed to be in charge introduced himself as Detective Michie. He didn't introduce the other two.

There was a soft clunk when the spade hit wood, and even in the moonlight she could see a brief twitch of excitement on the detective's face. The constable extracted the box, brushed the dirt from the lid, and held it out for the detective to open. The other man shone his torch on it – a bright, forensic beam – and he lifted the lid, removing first the doll. He shook it beside his ear before pulling off the head and holding the inside of the body up to the torchlight. On finding it empty he threw the two pieces on the grass and carefully unfolded the handkerchief, clearly expecting something to be wrapped inside. After shaking it in a slightly disappointed way he scrunched it into the corner of the box and fingered the necklace. Then finally he picked up the photograph and scrutinised it, looking closely at Fraser's face like he expected to recognise it.

He cleared his throat. 'Right,' he said. The other man handed the torch to the constable and tried to put the head of the doll back on the body, when that failed he threw the two pieces back into the box, closed the lid and dropped the whole lot back in the hole. None of the men looked directly at her.

'Let's go inside,' Detective Michie said.

In the kitchen he formally asked her name and address and

172

wrote in his notebook. She found the words hard to say, felt anxious about getting it wrong. The constable stood behind the detective, with his hat under his arm, and the other man walked around the room poking at things, opening doors and lifting lids. She was asked if she was the only one in residence, and she said yes. The detective showed her the warrant and explained they had reason to believe there were drugs on the premises and they'd be conducting a search.

'Drugs?' she said, half-relieved. Or was this some sort of complicated nods up from Fraser? She steals his car on a crazy whim, so he retaliates by sending the police in on a contrivance to give her a scare? She thought she might be blushing. Would they interpret this as indicating she had something to hide? Was that irrational?

Not even trying to keep the natural condescension out of his voice, the detective began to explain they would be bringing a dog through the premises and she'd be asked to wait outside with the constable. The other man went out and came back a few minutes later with a serious-faced Labrador on a lead.

The constable led Simone to the garden. They stood facing each other in awkward silence for a short time. He looked young and apologetic. She walked over and started kicking dirt back into the hole. Clouseau was whining now, in the shed.

'What's your dog's name?' he asked.

She didn't want to say it. 'Um, Inspector Clouseau.'

'Like the detective?'

'Yes,' she said quietly.

Somewhere in the far distance a morepork started calling plaintively, its cry clear and definitive above the ambient rumble from the beach. Through the windows she could see lights flicking on in succession as the two policemen and the dog moved around the house.

'Go for a swim much?' the constable asked. She thought she could hear, in his friendly attempt to make conversation, a preference for believing in innocence. He hadn't been in the force long, she thought.

'No,' she said. 'It's too cold.' She didn't really want to chat, was too nervous of what she might inadvertently say.

'S'pose it is,' he said, and he started whistling under his breath.

It was strange, she thought, how you only ever heard one morepork. Like they each had an allotted territory, and in calling out were just letting the underworld know they were there, doing their regular shift.

The detective came outside and indicated for her to follow. He took her through to the kitchen where the dog was sitting facing a cupboard door. 'What's in here?' the detective asked.

'Um . . . I'm not sure.'

'What do you mean *not sure*?'

'Well it's not my house.' She explained she was house-sitting, and he licked his bottom lip and wrote down all the details. The only time she'd ever looked in that cupboard, she told him, it seemed to be full of the usual kind of junk that was everywhere else in the house.

The dog handler swung open the door, and while he held tightly to the leash, the dog scrabbled to get at the back of the cupboard where there was a rusty blue cake tin with a windmill printed on it. The handler reached past the dog to retrieve the tin and handed it to the detective. Inside were a couple of objects that, at a glance, Simone thought might be the pupal casings of a bag moth.

'Are these yours?' the policemen asked, and on a closer look she realised they were more likely to be two fat joints, twisted at either end, and rolled so long ago the cigarette paper had turned brown.

'I never even knew they were there!' Simone protested meekly.

'Whose do you think they are then?'

'Honestly I have no idea. I mean they could be Alice's but I doubt it, she's pretty old.' Was it okay to point their suspicion towards Alice? It's not as if they were going to be able to question or arrest her. What was the big deal anyway?

'You'd be surprised,' the officer said, narrowing his eyes and observing her closely as he passed them under his nose. He made eye contact with the dog handler, and pulled a plastic bag out of his pocket to contain the evidence.

They asked her to remove the dog from the shed so they could check there and she went out and dragged Clouseau to the laundry. On the way Clouseau twisted his head to growl at the police dog, which sat beside its handler, professional and cool, eyeing Clouseau like he was a pitiful degenerate.

She sat down at the kitchen table, trying to think. Was this just a coincidence after all? Have they got the wrong house, perhaps? Was she responsible for the drugs they found? Would they care that much about two joints? Whose were they anyway?

The detective came back into the house and she found herself sitting up straighter as he seated himself opposite and stared at her for a long intimidating moment. He almost seemed to be trying to imply that a few minutes of observation under his well-honed eye would be enough to determine, once and for all, where she sat on the scale of innocent–guilty.

'Right. I want to thank you for your co-operation,' he said. 'We'll take the evidence in for consideration and if there is any further action we'll be in touch. We could give you a citation for possession, but as you are not the permanent resident here, and there seems to be some reasonable evidence they may not be your drugs then it is unlikely any charges will be laid at this time. All right, young lady?'

'Yes, thank you, officer,' she said, with the obedience of a child.

25

At first Simone wondered why the alarm clock had suddenly decided to set itself off. It took a few minutes for the flux of sleep to clear enough to register it was not the chiming bedside clock but the ringing telephone which had woken her. By the time she'd struggled out of bed the telephone had ceased, and it took a few more moments to reassemble herself enough to remember why all the drawers in the house were spilled open, like out-turned pockets. She'd collapsed into bed the night before, unable to find the energy after the police left to close a single cupboard. Now she saw she hadn't even thought to shut the front door and the floor in the hallway was crunchy with blown-in leaves.

In the kitchen she found Clouseau already up and eating, munching on a bowl of dog biscuits with a hearty urgency, his tail wagging.

Waiting for the kettle to boil, Simone opened the window above the bench to let out the steam, and the net curtains Alice had hung there began to dance about in a gentle draught. She had a sudden recollection of her mother getting annoyed with her on a road trip they had taken in Australia. They were in her mother's new car, on the way to meet her new husband's family, and Simone kept winding down the window to feel the breeze on her face but her mother insisted the windows had to stay up, and more than once used the controls on her side to reclose it. When they finally got to their destination she leant across to open the glovebox and showed the page in the manufacturer's handbook that advised the windows must be up for the air conditioning to work properly. Later that night they'd had a family barbecue and Simone had thought her mother looked happy, fussing about, getting everything just so. She'd spent her first few years as a widow lunching with friends. They were of an age where grandchildren were a popular topic of conversation. Simone's mother liked to keep up but she hated not having any contribution of her own. Occasionally she'd make restrained but wistful remarks about it to Simone and eventually she seemed to be suppressing a gentle resentment. She felt she was missing out, and it was Simone's failing. Over one lunch a friend introduced her to an Australian cousin, an aging widower with five children. She married him within a couple of months and shifted to a big, immaculate, concrete and glass house on the Gold Coast, where they hosted a barbecue every Sunday for his children and grandchildren. She'd found her place now, with her newly affiliated role in the grandparent society.

Simone opened the freezer door and looked inside, half expecting the condom to be gone. Did the police notice it? What would they have made of that? Maybe they passed it under the dog's nose and it had gone – *nah, interesting maybe, but not punishable*. The thought made her blush. Perhaps she should just do it. Get rid of it. Take some folic acid. Wait until the next right time. Try it out, that slim chance.

Just as the kettle was beginning to bubble the telephone started ringing a second time and when she picked it up it was Clara, sounding skittish and excited. 'Did they come to you?' she rasped in a low undertone, as if she thought *they* might be listening.

'Yes.'

'Did they find anything?'

'Yes.'

'Better come over.'

Charlie was accommodated in his favourite chair in the living room with a cup of tea and something on the stereo while Clara and Simone sat at the kitchen table, talking in low voices like two schoolgirls not wanting Dad to hear. .

Clara told her the police had been to their place too. 'I was lucky,' she said. 'I saw them coming up the path so I sent Charlie to the door while I went and flushed what I had down the toilet.'

She said this with such impressive smoothness Simone began to wonder at how regularly the local police conducted drug searches up and down this street. Was this something she was already accustomed to?

'Whenever Charlie goes to the door he always tries to make a good fist of it,' she went on. 'It took them a few minutes to realise he was a bit confused. He told them a policeman had come to the door only a couple of days ago and he was going tell them what he told that chap – he didn't know anything about any sheep rustling across the road! Once I'd got rid of the stuff I came to the door smiling like the dear old lady I am. "What can I do for you, gentlemen?" I said. They didn't stay long.'

It was clear some part of Clara was thrilled at her own cunning. She liked to think of herself as something of a rebel, although there must be few enough opportunities for mischief in the life she'd now come to. This incident, though, had her eyes shining with adventure.

'What made them come do you think?' Simone asked. 'I've never heard of the police doing a house-to-house like that. It's so weird.'

'Well they may have had their reasons,' Clara replied cryptically. She gave Simone a look, like she expected her to know something. And even though nothing had been suggested by the police, and nothing was being directly suggested now, Simone couldn't help entertaining the idea she might've been responsible for drawing the spotlight to this part of the earth.

'What are you saying?' Simone asked. If Clara had some hunches she wanted them in the open.

But Clara's strange expression had nothing to do with Simone's behaviour. 'Toss was charged with cultivating cannabis,' she exclaimed with equal amounts of dramatic effect and appropriate neighbourly concern.

'What? Our Toss? How much did he have?'

'Just a few plants he was growing hydroponically in his back bedroom,' Clara said.

'So they sent three men and a dog for that?'

'I know. It did seem a bit excessive.'

'And how come they got warrants for the whole street?'

'I don't know.'

'Perhaps there was a mix-up and they just happened on Toss's plants?'

'Well Toss thinks they had some kind of tip-off.'

Simone was finding it all a bit hard to take in. Toss? Arrested for growing hydroponic weed? That was a bit like finding out Clouseau was the secret sheep rustler. 'You don't think it was me?' Simone asked, laughing slightly.

'Well *I* don't, obviously, but I'm afraid your name has come up once or twice. Being the newcomer, and everything.'

'But Clara, how could it have been me? I didn't even know about Toss! And besides, I'm not the sort of person who'd do such a thing.'

Clara patted her on the arm. 'That's exactly what I said.' She offered her tea and went to the kitchen to make it. The morning sun was streaming in through the dormer window above the bench and Simone could hear Clara humming quietly to herself. When she sat down again with the teapot and the cups Simone asked her what was going to happen to Toss.

'Lord knows!' Clara said. 'They seemed to think a fine of some sort. Perhaps community service. It's not like he's selling it to little kiddies or anything. It started when his wife got sick. She had a lot of nausea with the chemo and they tried a bit to see if it helped. After a while we all tried it. It's actually very good for arthritis. And a little bit of Toss's oil in milk at night helps with sleep. Poor Toss.'

'When you say we, you mean . . . ?'

'Well not Marjorie, obviously,' Clara informed her. 'But the rest of us. Zita has terrible arthritis. And Alice used to have a smoke now and then. Obviously,' she added.

'So you lot were a kind of drug ring?'

'Yup,' Clara said, playing up to the idea. 'That's us, delinquent pensioners.'

'Just as well they caught you in time. Next thing you know

you would've got onto the hard drugs and had to find ways to supplement your pensions to support your habit.'

'That's right. We all would've been flogging off the Queen Anne furniture and denying our heirs the satisfaction.'

Simone laughed, but even as she did so she felt a weird kind of pressure. The last few days had required her to take in too much information and her insides felt coiled and twisted, everything aching. 'Did they go to Zita's?'

'Yes. Didn't find anything. She must have got rid of it somehow.'

Zita's odd behaviour came to mind. 'But how did the police find out?' she asked.

'Who knows?' Clara said with genuine mystification.

Simone mentioned her visit to Zita. 'She was acting pretty strange. You don't think . . . ?'

'No, she definitely wouldn't have,' Clara said emphatically, 'She'd never do that to Toss, and she liked it too much.' After a thoughtful pause she said, 'What do you mean strange?'

'Well, I wanted to help fix her sticky front door and she wouldn't let me in.'

'Oh,' said Clara. 'Actually I know what that's about. She's a bit down on you.'

'Why?'

Clara hesitated, and then said, 'She doesn't really approve of you having sex with that young boy.'

'You mean Ollie?' Simone asked, blushing. 'Why? I mean he was pretty young but he was old enough. I mean it's not like it hurt anyone.' She could hear the whiny self-justification in her own voice and felt a distinct pang of dislike for Zita for making her account for herself in this way.

Clara sat back in her chair and grinned, 'Ollie? Who's Ollie? I meant the other one.'

'What other one?'

'The boy who was staying with her.'

'Ravi?'

Clara nodded.

Simone was incredulous. 'You've got to be joking. I never did. Well, I mean, he asked me to but I sent him packing. Did he say . . . ?'

Clara nodded again, delighted. 'Told Zita's son.'

'Cheeky little shit.' But why on earth would he do that? Why would he say she had sex with him? And to Zita's son, of all people. That was just plain weird. No wonder Zita was off her. *Quick, lock up your grandsons everybody, here comes Simone. Probably the drug fink too.*

In the rearrangement this required, Simone suddenly remembered something else which was not as solid as she'd thought. It had been in the back of her mind but she hadn't let herself think about it yet. The magazine article. The mutual friend. Lexie had let her think coming here was a simple favour, but, no. 'A mutual friend had assisted in moving her on,' Fraser had claimed, or something like that. Like they were co-operating in managing a small brush fire. The thought of it made her want to go back to bed and sleep and sleep and sleep until everything was hazed and distant.

She looked at Clara, struggling, totally confounded by everything, and Clara snorted. If she hadn't just mentioned she'd flushed everything down the toilet, Simone might've suspected she was a little high, but perhaps it was just the thrill of the dodge.

There was a soft thud out on the front path, the sound of the local paper being delivered, and as Clara went out to fetch it Simone thought how strange it was that some important things registered immediately, and others took their time to come to full existence, like spring shoots. It was too brain-twisting to think of Lexie in cahoots with Fraser, so much would need to be rethought. How far back did it go? How deep did it go? This was something she'd subconsciously put aside, and now she'd have to choose to consciously rest it because to deal with it properly now would be to effectively make herself homeless.

Clara was laughing about a new idea when she came back in through the door. She speculated about whether there might be a story about the raid next week. '"Pot-smoking pensioners exposed"?' she suggested.

'"Cul-de-sac cartel busted"?' Simone offered.

After some thought, Clara added triumphantly, '"Ganja Granddad nabbed"!'

Her amusement was interrupted by the record catching in the next room. She put the paper down on the table and moved to stop it repeating but as soon as she was through the living room door she wailed, 'Oh no, he's gone again.' She turned back with a helpless look on her face, her confidence instantly evaporated, and for the first time Simone saw how close to surrender she truly was. It was easy to believe in her good grace, her continuous serenity, her stoicism, but Charlie's disease was a persistent and difficult adversary, and sooner or later a limit must be reached.

'Don't worry, I'll go,' Simone said. 'He can't have got far.'

Once outside Simone attempted to whistle up Clouseau but he didn't come crawling out from under the verandah, where he usually liked to wait for her. He's out there with Charlie, she thought, and with this realisation came a brief feeling of relief, as if Clouseau had the necessary credentials to nose Charlie away from danger. As she ran down the street, scanning the far distance, she had visions of the kind of trouble Charlie could get himself into – wandering in traffic, entering the sea, unkindness of strangers. But then again he wasn't a toddler. She should give him more credit. Just because your capacity was falling away it didn't mean you lost your acquired instincts about things like road safety and water sense.

As it turned out Charlie wasn't hard to find. She ran down between the dunes and there he was sitting peacefully on a log with one hand rubbing under Clouseau's willing ear.

Often, on the very bad days, Charlie's face had the look of an abandoned room. And sometimes the look of a rougher vacancy, like a building that'd had tear gas thrown through the windows to clear all inner activity. His mouth would hang a little, his eyes wouldn't really see, his battle for control of his mind was lost and he was nothing more than the slowly expiring ruin. But sometimes, like at the moment Simone sat down beside him, he'd seem freshly reinhabited. As if he'd found light again, had fought his way out through all the hanging cobwebs and treacherous sinkholes within. Perhaps it was the activity – the singular mischievous ambition, the quiet escape from the house, the rush of fresh air, the working of his legs, the exercising smell of salt rising in his nostrils. Or perhaps it was a sudden awakening, finding himself sitting on a log on a beach with no immediate history of his path there. But whenever and however it happened it was easy for anybody to see that in those moments he wanted only one simple thing – to be himself again. Not even the best of himself, but the natural thinking, not-anywhere-near-perfect being he once was.

'I wasn't always such a fool,' he mumbled, his eyes still on the horizon. Simone knew enough from the photographs in Clara's house to know this was perfectly true. He plucked his double bass and people danced. He was the Brylcreem hero up on the stage, providing the rhythm and swing. He was the steady backbone of all that was shifting around him. In the group photos he was always the one staring straight into the lens with the big solid grin. Always with the look of a man who liked to be liked, who couldn't believe his luck.

'It just used to come to me,' he said. 'Not even something you had to think about, but now it gets all tangled.'

Simone wanted so badly to say exactly the right thing. But what was the right thing to say to man whose floating moment of insight made him see more clearly his sanctum had been plundered – and his source of all power, his very manliness, was wrecked. 'I still think you're a pretty cool dude,' she tried, but he turned his head and looked at her, and she felt as anyone would when a person had bared their scarce and precious truth and all you could find to offer in response was a token.

'Oh, have we met before?' he said.

26

It wasn't until Charlie had been safely returned home, and Simone was walking back to her house, that it occurred to her it was possible there had been some real intention behind Charlie's escapade. She'd assumed Charlie had just wandered down to the beach and she'd happened to find him sitting grieving for his lost self, but maybe that wasn't it. Maybe he was thinking of his future. Maybe if the clouds parted just enough for you to see that all your tomorrows contained little more than a sad and increasing dependency, you'd seize that opportunity to consider the alternatives. Who would not begin to think, in that rare moment of clarity, a quicker death might have more dignity? Maybe he'd been sitting there plucking up the courage.

Simone was so lost in the terribleness of this thought she wasn't quite equipped for a car pulling into her driveway, from which two men emerged. At first she thought it was the police returning. But after a moment she recognised Joey, and then realised they'd arrived in Lexie's mother's station wagon. The other man, she could see now, was Alice's son, although he didn't live up to the idea she had of him. Taking her cue off the photo on Alice's wall she'd imagined her forthcoming visitor would be more conventional. She'd expected him to arrive wearing a suit and tie, or at least a polo shirt, looking serious, perhaps a little grave, in his neatly clipped hair. But even as he stood leaning on the car, with his big arms folded, watching her come up the street, she could detect something wayward about him. Perhaps it was the gingery sideburns that almost met at his chin. Perhaps it was the black beanie on his head with *Metallica* embroidered across the turn up. Perhaps the unapologetically appraising way he was watching her, with eyes that seemed to be able to look in two places at once. He was not, after all, likely to be a professional accountant, or a funeral director.

And there, standing on the other side of the car was Joey. Joey, who had kissed her and left. An awkward moment followed, where she had the familiar dilemma of not knowing quite how to greet him – a quick peck on the cheek, or just say hello? She thought at first he'd cut his hair short since she last saw him, but now realised he'd just tied it back off his face. His usual reserve made her stand back from him, and he took that moment to introduce the other man. 'Ethan,' he announced, in exactly the same low-key manner his nephew Billy, when he was a toddler, used to point at any passing animal and say *dog*.

Clouseau went up to them and sniffed with interest at their crotches. While Joey pushed him away with his knee, Ethan squatted down, a little awkwardly, and started rough-housing him, letting him lick at his face. 'Good boy,' he was saying, 'Good boy.' Simone looked on, liking to see Clouseau respond to any attention with lavishly returned affection, but then she realised how quickly she'd become used to relying on Clouseau's constancy, thinking of him as her dog. Now might be the moment she loses him.

She led the two men inside but as they went through the door she remembered she hadn't yet tidied up after last night. Ethan and Joey stood in the kitchen looking around. Joey scratched the back of his head.

With friendly mockery, Ethan said, 'Well. You're not much of a housekeeper are you!'

'But I didn't make this mess,' she protested too earnestly, rushing to start shutting the drawers, closing the cupboards.

'What's the story then?' Ethan asked. He had the kind of accent you get when you've been living overseas for a while. Not quite recognisably British, but cleanly enunciated. And now he was looking directly at her she noticed his eyes were very subtly out of alignment. Not so much that they were conspicuously damaged, but enough to induce a tiny amount of uncertainty about how to meet his gaze.

'Um, the police came,' she said, thinking as she said it that

185

perhaps she should've made something up. She saw the windmill tin and tucked it back into the cupboard.

'The pigs?' Ethan exclaimed, exchanging a glance with Joey. 'What the hell for?'

'Um, it was a drug bust.' This sounded so ridiculous she couldn't help smiling. They looked at her as if she was having them on.

'For real?' Joey asked, bemused. 'Did they find any?'

She nodded. 'Couple of joints.'

'Yours?' Ethan asked, impressed.

'Um, no.'

'Well, whose then?'

She shrugged. Who was she to tell him about his ailing mother's pot habit?

'Man, that's weird,' he said, with a slight note of paranoia.

Joey sniffed loudly and said, 'Did they take it away?'

She nodded.

'Bummer,' he said.

She offered them some tea. Was tea what you offered here? Suddenly she felt overshadowed, inside the house the pair of them had such an enormous presence they seemed to take up all the air. She felt small and shy and girlish and could barely look at Joey. Did he even remember? He was pretty drunk at the time.

While the kettle boiled Joey went outside to have a smoke and Ethan wandered through the house, looking about. She caught up with him near the bedroom door and explained she hadn't been sleeping there but on the daybed in the sun room. He slipped off his jacket and tossed it down on his mother's bed, staking his claim. 'Do you want me to leave now you're here?' she asked, staying near the door.

'Nah, you're all right,' he said. 'I don't really know how long I'm gonna be here anyway.'

They all sat at the kitchen table while she poured out the tea from the pot. 'Shall I be mother?' she said. They smiled weakly, but it wasn't really the kind of joke that amused them.

She wished she hadn't said it. She wished she wasn't tinkering around with mugs and milk and teapots, serving them. It would've been cooler not to have offered them tea at all. She glimpsed at Joey's face, but he sat waiting with an expression as impenetrable as a locked door.

After a couple of sips from his cup, Ethan looked at Joey and said, 'Spot of fishing this afternoon, mate?'

Joey said, 'I was thinking we could check out the surf.'

'Okay. But dunno if I'm up to much,' Ethan said.

Joey nodded and said, 'Oh yeah, I keep forgetting about the . . .'

Ethan shot him a warning look, and he didn't say any more.

She told them she was due in at work

'Okay. Whatever,' Ethan smiled. 'See you later then.'

To Joey she said, 'Do you think you'll still be here when I get back?'

He just shrugged.

Glancing back through the window she saw them still sitting at the dining table, looking like two men who understood each other easily.

27

When she got home late that afternoon Ethan and Joey were out, but they'd left behind the smell of fried bacon, and a small stack of dishes in the sink. There was a sleeping bag on the sofa in the living room so it looked like Joey might be staying the night. Glad they weren't home, she went and stretched out on the daybed, in the silent house, and closed her eyes, trying to think about her day.

On her way in to work she'd noticed Toss sitting on his front porch, wearing a singlet and his usual pair of soft brown corduroy trousers. His woollen-socked feet were stretched out in front of him and he was holding on to a mug of tea and gazing distractedly into his garden. He looked so bereft she was drawn towards him. His front gate creaked as she opened it and as she came up the path he said, 'Simone, lovely, sit yourself down on the steps of the house of ill repute. I think this old man has a bit of apologising to do.'

She stepped onto his weathered porch and sat, leaning her back on the balustrade, and Clouseau settled himself down between them. Toss indicated his mug and said, 'Think there's still a bit left in the pot. I'll just go inside and get you a cuppa. If you've got a minute.' She told him she'd love one, and when he came back out of the house a couple of minutes later he said, 'I'd offer you a hash cookie to go with it, but it appears I'm all out this morning.'

His expression was dry, unreadable. 'Is that what you used to do with it? Make hash cookies.'

'Sometimes. I did a bit of experimenting around with recipes but I found the best was the Anzac biscuit recipe from my wife's old Edmonds Cookbook. She probably would've had a conniption about that, but they went down pretty nice.'

The tea he handed her was milkier than she would've liked,

with floaters on the surface. She'd already had a lot of tea that morning – with Clara, with Joey and Ethan.

'Some of the older ones used to have trouble smoking it, you see,' he told her. He gave her a thin smile which showed signs of strain. She noticed that the silvery stubble that most often graced his chin was gone. One of the first things he'd done this morning was to clean-shave his face.

'Have you worked out who reported you?' Simone asked, hoping that by now she might have been crossed off the top of the suspect list.

'Actually I was just sitting having a bit of a contemplate on that.' He reached for his tobacco pouch and began rolling a smoke. 'I reckon I was getting a bit cocky about it all. I was just sitting here thinking about how my father used to be. He grazed a few sheep in a wee paddock behind the house, see, and now and then he liked to invite people around for a Sunday roast. All through the meal there'd be, beaming with pride, waiting for somebody to say how tasty it was so he could boast that he raised the best hogget for miles around.' He paused to lick along the edge of the paper. 'I reckon I was getting a bit like that myself. Couldn't help skiting about the quality of the stuff. I never sold it to anyone though. Never even gave it to anybody who was not on a pension. Hard to see where the crime was really.'

He put the cigarette between his lips and lit it, and for a moment they both gazed out over his vegetable garden, their eyes drawn to the restfulness of its rows. 'Whoever it was had the wrong end of the stick though,' he told her. 'Those fellas weren't too impressed with the size of the yield. You could see the disappointment all over their faces. Reckon they were expecting more. I tried to give them a few lettuces to take home to their missus to make up for it but they weren't having that.'

'Their loss then.'

'Mmmm,' he agreed, almost beginning to grin as he took his next draw. 'Did it give you much of a fright?' he asked without looking at her. 'When they came?'

'A bit,' she confessed. She told him they'd found her out in the garden and Clouseau had tried to scare them off. She would've liked to have made a funny story about the cops digging up her buried box, but then she would've had to try and explain what was inside the box and that would get around everybody else too.

'I'm sorry. I don't know why on earth they got onto you like that. Or the others.' He let out a slightly defeated sigh. 'I expect it'll all come out in the wash one day but . . . well . . . is there something I can do to make up for it?'

She reached across Clouseau to lightly pat his arm. 'It's fine, Toss. It's okay. One of those things. Soon it'll be quite funny.'

He grimaced. 'You reckon? I hope you're right. But you know, I've never even had a fine before this. Now I'm about to go to court and be a bloody criminal.'

She glanced at the side of his face as he took a long, deep drag and wondered if he'd felt like a different man when he'd looked into his shaving mirror that morning. *Now I am a criminal.* There must have been other more important moments in his life, though, when he'd got up in the morning and stared into that mirror feeling for the first time like a changed man. *Now I am a husband. Now I am a father. Now I am a widower.* These were the only things she really knew of him, and in a lifetime they weren't all that much. And he knew little of her, yet on face value he almost immediately sought to befriend her, in his way.

'It's not so bad. Maybe they could give you diversion,' she said. She wanted to say something else. It was like a pressure, waiting to burst forth. I've committed a couple of crimes too, she wanted to say. It's not so hard to achieve, all you need is a little motivation.

Occasionally she studied photographs of serious offenders, rapists and murderers, in the newspaper and tried to see what it was in their face that could give them away. Often they were dressed in their best clothes, for their court date, and it was hard to distinguish them from the photographs of the people

190

on the business pages, except that shame and an awareness of public scrutiny made them appear more often in a humble posture. Stripped of their crime-doing demeanour the faces of the men often looked quite handsome. She could imagine them leaning over the café counter asking for the sugar and appearing quite desirable. The only thing she ever learned from that kind of scrutiny was that looks are deceptive, it's always all in the accumulation of facts and evidence. Nobody would've looked into Toss's garden – with its neat little lines of veges and its chummy old occupant – and imagined marijuana was growing in the back bedroom under lights. For all she knew he had boy scouts buried under the floorboards, a taste for snuff movies, and a tendency towards violence when pushed, but she would never look into that salty old face and suspect it. And nobody would look at her face and think the worst – car thief, vandal, cautious seeker of vengeance.

In reality she didn't have the honest inclination to see herself as that corrupted, just somebody who had responded extremely badly under testing circumstances. Even Fraser was apparently able to see it in the light of *feistiness*. Now that her overall temperature had dropped back to something approaching normal she could begin to rationalise what had been so unbalancing back when it started – mostly that Fraser had appeared so unharmed, even quite happy, while she was so pained. She saw now that her actions might've been about wanting him to feel loss as well. But then, was that any justification? Those terrible men in the photographs probably had all manner of ways to rationalise their misdemeanours too. And while they were being made to atone for their crimes, behind bars or whatever, they probably found out the same thing she did – trying to inflict your own pain onto others is no solution for living.

Once she got in to work another thought occurred to her and she began to feel quite paranoid. Clearly Fraser knew it was her that had stolen the car. He'd talked openly about it, revealing her embarrassingly to anybody that knew them personally, but was it also possible that he'd reported it? She remembered the police writing down her details the night before and began to wonder if her name was on some database somewhere. Maybe they'd been delivering the warrants for her arrest to her last address. It was quite possible they hadn't known where to find her until now. All day the hair on the back of her neck had prickled every time somebody opened the door to the café, and it was only now that the day had passed without incident, and she was home lying down, that she could let some of that worry slide away from her.

Clouseau padded softly in and lay down on the floor beside her and she dropped her hand to rest on his stomach, feeling the movement of his breathing, like the swell and fall of loyal assurance. After a little while the phone rang and she dragged herself to the kitchen to answer it. It was Lexie.

'Ingrid told me,' she said.

Simone felt her mouth form an *oh,* but no sound came out.

There was a too-long silence before Lexie said, 'There's something I want you to know.' Her voice was quiet and calm. 'That magazine story. It wasn't quite the way that stupid idiot made it sound, you know. He came in to see me at my work, around the time of your birthday.'

Simone slid down the wall she'd been leaning against. As she sat she could feel the coldness of the kitchen floor through the material of her jeans. 'And?' she whispered.

'Exactly?'

'Yes, please, tell me exactly.'

'Well to use his exact words he just said to tell that *nutbag* he'd changed the locks.'

'Nutbag?' Simone repeated. So this is what she is to him now. Just a woman to whom he feels he can legitimately attach labels. Stalker. Nutbag.

'I know,' Lexie said. 'Bastard. But he did say it in a kind of affectionate way. And that was about all. I mean he must have known about the car then, right? But he didn't say. I only found out about all that from Ingrid yesterday.'

192

Simone looked at the floor in front of her and had the sudden urge to lie down and put her hot cheek on the cold, dirty brown lino.

'I didn't offer you the house as a favour to him,' Lexie said. 'I wanted it to be a favour to you. I wanted you to have the chance to breathe – but as soon as we got there and I saw it . . .'

'Was he really, really mad at me?' Simone whispered into the telephone, realising she wanted him to be. She wanted him to be so mad he'd come and yell at her. She wanted to have a fight with him. A dirty, slapping, physical fight.

'Not overly. Considering.'

For a little while there was only the sound of breathing on the line. 'I'd probably do a lot worse if Anton did what he did,' Lexie said eventually.

'Well if you ever suspect him let me know,' Simone said. 'I'm thinking of hiring myself out.'

She didn't hear any response, not the brief acknowledging laugh she was expecting, just a slight fizzy crackle in the line.

'Should I have done more?' Lexie asked. 'I should've, shouldn't I. I could've tried to talk to you more. You weren't quite yourself after . . . well . . . from when you lost the baby I guess, you were all sort of clammed up and I didn't quite know how to talk to you about it. Ingrid and I, we both just sort of tried to be around. And I guess I kind of thought you'd talk in your own time . . . and then Dad . . . but maybe if I'd tried harder you wouldn't have . . .'

'No Lexie. Please stop that.' Had she? Clammed up? If she had it wasn't Lexie's fault. 'It's not like I didn't know it was . . . off, all that stuff I did,' she admitted. 'I couldn't think straight. He tipped me on my head but I just missed him. And I was suddenly so alone. And I didn't want her to have him.'

'I sort of miss him too,' Lexie said. 'I realised that when I saw him. He's sort of feckless but he has something – you always feel like something interesting's about to happen around him. Do you remember that time he turned up at one of Billy's birthday parties dressed in a gorilla suit and got all those little boys so whipped up they were practically peeing their pants with excitement?'

Simone fiddled with the cord on the telephone and felt her eyes begin to prickle. She didn't think she could bear to talk about what was good about Fraser.

'Sorry,' Lexie murmured.

'Do you think he could be happy now?' Simone asked. 'With her? With a baby on the way?'

Lexie didn't answer immediately. 'Do you remember Jimmy? Jimmy from the band?' she asked. 'Well the other day I heard he got some girl pregnant. And it made me think about guys like him and Fraser. They go around causing heartache here and there and everywhere because they believe in some kind of stupid idealised perfection which mostly just makes them shit at relationships. But then they start to feel their age creeping up on them and they suddenly realise they can't resist the fact that they love their own sperm and so they just grab whatever girl is handiest and get her pregnant.'

'Poor girl who ends up having Jimmy's baby.'

'Hey. Shut up. Once I wanted that to be me,' Lexie said, laughing a little. 'And you know what? To somebody else looking in, it doesn't look like such a good prospect having Fraser as the father of your child either. He was never exactly mister reliable.'

'I guess,' Simone said. Not able to let herself picture it, realising she'd never particularly aspired to reliability as an uppermost quality.

Softly Lexie asked, 'Are you all right? Will you come back to us soon? Did I tell you about crazy Georgia?'

'What's she been up to now?' Simone asked. She felt a spooky sense of relief, like a storm of swallows had flown into the house and then suddenly departed again through the back door, leaving nothing but a staticy aftermath in the air. She and Lexie returned easily to their default positions, and Georgia could be relied on to generate something diverting. It might be all right.

'She's had crabs, and I don't mean for dinner.'

'Crabs! Ker-rist, I thought they were well in the past. How did that happen?'

'She said she must have picked them up in a public toilet,' Lexie told her, 'but it's pretty obvious what's going on.'

'She's not the only one her lover is fucking?'

'I know, revolting isn't it. But she's been having the time of her life sex-wise and doesn't want to give it up so she's not asking any questions.'

'She's a nutbag then.'

'Yeah, there's a lot of that going around,' Lexie said.

Clammed up? That was the kind of thing people said of Jean Batten in that book she'd been reading – *The Garbo of the Skies*. People said that in her later years she was emotionally shut down and unapproachable, but so little was known of her inner life. She'd been forced to stop flying during the war, had never had children, and had ended up living a good proportion of her life with her mother. People tried to put her behaviour, her emotional inarticulateness, down to something quite singular – her disappointment in the loss of limelight – but these things tend not to be singular, they occur more as a sequence, a gradual tightening that becomes a consequence in itself. Simone remembered a distant day when she was lying in the sun on the living room floor reading a magazine, and Fraser's old tabby cat climbed onto her back and nestled itself down within the hollow of her lower arch. Fraser came into the room, returning from somewhere, and at that moment both she and the cat swivelled their heads to look at him. He laughed and said, 'And how's my little family today?' She smiled up at him, and then they found they had to avert their eyes from each other. There was a sense they both knew they desperately needed a fresh face around the place. 'Maybe this month,' she had secretly thought to herself – that constant stalling hopeful thought, drawing her down into its murky chamber.

*

The quietness of the house had an anticipatory feeling, a sense of imminent change, like a parked vehicle awaiting a foot on the accelerator. She was in bed when Ethan and Joey came clomping in. She pretended to be asleep and heard one of them pull the door closed between the kitchen and the sun room. She caught a whiff of beery pores and smoky clothes. She could hear them moving about in the kitchen, opening drawers and shushing each other. She heard the sound of a bread knife cutting through a loaf. Of lids being screwed off jars, and the fridge being opened. And then there was a silence, where she imagined the two men sitting opposite each other at the table, eating, like two tired wildebeests just in from the plain.

'Good night, huh,' she heard one of them say.

'Yeah.'

'How's that guy at the pool table.'

'Yeah. Uptight little nostril!'

'Yeah. You sorted him, but.'

Nothing else was said and soon she heard them go off to bed. From the living room came the sound of somebody, presumably Joey, rustling into a sleeping bag, and after just a few moments, snoring. She lay there, unable to sleep, listening to the sound of it. There was a quality about it that was very definitely masculine. His exhales seemed to harden the air.

What was it about Joey especially that made her so uneasy? She was precariously drawn to him and certainly that kiss had confirmed there was some kind of physical appeal, but she had no instinct for knowing how he felt about her. He had that male evasiveness, but both he and Ethan were different to Fraser. They didn't have his easy charm, but also they didn't appear to need people to like them particularly. There was that take-it-or-leave-it quality about both of them. And there seemed to be something dangerously unfathomable about them, as if underneath they could be swarming with fetishes and fixations and some kind of unquiet stream of rage. But she knew too their tough exteriors were a shelter for something else, something far less certain – one of them, at least, was

196

a man with a slightly sentimental regret for his unachieved ambitions.

She felt stirred and curious, drawn and repelled all at the same time.

In the morning she was woken by a loud, unapologetic blast from the next room. She should've been disgusted but for some reason she wasn't. The essential freeness of it made her want to laugh, in the same way you could find yourself laughing at a really bad joke. She quietly pulled on her jeans and a sweatshirt under the covers, swung her legs out, laced up her shoes, and left the house with Clouseau.

It was early, just getting light. A mist hovered over the sea and oyster catchers were raking over the shore. Further down the beach she saw a man out walking with his dog, and she thought sometimes it might be good to be a certain kind of man, walking around feeling your cock rubbing on the seam of your pants, supposedly thinking of sex every eight seconds, being strong, being unafraid, being able to fight, letting out that big rollicking night-time snoring, stinking up the bed with man-sweat and farts, pulling on the same underwear as yesterday, standing while you piss.

She'd once attended a workshop at the network run by a tall, rangy, power-loving, speed-talking consultant. He was working on improving their *cross-departmental communication*, a previous survey having found a problem in this area, and chose to start off the day with something he referred to as a fun exercise. 'Stand up if the answer is yes,' he instructed. It had started out easy – *Do you have more than one sibling? Do you eat breakfast in the morning?* – and then moved into more ambiguous areas, with the questions coming faster and faster. *Have you ever told a lie at work? Have you ever taken a sickie?* There was no time to think about the answer, and when they were finally asked if they peed in the shower every man in the room and only one of the women jumped to their feet. The remaining women were left looking at each other, expressions of amazement on their faces, realising they'd truly learnt something that day.

Simone walked on to the café, and then around and beyond it for the twenty-minute walk towards the shopping centre. On the way she passed a clay bank from which she heard a soft, enquiring noise – a gentle *kree, kree*. Looking around, wondering where it had come from, she noticed a small round hole dug into the clay. She squatted to look down into it and it took her a moment to realise she was staring into the snug lodge of a quietly nesting kingfisher. She moved quickly away, not wanting to scare the bird any more than she already had, with her big monster eye.

She began to wonder why she'd never had any desire to explore the shops before. She'd been happy to narrow her needs, and liked the idea of rejecting the quagmire of wants and temptations she might find there. It lacked the curiosity she was raised with though, her father's tendency to always nose the car down any unknown laneway just because they'd never been before.

The single street of shops was quiet and closed, so empty there was no movement other than the wind kicking a few leaves about the streets. And despite herself, she was drawn to the beautiful things displayed in the windows of the little boutiques. Cloth sunhats and nice sneakers and embroidered skirts and hand-moulded chocolates and ready-to-go picnic sets. And there were other more practical things – sun creams and mosquito repellent, can openers and towels. There was a bakery that promised to sell the southern hemisphere's best Cornish pasties. There was a butcher's, a fruit shop, and down the far end, a small supermarket. There was a place to get your films developed and a couple of cafés where you could expect white-bread sandwiches and cakes with pink icing. The whole little shopping centre had a sort of cheerful obliviousness to the march of McDonald's franchises and Warehouse megamarkets going on elsewhere.

At the far end of the line of shops was the gallery. She

stood against the window, sheltering her eyes with her hands, pressing her nose to the glass, curious to see inside, to see the things Marjorie's lot offered for sale. There was a slight movement at the back of the shop and she realised somebody was waving at her. Marjorie. She came bustling over to open the door. 'You're up with the birds!' she said. 'I was just making tea. Join me?'

While Marjorie went out the back to fill the kettle Simone was left to look around the shop. She was conscious of feeling guarded, hoping this visit wouldn't be made into a sly scheme to induce her into a voluntary job she didn't want. Most of the items were made from traditional crafts, crocheting, knitting, quilting, embroidery, some unglazed pottery. Fraser would've dismissed it all as dull and uncreative but in their own way these things had a kind of ticking integrity that reminded Simone of clean kitchens and home baking and everything that was sunny about nostalgia. There was something lovely and naïve and limited about it, a display of expended effort, the work of good women facing a kind of extinction.

'Wow,' Simone said when Marjorie came out with a tray and put it on the counter. 'Everything here is so . . .' Just then her eye was drawn to a wall display of photographs, hung so high she missed them at first, and even these had a particular domestic quality to them. The Russia Marjorie had captured through her lens was not the juxtaposition of communistic poverty against gilded structures that might be the expected symbolism of that period. She'd documented instead the daily lives of women. Their crafts, their food, their shopping trips. A kind of quiet continuity. The anachronistic nature of them suited the shop. There was one portrait of an old woman looking into a gilded mirror as she tied a scarf around her head – her fingers were all bent and twisted out of shape, her hair was negligible, her eyes retreated so far they were almost shut, and yet she was laughing in recognition of herself. Looking at this Simone suddenly found herself having to reconcile her idea of the woman behind the camera – who'd framed this moment with such kind curiosity – with the woman she thought she was getting to know.

'Alice started it all off, you know,' Marjorie told her, standing at the counter moving the teapot around in a stirring motion. 'At first she set up a market on the weekends over summer, and then later we all got a collective going and opened this place.'

'What did Alice make?'

'Oh, never the same thing twice. But mostly doll's clothes. They were such dear little things. And then of course later there were the dioramas.'

'Dioramas?'

Marjorie looked around as if she expected to see some on the walls. 'Oh,' she said. 'Goodness, there are none left any more.'

Simone had always believed that whatever Alice did with all her junk was something bordering on an obsessive compulsive disorder. She'd thought she probably made crackpot gifts people would accept politely and put into a cupboard until the next time Alice was due for a visit. It hadn't occurred to her there could be some kind of legitimacy, that people could've actually wanted to buy the things she made. At that moment she would've given almost anything to see one of Alice's creations.

'What were they like? Her dioramas? What were they of?'

'Oh all sorts,' Marjorie said. 'She was very creative. And she had a magpie talent for the details of other people's lives, even little things. Once there was a time I told her a story about my son . . . oh wait a minute . . . I may still have that one here. I think it's out the back somewhere.'

Marjorie went to find it and Simone was left thinking *son?* She hadn't known about him before, but then again she'd never asked. 'Here it is,' Marjorie said, placing a small three-walled box down on the bench and swivelling it around for Simone to see. She lowered herself down so she could look directly inside, and for a moment was so amazed she had to make a small gulp for breath. It was an involving little scene – two dolls sitting down to tea, while one had her hair combed by a little doll dressed as a small boy. Alice had layered clippings from home decoration magazines to create a dimensional effect on the walls. On the table in front of the two dolls was a collection of tea things – cups and saucers and a tiny teapot, and a plate with tiny pastries all made from painted clay. The two female dolls were dressed in sixties-style clothes. One had an elaborately high beehive hairdo, while the other was having her hair teased up by the boy standing on a chair behind her. The boy doll was much too small, and the other two seated dolls didn't quite match each other in size either but she'd twisted their limbs in such a way they appeared to be quite animated in gossip while they were having their hair done. Suddenly what had once seemed to Simone like nothing more than a set of unfocused idiosyncrasies now swarmed and resettled into a recognisable talent.

'Once I told Alice about how when my son was a little boy the other expat wives and I used to pay him pocket money to tease our hair up into beehives,' Marjorie said. 'It was the fashion then, of course. She tucked that away in that busy mind of hers and later she presented this to me on my birthday.'

'This is a real treasure then,' Simone commented.

Marjorie smiled a little doubtfully.

'And where is he now? Your son?'

'Oh did I never mention him to you before? Owns a very successful design shop in London. He lent me the money to keep our little bach, after the city house had to be . . .' She caught herself, and instead of continuing on picked up a sachet of sweetener and shook it into her cup, her gold bracelets jangling on her arm. Without looking up she said, 'He's . . . you know . . . lives with another man.'

'Oh.' Simone was so surprised she couldn't immediately think of anything else to say.

'I never took this one home,' Marjorie told her, turning the box back around so she could look at it herself. 'My husband wouldn't have approved.'

'Of you telling Alice the story?'

201

'No. The hair. Afterwards . . . later . . . he said we were to blame.'

'To blame?'

Marjorie looked for a moment as if she wasn't sure she'd say anything more. At some time in her life she'd developed a habit of maintaining her composure by pursing her lips and refusing to acknowledge any inconvenient enquiry. But she forged on: 'That our son turned out . . . you know.'

Simone had always had a notion she might find Stanley to be something of a charming rogue, but now she suspected she wouldn't like him at all. 'But of course that's just . . . absurd,' she said.

'Yes, you're right,' Marjorie agreed with a quick uncomfortable laugh. 'He was rather keener than a boy should've been, even back then.'

A large delivery truck rattled past the front door of the shop, on its way to drop off the morning's bread at the supermarket. Simone blew at the steam rising from her mug. 'So do you always start this early?'

Marjorie explained somebody else was doing her turn for a week or two and she'd just come in early to get things all nicely set up. When Simone asked what she was doing with her time off she didn't answer, instead busying herself with rearranging the display items.

'Holiday?' Simone prompted.

A lot more shifting and tidying was found to be done behind the counter. But there was something different about Marjorie this morning, a slightly edgy vulnerability, like she didn't quite have her usual grasp on that busy, bold energy of hers. And while she probably didn't have any intention of letting out what was bothering her so, in the end she couldn't quite contain it either. 'Well I guess you'll hear about it soon enough,' she said briskly. 'I suppose you know where he's been, don't you?'

'I think so,' Simone replied, hoping she wouldn't think she'd been whispering about her.

'Yes, well he has a parole meeting and they're deciding

whether to let him out with one of those leg thingies,' she said, slightly grumpily, as if this admission had been forced out of her and she wasn't to be held responsible. 'I'm going to do my part.'

'Oh. He's coming home?'

Marjorie picked up the milk and took it back out to the fridge in the rear of the shop. When she came back she said, 'Have you seen the paper today?' Simone shook her head and Marjorie told her there was a small story about the raid. Just a paragraph reporting that a local man, no names, had been charged with cultivation of cannabis and would appear in court next week.

'Silly old Toss,' she added. 'At his age, too. I always knew that business would end in trouble. And look what happened – the police at everybody's doors. Involving you in it all too. It's just lucky the whole street isn't going to court. I warned him so many times. Warned them all.' For a moment there was that small jut of the chin, that familiar surety in the set of her mouth. But now it seemed less a tendency towards imperiousness, more just a kind of self-preservation. After all those years in a world where propriety was held in high value, the only leftover asset she had to call on was her own resilience. Everybody had something.

'Still,' Marjorie added then, 'You can't put the toothpaste back in the tube, can you?'

'Exactly,' Simone agreed.

203

28

There was escalating talk about the raid in the café. The five elderly women Simone had seen on her first day, and never again since, now sat at a table in the corner. They were loudly swapping misinformed theories, overexcited at their own proximity to *news*. It was a big operation, they agreed. People were hauled off to jail. There was the manufacture of drugs. Gangs were involved. A lot of comings and goings had been noticed. Kitchens had been converted into crime labs. Innocents had been duped. What was the matter with youth today?

As Simone set down their coffees she knew she could easily put them right, but it wasn't possible without admitting some knowledge of the facts, and that would've only redirected their misguided enthusiasm towards much dearer ground.

When Ethan and Joey pushed their way in through the main door a sudden stillness fell upon that table.

'You were up early,' Ethan commented sunnily to Simone, while Joey went straight to the business of piling a plate with food. They each ordered a coffee, and as they moved off towards a table by the window Simone noticed Ethan had quite a pronounced limp. On the far side of the room vigorous assumptions were now being aired.

Hanife came and stood beside her. 'And?'

'Alice's son,' Simone explained.

'And who is the other big handsome one?'

'Joey, his cousin.'

'And they are staying at the house?'

Simone nodded.

'Well . . . a lucky new turn for you, huh,' Hanife said, her approval seeming to be against the overall consensus from the women in the corner, who already had Ethan and Joey deeply

204

implicated in shady proceedings – that being a general injustice that men with flourishing facial hair and tattooed sleeves were bound to attract from some quarters.

Ethan and Joey took their time over their breakfast. They spread the paper out in front of them and spent a lot of attention on the sports pages. They ordered second and third coffees and initially didn't seem to notice their general leisure was taunting certain other customers. However, gradually it started to bother them that they appeared to be under observation. Joey's response was to slump further down in his chair, his baseball cap pulled low over his eyes, his feet planted widely on the floor, and his general demeanour suggesting he was highly aware of the exit. Ethan, though, played up to it – smiling across at the other table where eyes would flit away as soon as they realised they'd been noticed. With an element of playful incitement he threw back his arms in a stretch and let out a loud attention-winning yawn.

'Some people easy make themselves at home,' Hanife whispered. 'His big open mouth remind me once I hear about a circus accident in China. Some dwarfs was doing acrobatics and one flips up and lands in mouth of a hippo in the middle of a big yawn. The hippo swallows and the crowd cheer and clap. They thinking it was part of the act.'

'And what happened to the dwarf?' Simone asked.

Hanife shrugged, 'Out the other end maybe?' She immediately went back to cutting sandwiches but Simone could see there was a slight lift in her movements, some seasoning in her day.

Ethan and Joey were still at the table when some shy Japanese tourists came up to the counter and pointed to Clouseau out on the deck and then to their camera. It was a helpless kind of pride that sent Simone outside along with them to get Clouseau to pose prettily for the picture, but once she was out on the deck they indicated they wanted her in shot too. She tried to resist but they were politely insistent so she found herself squatting and smiling alongside Clouseau, aware of Ethan and Joey watching from the window. As she was re-entering the café, she passed them leaving and Joey said mockingly, 'Did you ask for a copy for your Mum?'

She turned and watched them walk off the balcony and head down onto the beach – Joey with mild disdain in his low-back swagger, and Ethan with some effort in his step – and when she swung back around her she saw how many other eyes were still on them. The five women, the dog, Hanife.

As other people came through the café it began to make her subtly uncomfortable that somebody she didn't know could display a stupid photograph of her in a faraway country. She'd seen an article recently listing the ways in which people's movements are systematically recorded – cellphone calls, credit card use, in-store cameras, video rentals, street surveillance, computer browsing, speed cameras, loyalty cards. She'd mentally ticked through them all, noticing with satisfaction the unintended efficiency in the way she was sidestepping all kinds of involuntary subscription. Although, thinking about it, she realised that since then she'd lost some comfort in that anonymity – in a short space of time she'd become the unnamed stalker in a magazine article, and the unwitting insider to a minor drug crime. Even the silent privacy of her home had been encroached on. But if she was unsettled it was probably nothing compared to what poor old Toss must be feeling with the kind of public exposure he was now facing. This was probably the worst bit of it all for him, this period between the incrimination and the conviction.

Hanife was able to resist any questions only until the lull after lunch. 'So that one Joey,' she asked with such forced casualness Simone was alerted. 'You like him?'

Simone shrugged. 'I don't really know him. He's the kind of guy you could know for a while but not have a clue about the thoughts going round in his head.'

'Maybe a stubborn kind of man. He looks out the side of his eyes, like he's thinking he knows all about how to unstitch you.'

For a moment Simone felt a stupid confusion over the word *you*. Did Hanife mean it in a general sense, a personal sense, or did she think he knew all about how to unstitch her? 'Do you think that's good or bad?' she asked.

'It's good and bad. I think a strong man is best,' Hanife told her. 'My husband, he always let me do everything I want. At first he keep saying he adore me and he just want me to be happy and so everything I want he give in to. So sometimes I start to want unreasonable things, to see if he still give in. And he did.'

'And you disliked that?'

'Wouldn't you? It make me behave worse and worse. Like testing him or something, and then when he forgive I hated him. So I made horrible moods, I got lazy. It begin to panic me what I could turn into with him. He was too easy. Too tolerant. You understand?'

Simone thought that, if anything, she understood more about what it was like to fall on the parallel side. She'd once mentioned across the lawn to Caroline, who was then still just a neighbour and was out weeding her flowerbeds, that she was on a mug-gathering trip around the house and garden because Fraser never brought his coffee cups back to the sink. Caroline had commented abruptly that she wouldn't put up with that kind of behaviour. It had caused Simone to flinch for a moment, thinking perhaps she *was* too tolerant, and then she'd thought it was easy for Caroline to say when she didn't live with someone as distracted as Fraser, who'd turn you into a harpy nag if you insisted on his tidiness. But maybe that was the thing exactly. Caroline was single-minded and stroppy, firm in her wants, while she was loosely indulgent. Maybe in the end he felt that stroppiness, in all its lack of permission, gave him something more exciting to work against.

It got busy again in the afternoon, and Simone stayed on later than usual. She wasn't in any hurry to go home anyway, the idea of bumping around in that little house with Ethan and Joey vaguely exhausted her. She was still there when Hanife locked up the till and pulled two beers from the back of the refrigerator, 'You want one?'

They went outside and sat on the deck, leaning against the front wall of the café. Hanife flipped off both caps with the opener on her key ring and Clouseau got up from where he'd been lying and flopped himself down again with a sigh, closer to Simone's feet. The sun was just above the horizon in front of them, radiating its long orange fingers across the surface of the sea.

'You know sometimes I'm so bored here that after work I check available men on a dating website,' Hanife said. 'I find one who look quite handsome in his picture, and then you click on his information about hisself, and he says he's a foot fetishist, just like that! He's good-looking though, and for a minute I'm thinking I should invite him around, give my feet a good going over.' She let out a wry little smile. 'Not really though. Just like to look at what's available sometimes. I could never make contact. Too scary, what you might get. Maybe perverts, stalkers. And around here, maybe someone you recognise too much.'

They sipped their beers, watching the gulls padding along the edge of the outgoing tide, pecking and sweeping about, like a team sent in to clear up after the big game. The idea that Hanife might be lonely had never quite occurred to Simone before.

'And sometimes when I stand at the counter,' Hanife continued, 'I look at the men drinking up their coffee and I play a game with myself – which one would I seduce to make a baby with.'

'You want a baby?'

'Some days yes, some days no.'

'But some days enough to think about just grabbing some guy and shagging him for a baby?'

'A young surfer maybe?' Hanife said.

Simone felt her stomach tighten. Hanife had a knack for randomly scaring people into believing she knew their every secret.

'You know a few years ago I did a blood test for DNA,' Hanife told her. 'They were digging up bodies at home and need a relative's blood. The blood of the children is not best, better to have parent or sibling, but for my father there was nobody but me. And so lately I go a bit mad thinking about it, about how if I have no children then will be the death of his whole strand of DNA.' Her voice had become slow, serious. She paused to put the bottle to her lips and swallowed some of the beer, keeping her eyes on the sinking sun in front of her. 'But see there is another side also. If you start to think about these DNA things then you must think too about who you mix yours up with. And if you just take it from a stranger, without the proper permission, then there is some part of stealing in that. Don't you think?'

This notion made Simone feel stirred to defend against it, needing to try and step up in some way. 'I read somewhere some scientist, I'm not sure who, maybe Carl Sagan or someone, once said we're all made of star stuff – the iron in our blood, the oxygen we breathe, the calcium in our bones – it all comes from things that happened in the universe before our solar system was formed. So maybe the science part is really basic – DNA is just a measure of genes and genes are just a set of inherited traits and those traits can be good and bad. People always assume children will inherit the best of the genes, but it's more random than that isn't it? So maybe its better not to think too hard about the science, it's got more to do with what you personally can and can't live with. Isn't it?' Having got that out Simone wasn't exactly sure of what she'd said, or if she'd succeeded at anything or not.

'So you think its okay to be random?'

'I'm not sure I'm the right person to ask.'

'Well, let me ask this.' Hanife said. 'If God comes and asks you pick between a baby and the great love of your life what you choose?'

Simone considered her response. If she was asked the same question a couple of years ago her answer may have been different. Her desire to have children had once been quite intense and animal. To choose a life without children is to allow yourself to be diverted from some rudimentary path, to step outside the generally accepted league and deny the instinct for continuity. The possibility is you could end up like Jean Batten, aloof and alone in a hostile world, dying quietly of an untreated dog bite in Spain, completely unrecognised in any kind of close way. But also she was beginning to suspect children were sometimes not enough to compensate for the absence of a good, equal love. Or perhaps she just needed to believe that. She thought of that sad-eyed goth girl who came into the café, spending endless days in the lonely company of her wordless, slow-growing boy. She thought of the groups of mothers who complain so loudly but could never admit they would give anything for some of the quality of attention they used to get from their partners. And she thought of Marjorie, sitting up alone at her breakfast table, not quite letting herself enjoy her only son for who he is. 'The great love,' she said.

'Me too,' Hanife said. They clinked bottles and briefly their eyes met in a moment of recognition. Even though they were born into different worlds, had travelled different routes, they had arrived at the same place – working hard to reconcile themselves against all the human possibilities that were starting to slip their grasp. As were, each in their own way, their role-deprived mothers. As were too, in many different ways, nearly everyone else Simone knew. This seemed to be a simple fact of living, at some point you found yourself swimming along in the ebb of attainment, reaching out for buoys along the way.

29

When Simone drifted in she found Joey beached on the sofa watching a rugby game in the living room and Ethan sitting in the kitchen working on a laptop, with a bottle of whisky and a half full glass at his elbow. The expression on his face suggested there was a medicating quality to his consumption.

'What are you up to?' she asked.

He told her he was emailing his aunty about his mother. She sat down and he began talking about his mother's illness. Mostly, he told her, she was in a semi-comatose state, paralysed down one side. The first stroke had robbed her of her ability to talk, but then a few weeks later she'd had another one which had taken away her comprehension of words so she was currently unable to understand even simple commands, although occasionally she softly babbled something unintelligible. She seemed to be hovering in a state between deep sleep and wakefulness and the doctors could tell him nothing, except that she was stable for now, had little hope of recovery, and could go on for months if not longer. Her two sisters came and sat with her every day, knitting and gossiping as if they were at a normal family get-together and she'd just dropped off for a doze in the corner. 'They've all lost their husbands and they have some kind of talent for sickrooms,' Ethan said, admitting that after a week and a half by her bedside he'd reached the stage where he couldn't bear it. He'd rather be working.

She asked him what he did back in London.

'Engineer, a kind of concrete slab specialist,' he said, and immediately she could see him as a man who would be successful in the world of men and tools and very heavy construction. He had big honest hands and a general firmness about him.

'So you're going back to that?'

'Not yet. And I dunno. I'm getting a bit sick of the fuckers.

It's the friggin' league of nations on those big building sites these days, and they all hate each other. I'm sick of all the scrapping just to get things done,' he said. 'And I'm tired of living in a smoggy dump as well.'

'So maybe you're staying here?'

He didn't answer straight away but looked towards the window. 'Do you know why I didn't come out as soon as it happened?' he asked. 'I was waiting for my fitting.' He reached down and tapped his lower leg. It made a solid sound.

'You have an artificial limb?'

He nodded.

'How . . . I mean . . . ?'

'I was saving some little kiddies from a runaway bus in London.'

'Really?'

'Nah,' he said, looking as though he was making a mental note about the potential usefulness of her gullibility. 'Just a motorcycle accident.'

He pulled up his jeans slightly and she saw stainless steel above his shoe. 'Does that creep you out?' he asked. 'I've been wondering what girls will make of my peg leg.' He looked at her closely, his eyes ready to gauge if her response might be a polite but meaningful lie. In that instant it occurred to her that *lazy* was a particularly apt description of what was wrong with his eyes, because in moments that mattered, like this one, he was perfectly able to bring both of them into central focus. She knew what she said next was important.

'I think it gives you a sort of mysterious rebel quality.'

He nodded in a quick involuntary way, pleased with that. She asked him when it happened.

'About a year ago,' he said. 'I never told Mum about it. I was in and out of the hospital for months and she never knew. Can't stand hospitals now. That place where she is gives me the shakes. I don't really want to go back but I know I have to.'

He told her the doctors had advised him he should consider signing a non-resuscitation order. 'You've got no idea what's

212

going through my head. I keep trying to make bargains with God and I don't even really believe in God.' He didn't have any idea about what his mother would want, because he hadn't even seen her for five years. 'Who am I to make that decision for her? I should've talked to her more. I've decided to give myself a few days to get my head together, and maybe go through her stuff and get to know her a bit that way, and then I'm gonna bite the bullet, go back, talk to my aunties, and try and hang with her for as long as it takes. Could be months.'

Simone told him having a last chance to talk to her, even if he didn't know what she could take in, was worth a lot. She told him about her own father's death. How she was just starting out as a journalist back then and she'd been sent away to cover an election tour, trailing around after the leader of the opposition. Her father had a slight heart attack and had been in hospital for twenty-four hours but her mother had resisted calling her. 'I wasn't sure if I should interrupt your important work,' she'd said later, slightly drawling the word important. The thing Simone didn't mention was how she'd never really been able to forgive her mother for not contacting her, even though nobody had expected that he would have the second massive attack that killed him.

Ethan gulped down a shot of whisky and then went to refill his glass but stopped suddenly. 'Oops, manners. Want some?'

She nodded.

He stood up and got another glass off the shelf. 'Straight?' he asked, 'Or maybe there's some ice. I'll check.'

'Straight,' she said urgently, but he was already opening the freezer door. She held her breath hoping he wouldn't notice. 'What on earth?' he said, turning to her, pointing to the condom. 'What's this doing here?'

'I dunno,' she tried. 'What is it?'

'It looks like . . .' he attempted to pick it up but it was stuck to the ice at the bottom of the freezer and he had to tug at it. The latex stretched a little then flicked into his fingers. 'It is. It's a condom. With stuff inside.'

Unable to move or speak, she watched him inspect it. 'Christ, definitely looks like frozen spunk. Yuk,' he said, dropping it onto the table and then picking it up again between the very tips of his fingers as if it was a live mouse. 'What the hell? And you know nothing about this?'

'Nothing,' she said in a tiny voice.

'Hey Joey,' he called out to next room. 'Joey, come here and check this out.'

Joey sauntered in. 'Eww, what are you showing me that for? You should get that in the bin, buddy,' he said.

'I found it in the fuckin' freezer.'

'Fuck that,' Joey said. 'That's out of it.' He turned his head to stare at Simone. 'Why would somebody do a thing like that?'

Ethan said, 'It's not hers.'

'She reckons, does she?' Joey said, looking intently at Simone. 'So what then? Maybe Aunty Alice acquired it on one of those drug-fuelled binges of hers? Do you think, Simone?'

He had a mean streak, she could see that now. It wasn't unexciting though.

Ethan flipped open the lid of the bin and tossed the condom in. Scratching the back of his head he said, 'Christ, Mum liked to collect lots of mad things, but surely she didn't . . .'

Later Simone reminded herself she'd never really seriously entertained the idea of defrosting the condom. At best it was probably only ever a souvenir of an afternoon when somebody breezed into her life with some sunny appreciation, and moved her a couple of steps out of the wreckage. The actual reality of messing around with what was inside was kind of revolting, and as Hanife had indicated, morally dubious, and a long way removed from the satisfying act of obtaining it, or the simplicity of choosing to throw it into the freezer. It was more that she'd just liked the idea there was an option on hold, just in case she was overcome and even the remotest chance seemed necessary to try.

She'd once heard about an experiment where some scientists had placed a rat on a rat-free island, and then monitored its reaction via a transmitter. For the first few days the rat had run all over the island from one end to the other and then it settled in one particular place for a few weeks. The transmitter signal then disappeared from the island, and researchers were astonished to have it turn up on an adjacent landfall, a considerable distance away. So strong, so innate had been the rat's desire to reproduce that it did something previously thought physiologically impossible. Simone had wondered how many times that rat had stood at the edge of the sea before it decided the risk was worth it, and every time she opened the freezer door she always used to wonder when the day would come that some beating instinct might override her doubts.

Over the next couple of days she felt especially uncomfortable at home because Joey kept giving her looks that suggested he had the measure of what she was – a dangerously ovulating woman out to trick any unsuspecting member of the male population if they didn't keep their wits about them. He was spending a lot of time lying on his stomach on the sofa, and Simone began to notice there was something stiff and painful about his movements. Ethan mentioned that Joey was in the process of getting another epic tattoo on his back, from an old guy who lived a couple of towns over and specialised in sailor-style *trad* work. They would be staying around until it was finished. 'Takes a bit of careful skill to get the action of the sea right,' Ethan said.

What Joey couldn't begin to discern is that the incident with the freezer had created a shift within her and he possibly *was* in a kind of jeopardy, but for reasons other than the ones he suspected. The stored condom had kept her, ever so slightly, tied to the idea that having a baby might still be a plausibility. But what if, she began to think, she really did just relinquish the prospect, let it melt away and be gone? A certain kind of tyranny is ended then, and a person is able to float free. Instead of the rat on the shoreline they become instead the defector who firmly decides they don't fancy a swim, leaving more space for entirely creative, maybe even quite wanton, thoughts about other creatures.

That evening Ethan cooked up a meal from ingredients he'd bought from the supermarket. She'd allowed herself to become almost ascetic in her food consumption, and the sight of big fat steaks frying in a pan was unexpectedly wonderful. She helped him set out the cooked steak and salad and roasted potatoes and they all ate together, with Joey sitting backwards on his chair to save his back. She started asking about the tattoos. She knew she could never get one herself because she didn't think she'd be able to decide on a design she would want for her whole life. The minute the needle was placed on her skin she'd begin to hate whatever she'd chosen.

Joey told her he never lived anywhere long enough to have art on his walls so he chose to have it on his skin. She suspected it was really more basic, more about projecting some kind of refusal to bend to convention. She asked him if she could see them and he didn't say anything for a few minutes. 'Can I?' she said again.

He told her the one of his back was covered in petroleum jelly and wrap at the moment, and as for the others, 'Well I've got one on my dick,' he said with a long slow drawl, the corner of his mouth curling up into a dare. 'It's a fish. For good Catholic girls who don't like to eat meat on a Friday.'

Ethan said, 'Steady on mate.'

Simone felt a twitch, the kind of reckless low-down flutter that is experienced involuntarily. She didn't let it show on her face. 'Actually I've never really liked fish,' she said with a tinsel primness.

Joey laughed. 'Just as well.' He reached forward and grabbed the last potato from a plate in the middle of the table. 'Ask him to show you his secret one,' he suggested, nodding in Ethan's direction.

'Shut up, Joey,' Ethan said.

Alone in her bed she found herself thinking about what it would be like to trace around the lines of Joey's tattoos with her finger, with her tongue. His testing her, trying to find out if she was dangerous enough, made her feel hemmed in by the scent of something. The tang of hellfire and sin. She could still fall for it, just as easily as the next girl. Fast drinking. Slow talking. Tough nut. Bad men. She was tired of lying around in her little patsy-girl despondency. She wanted to be bad. She wanted to be used. She wanted somebody to hurt her in some way she could understand. But still she couldn't bring herself to get out of bed and go to him. She was scared she'd reach out and he might just look at her and say she wasn't exciting enough for him.

30

Simone began to notice that whenever Ethan and Joey arrived at the café Hanife's hand would slip to her hair and she'd rearrange herself very slightly before they got to the counter. And when they didn't come in she would sometimes say something like – *and what's happening with those two?* – as if they were a little problem she was helping out with. Her interest was disorienting. Simone thought if it did actually come down to a competition between them, and she wasn't yet committed to the idea she wanted the spoils, then the woman that had once been touched by unimaginable barbarism and survived probably had the superior right.

Even Clara was fascinated by the two men, but Ethan in particular. Mostly he'd been overseas for as long as she'd known Alice, but in her curatorial way she'd got chatting to him in the street, and had invited him in for a drink and a conversation about his mother. Once inside he'd fallen on Charlie's record collection. Every day since he'd gone over for a couple of hours and sat beside Charlie in the living room, both of them swept up in whatever was turning on the record player. He had a way of asking Charlie questions that sometimes stimulated his early memories, she said, and he was so nice about her slipping out of the house for a while when he was there.

'He's quite the music aficionado, that one,' Clara told Simone, leaning on the café counter. Hanife was hovering nearby, trying not to look like she was lapping up every scrap of information. 'He knows all those early artists, from way before his time. Today when he came in Charlie said something like, "Don't forget you'll need a black dinner suit for that wedding gig tonight," and Ethan just said, "Righto, mate, I'll get that sorted."'

Clara had done a round of visiting on the way to the café.

Toss, she reported, was feeling contrite and foolish and had his court date set for next week. And Zita was in a grumbling, complaining mood. Her birthday was coming up and her oldest son had told her he wasn't going to be able to visit because he was booked on a 'non-negotiable' business trip to Hong Kong. Clara thought she might've secretly been hoping they'd have a party, but all her other son had said was that he and his family would be able to make it over for a visit.

'Do you know what she said to me?' Clara said. 'She said she thought she was dying. Of course I was quite alarmed and I said, "What do you mean, Zita? How do you know you're dying? What does it feel like?" And she snapped back at me how should she know what it felt like, she'd never died before!'

'Cranky,' Hanife responded admiringly.

'I'd like to organise something for her,' Clara said. 'She's going to be ninety after all.'

'Ninety! That's a big number!' Hanife commented.

'We'll have a party at my house,' Clara announced.

'And we could help,' Hanife offered.

Simone glanced at Hanife's face, a quick fact-gathering look. As far as she knew Zita had never come into the café, and Simone was fairly certain they hadn't ever met. While Zita was exactly the kind of person Hanife liked to adopt, it seemed most likely this unusual enthusiasm was rising from some other source. They began to discuss the food and the invitations and Hanife said it might be easiest to have a surprise party at the café after closing time.

'Splendid,' Clara said. 'And music. We might need some music. Perhaps we could ask Ethan to do it.'

'And Joey could be the decoration,' Hanife suggested. Simone glanced at her again but she acted normally.

'I'll ask but I'm not even sure if they'll still be here,' Simone said, noticing how both their faces fell.

Later when she told Joey and Ethan about the party, Joey said, 'Not that keen on old ladies. Besides Lexie keeps texting me to bring Mum's car back.'

'Your tattoo is finished then?'

'Nearly,' he said. 'Bet you're dying to see it.'

She looked away from him.

Ethan said, 'Yeah, I suppose I'll have to go back soon too.'

She shrugged, trying to look as if it made no difference at all and Ethan said, 'Don't suppose she'll miss me for another few days though. It could be a laugh.'

'S'pose I'll have to stay on too then,' Joey said, opening the fridge door and reaching inside for a beer before going into the living room to turn on the television. Simone had never been aware before of how much motor racing it was possible to access on television but on a regular basis Joey was able to find some, drawn to it as a dog is drawn towards a moving ball, and he entered into an almost catatonic state in front of it, the only movement coming from the arm that held his beer. She was grateful for the rude spectre this raised of a future where he sat around with a big paunchy stomach demanding the regular delivery of beer from the fool who'd married him. Anything that caused a reduction in the ridiculous pulse-raising effect his physical presence had on her was a good thing.

It seemed now that he'd made slightly more effort around her in the city, and ever since he'd arrived at the beach he'd behaved almost as if he was purposely trying to repel her. It confused her but it didn't stop her from having to turn her gaze away whenever he fixed those puncturing eyes on her. It didn't stop her admiring how wide his shoulders were, or liking the strength in his posture, or enjoying watching him when he didn't know she was looking. And some surprising habits roused a genuine admiration for him too. Every morning after breakfast he sat down and wrote a letter for Amnesty International, and quite often when he returned from a trip to the beach he was carrying a sackful of rubbish he had taken the time to collect off the sand.

Ethan was spending the evenings working through his mother's things. He was throwing out some of her junk but Simone could see it was making him feel disloyal. She sat down

220

opposite him at the kitchen table as he sighed his way through a pile of invoices and bank statements and she mentioned what Clara had said about him being an aficionado. He laughed and said it made him sound like a bit of a spaz.

'Don't tell anybody but it started when my mother made me take piano lessons as a kid,' he said.

'And that's how you became an aficionado? Jeez you must have had a good teacher.'

'Nah, not really. At first I just plonked away on those turgid classical pieces and then one day I discovered I could get my teacher to show me how to play modern music so I started to send away for songs I liked.'

'Like what?'

'Oh. "Stairway to Heaven". "Angie". Shit like that. And some really terrible stuff.'

'Like what?'

'"Bad, Bad Leroy Brown". And then there was the one my teacher hated the most – do you remember "The Monster Mash"?'

'Christ!' she laughed. 'On the piano?'

'Hey. I was twelve.'

'Okay. Fair enough.'

'Anyway about that time there was a school concert, and a girl I liked. Trisha with the long dark hair. And she was mad about Robert Redford and *The Sting* had just come out. So I decided I would learn "The Entertainer". And do you know what I discovered in the Scott Joplin songbook?'

'The end of puberty?'

He laughed. 'Yeah that too. But also syncopated rhythm. It was much more fun to play. And from ragtime I got into blues and then jazz.'

'But what's with the Metallica hat then?'

'Might be getting a bit follicly challenged. Besides I'm not one of those finger-up-the-bum purists, you know. I appreciate jazz but that's more my secret private place. It's not the only thing I like.'

221

'Do you still play?'

He scratched the side of his face. It was something he often did. The skin was itchy under all that bristly hair. 'Haven't touched a keyboard for years.'

'And what happened to Trisha?'

'Well as I recall she did come up to me after the concert and said that was all right, but then she went off with Barry Murphy because he had a bike with ape hangers,' he said.

Some men had qualities that made it easy to imagine them as boys. Simone thought that even as a child Ethan probably had a kind of wilful strength about him. He probably would've made an enviable brother, having the sort of presence that made him both game and good company. If she'd had a brother like him there would've been no reason at all to force the poor cat down her windbreaker.

Neither Joey nor Ethan much liked lying around in bed in the morning. They were usually up before Simone, frying bacon in the kitchen. The smell of it drew Simone out to join them but while they appeared to regard bacon as a regular staple, it was more her idea of an occasional treat. She no longer had an appetite for it, a matter they found incomprehensible. She enjoyed more their obsession for coffee – a significant part of their morning ritual was to discuss the quality of the crema achieved with their rudimentary equipment. They liked to find the fine line between making it as strong as possible and being too bitter to drink, referring to the first one of the day as the defibrillator. Other little rituals developed too. Nearly every morning either Ethan or Simone would ask Joey to pass something and he would respond by saying he would but he'd just discovered he had a lash above his eye, a nail in his thumb, (or one time) a bone in his leg. They'd groan and he'd pass it anyway, and soon they began to say similar things themselves.

As Simone took a testing sip of this morning's brew Ethan pushed a letter towards her. 'Some mail came for you,' he said. It was a fat white envelope with the address written in Lexie's handwriting. She picked up a knife and ran it along the top edge. Inside there was another envelope with her name written on one side, and on the reverse, scrawled in Lexie's script – *Fraser asked me to send this on.*

Immediately she felt an unease, like when a letter comes with the logo of the court on the envelope. She was too faint-hearted to open it with anyone else looking on so she took it into the sun room and closed the door. Her hands were unsteady and she cursed the intensity of her reaction as she opened the second envelope but inside was nothing but the article, ripped roughly from the magazine. He'd scrawled *I'm Sorry* across it in red pen.

She sat down on the bed, looking at the red writing. What, she wondered, was he sorry for? Precisely? And was she supposed to be grateful? *I'm Sorry*. It was so neatly obscure. But then he'd always been inclined to throw his apologies up in the air, hoping he could get away with not bothering about exactness. She stared at the way he'd capitalised the *S*, it made the sorry seem louder somehow. *I'm sorry* might've been more sincere. *I'm Sorry* placed the emphasis on the first part of the word, like the way you might say it if you were being disingenuous. Even as she thought this she knew it was just plodding and vain to niggle away at the stroke of the pen, most likely he'd just dashed it off thinking more about the gesture than anything else – still now he'd gone to the effort of getting in contact she was surprised by how disappointed she felt. She realised that in a way she'd wanted to be summoned, to be invited for an accounting.

She screwed the piece of paper up and threw it across the room with as much violence as she could muster. When she went back into the kitchen Ethan and Joey looked up at her expectantly and she gestured roughly around her and said, 'Christ this place is turning into a bloody pigsty.' Joey, who had been sitting at the table with the paper spread out in front of him, disappeared as if into vapour. She wished they'd leave soon anyway. She wanted her solitude back. Even the dog was

223

beginning to annoy her, panting around behind Ethan, as if he reeked of adventure. It was like Clouseau had an instinct that he belonged more to Ethan than anyone else, and if she let herself think about that too much it made her ache. So she didn't bother calling him as she left for work. He could stay there if he liked it so much.

As she passed Zita's house she saw her sitting inside her conservatory. Zita gave her a little wave, trying to beckon her over. Simone had been thinking about stopping in there some time, trying to explain about Ravi. But she'd been a little stung by the way Zita had judged her, refusing to open her door, and that following the raid they'd all discussed the possibility it was her who had called the police. She didn't particularly hold it against them, supposing it was just one of many theories offered up in the confusion. But today, right now, she wasn't feeling wholly forgiving. She tapped her watch indicating she was running late for work.

It looked like it was going to be one of those perfectly fine days, an opening performance for summer. The sea was acutely, luridly blue – a flawless reflection of the wide infinity of sky. Where had all this blue come from so suddenly? This seasonal turn that was so obstinately in opposition to her mood? The strength of the sun's rays was already making the beach look distantly hazy. She could feel herself begin to overheat as she strode along the sand and she knew the café would be hot and busy all day. At this rate she'd have to take off her sweatshirt when she got to work, and underneath she was only wearing an ugly brown tank top which had moth holes all through it. She hadn't brought her sunglasses either, and the reflected glare bouncing off the sea was beginning to irritate her eyes. She passed the old wooden dinghy and missed Clouseau. It didn't feel right to be walking along the beach without him by her side.

Halfway to the café she felt a small tear slide down her face. She wiped it away with her sleeve, but there was another. She kept on walking and they kept on coming. Just sneaky little

224

tears, no more consequential than beads of sweat, but they didn't seem about to stop.

She sat down on the sand for a while and still they kept coming. She tried to think of other things, lucky things. But there was a pile of horse dung nearby with blowflies hovering around it and it brought to mind an image from a surreal Spanish movie she and Fraser had once seen at a film festival. She couldn't immediately recall the title but it had begun with a close-up of flies buzzing around a body in a field. Afterwards they'd lain in bed discussing it and she realised he'd somehow missed the whole subtext of the plot. She pointed it out to him and as he'd begun to understand he'd become quite excited. The next day his friend came to visit and asked what they'd been up to lately, and Fraser said he'd been to the movies. The friend had seen the same movie so they began discussing it and Fraser told his friend about the subtext of the movie as if he had assumed it all himself. Later on she asked why he'd done that, and why he'd said *he* had gone to the movie and not *we*. He apologised for not acknowledging her to his friend but he didn't seem to realise that what she really needed was to be acknowledged for mattering in the first place.

But she was tired of resurrecting these unhappy moments, working them all over in her head, like the last lonely maggot on a carcass. Being angry at somebody for not loving you properly was not just pointless but stupidly impotent. She could do nothing about the tears. Something had temporarily broken, like a threadbare washer had finally inconveniently disintegrated.

She decided to return home and when she got to the house Ethan was sitting on the doorstep watching some sparrows and fantails peck at a half-loaf of stale bread he'd thrown onto the lawn. 'Back a bit early aren't ya,' he said. 'Forget something?'

'Not really,' she replied, ducking her eyes away from him.

She closed the sun room door behind her and climbed under the covers with all her clothes on, not even bothering to remove her sandy sneakers. She turned her face to the wall and let the tears soak into the pillow like nothing more than an inconvenient surplus the body had decided to purge. She didn't want to concede anything, especially not the cause of this.

Beyond the door she heard whispering, and then a scuttling about which she decided was probably a dutiful attempt at housekeeping. The possibility that discovery was only a twist of a door handle away puts some brakes on any full-on descent into self-pity, instead she hovered between an unhappy resentment at their proximity and a reluctant desire to have her misery interrupted.

After a short time Ethan knocked on the door and clumsily entered the room with a cup of tea. She propped herself up and he handed it to her, looking into her face and then looking away again. She thought about telling him it was only a touch of hay fever. He ran his hand through his hair, unsure if he should leave or not. She asked if he'd mind going and telling Hanife she'd be late.

She hadn't noticed Joey hovering just beyond the lintel until he said, 'I'll do your shift for you. I've worked in plenty of cafés before.' He turned and left immediately, eager to flee tears, she guessed.

Ethan lingered nearby. 'Was it something to do with your family?' he asked cautiously.

She shook her head.

'Some kind of boy trouble?'

Simone curled her feet up to allow him to sit down on the end of the bed. 'Sort of. My ex.'

'What does he want?'

'Nothing very much.'

'And what do you want?'

'Just to feel nothing I suppose.'

'Do you want to talk about it? We don't have to, if you don't want.' He sat on the very end of the bed, his back against the wall, keeping his face at right angles to her, not wanting to place her under any pressure by further acknowledging her tears. 'Why'd you split up?'

'He had an affair with the next-door neighbour and got her pregnant.'

'What a cunt!'

She was about to say it was much more complicated than that, but suddenly she thought maybe it didn't have to be. Maybe it was just that some people were not as good as you wanted them to be. 'Yeah, he was a cunt,' she agreed, feeling how satisfying the word felt in her mouth.

'Must have been crazy too,' Ethan said more quietly.

Clouseau came up and rested his chin on the edge of the bed, shifting his eyes from Ethan to her and back again.

'I went a bit crazy,' she confessed. She showed him the story in the magazine. She pointed to the line containing the word *stalker* and said, 'Me.'

He read the whole section then he said, 'Wrecked his car, huh. That reminds me of a story about this guy whose wife said she'd fallen in love with someone else and was leaving and she wanted half of everything. So he went out to the shed, found his chainsaw, and walked around to the front of the house and cut their car right down through the middle. "There's your bloody half," he said.'

'What did she do?'

'I dunno, but I know what he did next.'

'What?'

Ethan waited a beat before saying: 'He went out and bought a one-way ticket to England.'

She stared at him. 'You were married?'

'If you could call it that.'

He looked at her with a little half smile and then his knee moved, jerking up in what looked like a small spasm. His opposite hand moved automatically towards his lower leg with a will of its own to scratch at what wasn't there, and then in a more conscious movement he slipped both hands under his armpits as if he wanted to clamp them down.

'Do you miss it?' she asked. 'Your leg?'

'Nah,' he said. 'But I think it misses me.'

227

Later that morning Ethan used the old hand mower in the shed to flatten a little square of grass on the lawn on which he laid out the living room rug and some seat cushions from the sofa. He then urged her to go out into the sunshine. Chocolate biscuits were arranged in decorative circle on a dinner plate to accompany her next cup of tea. For lunch he brought out salami sandwiches, with yellow globby lumps so inexpertly spread they looked to have been prepared by a child with no previous experience of refrigerated butter. She ate what she could in appreciation of the effort. It was warming, this, to be the recipient of so much well-intentioned bounty.

In the afternoon he said he was expected next door and not long after he left Clara appeared in the garden holding a plate. 'Toss dropped some mussels off this morning – his special kind of apology I think – so I spent all morning cooking them up into these fritters. I'd just stuffed most of them down Ethan when he mentioned you were home so I thought you might like to try the last one.' She sat down on the edge of the blanket, placing the plate beside Simone and examining her face in such a way it was clear Ethan had mentioned there'd been tears earlier.

'Clever Ethan's busy installing some new locks on our doors,' Clara told her. 'He suggested we put on these special locks where you have to punch in a number code to open them. Charlie won't be able to sneak out any more. You can't imagine how excited I am about it, it's such a simple idea but I won't have to worry half as much.'

'Why didn't we think of that ages ago? That's such a good idea,' Simone said. She picked up the fritter and bit into it. 'Yum,' she uttered as the delicious combination of lemon, parsley, pepper and mussel hit her taste buds.

'Well I think it just happens that men are good for some things,' Clara replied.

'But you know I'm quite handy with a hammer. I could've put those new locks in for you, if we'd thought of it,' Simone said, feeling slow and remiss for not thinking of it.

228

'I know dear,' Clara said. 'But in the end it's quite nice to lie around in the sunshine and have a man do things for you, don't you think?'

Simone pulled out one of the cushions from underneath her and offered it to Clara who then lay down beside her. The grass around the edges of the garden was quite long and the activity with the hand mower had stirred up the insect life. Earlier a bright green grasshopper had leapt onto Simone's hand and bounced straight off again. And nearby a fat bumblebee was cheerfully working the flower heads. Clara wriggled around a bit to make herself comfortable and then folded her hands on top of her stomach. 'I'm beginning to wonder how much longer I can really manage though,' she said. 'Charlie and I had a silly scary argument yesterday. He wanted his dinner on the table but when I tried to convince him it was only two in the afternoon he didn't believe me and said I was lying. Lying! About that! But he got very angry. He hit me.'

'Hit you? Charlie?' Simone was up on her elbow.

'Not that hard. It didn't really hurt.'

'Oh Clara . . .'

Clara sighed. 'I know. You'd think with this . . . illness . . . the person would stay who they really are, and just sort of become less and less, but sometimes he's just a whole different, much more difficult person. It's like it's pressing against some of the worst parts of the brain – anger and paranoia. Yesterday I could hardly recognise him.'

Simone was trying to think of the most workable way she could offer help when Clara said, 'Sometimes I think he's lucky to have me. I quite often wonder what it would've been like if it was the other way around and I was the one that got sick.'

'He would've cared for you, wouldn't he?'

'Probably not.'

'Clara! Do you really think so?'

After a pause Clara said, 'Charlie wasn't . . . perfect.'

'Who is?' Simone said, but she couldn't be sure of the gravity of what Clara had meant. As far as husbands went around here there were existing standards of imperfect. Stanley for example.

'The thing that upsets me,' Clara said, brushing a fly from her face with her hand, 'is I always thought there would come a time when we were old and he would've given all that other rubbish up and he'd be all mine. But look what happened! It feels like I'm competing against the biggest affair of them all, but this one's really got her claws into him and is finally taking away everything he had left over for me.'

Clara so blithely revealing Charlie cheated on her felt a little shocking, like your own mother casually mentioning your father had other lovers. It was directly troubling to the romantic construct Simone had formed of Charlie. Having only ever had fleeting access to his real personality she'd allowed herself to enjoy an idealistic notion of their life together. In Simone's mind he had once had a powerful devotion to Clara, and this had been a source of her own fondness towards him. 'Does that make you feel upset at fate, or upset at Charlie?' she asked.

'Mostly fate. Sometimes Charlie,' Clara said. More softly she added, 'Poor old Charlie.'

The radiance of the sun was having a slightly narcotic effect, leaving Simone drowsy and depleted, and not very reliably composed. What Clara had said reminded her of Fraser's fighting tigresses. She saw now it was essential for Clara to feel she was putting up a good fight for this one because otherwise what had been the point of all the other struggles over Charlie?

Clara was lying with her eyes closed, and she yawned. Simone closed her eyes as well and heard Clara's breathing start to slow. Simone listened to the chirping birds, the relentless energy of the sea, the bustle of stirred-up insects, Clara's long raspy breaths – and before long she was having a sort of surface dream where Fraser had flown up and landed on the roof of the house and was mouthing the words *I'm sorry* across the garden, and in his arms there was a fat wriggling puppy.

A sudden snort from Clara jerked them both awake, and as if there had been no break at all Clara carried on talking, '. . .

but do you know what really scares me when I'm lying in bed at night now? There is no other layer underneath. No children. No nieces or nephews. Only the stepchildren. And if I got a bit past it I imagine they'd be quite happy to lock me in a cupboard and forget about me.'

'Not on my watch,' Simone said.

'Oh, daughter!' Clara replied and laughed lightly to show there was no real obligation.

31

It was not an easy thing to call him. Her hands trembled as she punched in the number. 'Hello,' he said into the speaker, cheerful, as if he'd been expecting a friend, something pleasant.

'Sorry for what?'

There was a silence so long she was able to heap shame and misgivings upon herself. 'Meet me,' he said finally. 'We should talk.'

They arranged to meet halfway. On the telephone they could only think of one landmark, a roadside café beside a river. Neither of them knew the real name, but the car park was always teeming with greedy birds, fat ducks and geese, which had stepped up the riverbank to spend their day harassing the customers for sandwich scraps. They'd always found it a source of amusement as they'd driven by in the past, referring to it is as the Doo Duck Inn.

She asked Ethan to take her.

'I would but . . .'

'But?'

He hesitated. 'Well it's just that I haven't actually driven a car yet, since . . .'

The accident. His leg.

'Sorry . . .' she mumbled, 'I didn't realise. I shouldn't have asked.'

Perhaps she wouldn't go at all. Actually she was afraid of meeting up with Fraser. She might be disappointed. He might not be sorry for the things that matter. Her heart might give out at the sight of him. He might want to have her arrested. He might hate her. She might hate him. She might love him still. She didn't know if she was strong enough. A meeting had seemed achievable if Ethan was there too, in the background, just for safety.

'I'll arrange it with Joey for you,' Ethan offered. 'We could all go. Family outing.'

Maybe it wouldn't be so bad. Maybe Fraser wanted to say he's sorry he hurt her the way he did. That he's sorry he's not still with her. Not having the baby with her.

He'd arrived before her. She could see him through the window, slouching back in his chair, looking preoccupied and slightly adrift. Joey and Ethan offered to stay in the car with Clouseau and she went inside and slid onto the seat opposite.

He had been staring into an empty cup and when she appeared he looked up and for a brief off-guard moment she thought she caught a look of pure pleasure at the sight of her. This immediately gave way to something more cautious, and she felt him look her over with careful interest, gaugingly, his expression now a more circumspect mixture of old fondness and wary distance.

She dropped her eyes to the shirt he was wearing. It was new, she registered, with some kind of overdesigned screen-print down the left-hand side. It wasn't the sort of thing she'd ever seen him in before, and it seemed inconsistent and jarring. He'd always had a kind of downbeat pride in his scruffiness, preferring to wear rips and stains and paint splatters with a cavalier indifference that marked him out as a man with his own special purpose. And now, for this meeting, he'd dressed in a shirt he'd clearly not bought for himself, and the idea he might have done this on purpose, as a subtly undermining indication of how transformed he was, wrenched the question from her immediately.

'Sorry? For what?'

It was too quick, too abrupt. He shrugged. He'd been sitting there, waiting, gathering, and she'd barely even scraped the seat. She hadn't even said hello. She felt undone, suddenly, waiting for his answer, and he took his time.

'Just for the way it all happened, I guess.'

She stared at him. That meant nothing to her.

'About the article I suppose,' he expanded reluctantly, leaning back away from her. His posture suggested he had come as a conciliatory gesture but now that she'd shown she was possibly still a little rabid he felt he could afford to be aloof and unresponsive.

She took a breath. 'Do you want another coffee or something?' she asked.

'Yeah, I'll get them,' he offered. 'Although prepare yourself for the worst brew you've ever tasted.'

He sauntered over to the counter to order, having to call out to get the attention of the sluggish girl who was busy deep-frying chips further back in the kitchen. Simone registered that the fat she was using was rank and needed changing and the god-awfulness of the place they'd chosen began to feel ominous.

When Fraser came back to the table he said, 'So . . . at last . . . The Doo Duck Inn, huh.'

'More like the Duck Doo Inn,' she said.

'Or the Mad Old Duckden,' he offered, smiling briefly. And it came to her then, drifting across the table towards her like a rapprochement – their familiar old rhythm, the addictive smell of him.

'I hadn't meant to talk about all that stuff,' Fraser began to explain, '. . . in that profile. It's just it had sort of got around, about the stolen car and all that, and the journalist was a kind of mate and we just ended up talking about what had happened. And afterwards, when it came out in the magazine, I felt sort of embarrassed . . . for you.' He gave her a hapless look, almost as if he *was* expecting gratitude.

'Embarrassed for me?' Simone replied steadily. 'For what? Because of the crappy way you were belittling me? Or because you turned something private and hurtful into a convenient story to make your crappy work of art more titillating?'

It was like she'd plopped a flapping fish down onto the table in front of them. She couldn't quite work out what was right and wrong here. She wasn't blameless, not at all, but she could see clearly in her mind the images of the two angry tigresses fighting, with the infuriating implication he considered himself to be the innocent bystander as a contest was fought over him. He made no move to answer or explain himself, so she added: 'Love fucking Lies Bleeding?' She may have said this quite loud, shouted it nearly, other people in the room turned their heads towards them. She hated how shrill her voice had sounded, how lacking in the cool reason she'd hoped for. The waitress came over and placed the two coffees on the table, giving Fraser a covertly flirtatious smile, the kind of passing attention Fraser, with his offhand handsomeness, attracts every day, a million times a day – so cheap to him he hardly seems to notice. The waitress then turned to Simone and said blandly, 'Do you want to order any food?'

'Just the coffee,' Simone replied.

When the waitress moved off Fraser leaned forward and said in a lowered tone, 'Christ, Simone, you can get mad at me but don't forget you destroyed our car . . . that was a big thing. You did this big thing to us. I'm entitled to have a response to it.'

'Why do you think it was me?' she asked, but knew she wasn't convincing in this pretence.

'Come on,' Fraser said. 'Who else? You'd been following me around. It's not like I didn't notice.'

It occurred to her then that he'd actually been quite unfazed by the things she'd done. It was another form of attention and in some way he might almost have enjoyed it, thinking it was not unusual for a person to have trouble getting over him, a perfectly natural reaction. He'd incorporated it into his work after all, his particular kind of trophies.

There was a water jug sitting on a side table and Simone went over to it and filled two glasses. Back at the table she offered one to Fraser and slowly drank the other, trying to win back some composure for herself.

'Tell me what you'd expected me to say here?' he asked. 'Sorry for what?'

'I thought you might be sorry because that was how I found out you were having a baby?' she said in a quiet voice.

There was a brief look of surprise on his face. It seemed not to have occurred to him that she didn't already know.

'I guess I am sorry about that,' he said, and she could see he really was.

'And I don't know, there's so much other potential,' she went on, unable to stop herself. 'Sorry I had an affair behind your back. Sorry I let you support me and then just slipped out the door when it suited me. Sorry I couldn't have been more loyal. Sorry that as soon as I moved on I treated you like dirt under my shoe. Sorry I didn't care you lost the baby . . .'

'I did care,' he said softly, gently, in a tone that suggested he thought he'd made it clear in the past. He put his hand across the table and touched her on the arm.

'Did you?' she said, nearly in a whisper. She felt a tear threaten and looked away from his face, out the window. She knew how much she'd given away, in that angry totting up of his love crimes, she wished she hadn't let him know how far off she was from being over him. Out the window she saw Joey and Ethan still in the car, waiting reliably, although she could see the ducks had them in their focus and were edging forward. After a little while she said, 'Nice way of caring.'

There was a long silence while he appeared to be trying to find the words to explain himself and then he said, 'I guess that's the point though, isn't it. I mean I did care, and I could kind of see you were struggling but, I dunno, I couldn't find it in me to try and be there for you. We were sort of . . . stale. I know that sounds horrible to you. But surely if I'd really truly loved you, I would've tried harder. So can't you see you're better off without me? You're such a great person. You'd be better off with someone who could love you properly. The way you deserve.'

Simone looked into his face, hardly able to take in what she was hearing, and she could see he'd thought about this – some part of him was obscurely pleased with the inarguability of this line of reasoning.

'Okay then,' she said, with barely smothered hostility, 'Well thanks so much for letting me off the hook then.'

He sighed. 'I have let you off the hook, in more ways than one.'

'What do you mean by that?'

'The car of course, the break-ins. I never reported it. I'm not sure I can stop Caroline doing something though, if anything else happens.' He delivered this last sentence almost as if it he had rehearsed it, or been rehearsed. This then, was what he had really come to say. Caroline had wanted him to issue this ultimatum, perhaps as a security measure, or perhaps more craftily to force him to display, once and for all, his fidelity to her. Simone fought a desperate urge to say *but can't you see I've stopped already, can't you see it wasn't me exactly, just a stumble under the weight of all that faithlessness?* But what was the point, to beg his understanding like that? His loyalty was now absolutely engaged elsewhere.

Having fulfilled his obligation, though, he softened. 'Are you okay now?' he asked. 'Are things working out for you?'

Just then his eyes swerved towards the door behind her, and Simone turned to see Ethan and Joey coming into the café. They took food trays in their big hands and bumbled about, sliding the trays down the counter, bumping clumsily into each other, piling plates with pies and cakes, and only briefly glancing her way. They couldn't help being a huge presence in the café but they'd prepared themselves, she could see, to pretend they didn't know her if that's what she wanted. Ethan turned to look at her again, as if he was casually surveying the room, and she gave him a little wave.

'Who are they?' Fraser wanted to know.

'Oh, just my friends,' she said, enjoying for a moment how they must look to Fraser. These two big tough-looking guys with their beanies, their dark jeans. The waitress was eyeing them suspiciously, but from Simone's perspective, perhaps because she knew them, they seemed to radiate a particular brand of decency.

'Was she pregnant when you left?' she asked Fraser quietly.

'Yes.'

'Did you know already?'

'Yes.'

'Did you plan it?'

'What do you think I am? Of course I didn't plan it. It was an accident . . . but once it happened . . .'

'So that was really why? Why didn't you tell me at the time?'

'I don't know. It was a shock, I guess I was trying to do the right thing.' He shrugged. 'What can I say here? It was a shitty situation. Would you've felt any less hurt at the time if I had told you I was leaving you because she was having my baby?'

He almost had a point there. She glanced over at Joey and Ethan. They'd seated themselves at the far end of the café. She hoped they couldn't hear any of this.

'So when you said that thing about feeling relief . . .'

'What thing?'

'Relief that I lost the baby.'

'I never said that.'

'Yes you did.'

He looked at her as if she was being irrational. 'No, I wouldn't have,' he said firmly.

'Yes. Why would I make that up? That last fight. Your exact words were – the only thing you remembered feeling when I lost the baby was relief.'

It seemed to come to him then – there was an audible intake of breathe. 'Did I?' he said. His shoulders dropped as some distant recognition occurred. 'Jeez, that was mean.' He looked down at his hands for a long time, trying hard to remember the moment. 'I don't think I could've meant it,' he said. 'I mean we were arguing, I guess, and I just blurted stuff out. Deep down you must've known that wasn't how it really was . . .'

She couldn't make any response. She couldn't rely on her voice, so hard was she fighting down a backlog of tears. He was right, in her heart she'd never really believed it was that simple for him.

'I mean I suppose if I'm really honest I did feel relieved in some dark kind of way,' Fraser ventured carefully. 'But that wasn't everything. I felt a tiny bit relieved but more just sad. Like when you were pregnant I felt a bit scared and also quite excited. I'm sorry if I said that – it might've kind of been the moment. You were putting a lot of heat on and I felt guilty and caught out. But I did care. Okay? It's not like I didn't. And it's not like I felt relief that I could go off with somebody else or anything. That just kind of happened . . . by accident. I'm really truly sorry if you've been thinking that all this time.'

Neither of them spoke for a long time. She began to admit to herself that maybe it had taken its toll on him too. In that brief period when she'd fallen pregnant he had seemed quite genuinely thrilled. They suddenly couldn't get enough of each other and had sex all the time. They'd always had a lot of sex but for those few months they had so much she felt guilt stricken afterwards, thinking it may have caused some damage. The burden of choice had finally been removed from him, and it freed him up to be completely loving. He was irrevocably in it suddenly. But afterwards, after everything, a new tone entered their love making – there had been something exhausting and maybe even futile about it.

She started to consider how this had all started, of Fraser looking across with longing at the playing children in the garden next door, and it occurred to her that maybe Toby – Caroline's healthy, athletic, energetic child – might have been much more important than she'd realised. Because if Fraser was searching for something to cement him down, if he'd become increasingly conscious of his own finiteness, if the question mark hovering over Simone had come to represent improbability, then perhaps Toby's very existence was proof of the alternate possibilities, proof of the potential for accomplishment – whether Fraser had realised it or not.

She couldn't look up at Fraser because that would almost

entail accepting his apology and some pain you inflict didn't deserve to be taken back too easily. 'So if you hadn't got her pregnant, would you've . . . ?'

He didn't speak for a long time and then he hesitantly said, 'Caroline is . . .'

Simone abruptly turned her head away. It wasn't clear what he'd been intending to say but she feared whatever it was. She realised she didn't want to know any more why he had been drawn to Caroline. She didn't need to know, either, if he was happy or not.

He stopped himself. 'Oh I don't know,' he said instead. 'What's the point in playing *what if?* Sometimes things just happen, your fate just intersects with other people. That's what makes life. It's just all about what you do at the time.'

He was always a person who felt more comfortable with fate than accountability. She'd known that from the moment she met him, just like, if she was honest, she'd always known he would probably leave her one day. She'd been drawn to him by some inextricable pull he possessed, but while she was with him she'd always secretly thought of it as borrowed time, a charmed date with the devil. 'Just fate, huh. Well don't even try and get all friggin' fatalistic on me. Because I might have something special to say about the way you manage your intersections.'

'Okay,' he said, smiling a little. And there was something in the tone of that smile that allowed her to suddenly change gear.

'I'm sorry,' she said. 'For what I did to your car, for those other things.' Saying the words was so much like releasing an air valve that she found herself offering him her own car as reparation, when it was out of its lease. He didn't accept though.

'Nah, it's okay. It was a pretty crappy car anyway, and besides I reckon in the big weighing up that I probably still owe you overall.' He picked at the edge of his fingernail for a moment and then added, 'If it makes any difference, I do miss us.'

She had nothing left now. Only a parting shot. 'Well I miss you about as much as the *Titanic* misses an iceberg.'

'That would be not at all then,' he said with a crooked smile.

She noticed every now and then Joey's eyes would flick over her in the rear-vision mirror, like she was a child, or a found roadside casualty, that needed checking on. There was something consoling in this – in being driven away from Fraser by two men, in their fraternal concern. It gave her a sense of belonging to something new. But the rank odour of the frying fat had clung to their clothes and followed them into the car, like a tailing scourge, and she began to think about how he'd said *us*. 'I do miss us.' Not *her* exactly.

Clouseau had his head out the window on the opposite side of the car and she opened the window on her side to stop the incoming breeze from creating an uncomfortable vibration. As the wind played in her hair she leaned back against the headrest and remembered the first time she'd travelled down this main highway with Fraser, when they had first christened the Doo Duck Inn, when everything had seemed funny to them. They were on a trip to meet his parents. As they neared the end of their journey, neared the house, Fraser became increasingly vague and distracted, like the house itself was emanating some kind of antigravity effect on him. As they came up to the driveway he was pointing out the permanent Santa grotto in the neighbours' front yard when he let the car drift off too far to the left, nudging his father's letter box askew. 'Whatever you do, don't mention this,' he'd said as he hurriedly reversed back, and she'd laughed.

She was introduced to his father in the back garden. He was wearing a weed-sprayer backpack and greeted her with the comment, 'So he got you here in one piece did he? Well at least that's something anyway!'

It wasn't until the next morning that Fraser's father discovered the damage. They were sitting at breakfast when he went out to collect the paper and she'd avoided any eye contact across the table, afraid she might giggle. 'Some bloody idiot's vandalised my letter box,' he spluttered when he came back and nobody said anything in response, which struck Simone as a probable inferential indication of guilt. Fraser's mother started an urgent clearing-up frenzy – restraining herself only until the last mouthful was up on a fork and off the plate, accepting no offers of help. They escaped up to their room. Simone was standing by the window brushing her hair when Fraser came up behind and slipped his hand up the front of her jumper and wriggled his fingers up under her bra. He was quite randy in the shadows of his parents' house and he put his lips to the back of her neck and was playfully blowing air out through his nostrils like a dirty old stallion ready for business, when they both caught sight of his father out in the driveway running his hand over their car's front bumper. She felt Fraser go still. 'Let's go fetch some walnuts to take back to town with us,' he suggested, and they raced each other down to the little garden gate at the rear of the section leading out onto the golf course.

It was a ten-minute walk to the river, if you cut across the green. They sat down on the bank, under the shade of the big old walnut tree and Fraser threw every nut within arm's reach into the water, one by one, and they bobbed off downstream, like a row of small hapless children. 'He's such a jerk,' Fraser said. 'Did I tell you about that time I came down in winter after my last exhibition . . . and I took the hammer off his workbench to hang a painting for Mum and when he found out I hadn't put it back straight away he went off his rocker. Like I was a little kid, not a grown man.'

He had told her about this before. It'd always made Simone think about how many times she'd asked him to hang his towel on the rail after he'd finished with it. And how he always borrowed her car keys and could never remember where he put them afterwards. And how he could hardly wash a dish without breaking it. She'd decided if they were going to live together in any kind of harmony she'd be better off to accept he was a bit of a woolly airhead about certain things. He was often so vague and self-occupied that sometimes it was like he'd burrowed down inside his own head. But then that was also part of what she loved about him – his dreaminess, his devotion to imagination. He sometimes wouldn't even respond when she called his name, but instead of letting this frustrate her she would deal with it by putting her hands around her mouth and speaking out in a crackly, megaphone kind of way . . . 'Calling all boats, calling all boats, come to shore, Drifter, over.' Clearly, though, his father still had enough hope of improvement to get mightily disappointed in him.

'Did it make much of a dent?' she asked. 'The letter box?'

'I dunno,' he said. 'I forgot to look. Christ, he'll never let this go now.'

When they returned to the house the expectation that his father could come into the room at any moment with an accusation was making the air uncomfortable. So when he stomped in and said instead, 'What do you think about giving the new boat a whirl today?' Simone responded by clapping her hands together and saying, 'Oh yes! Let's.' Then she saw Fraser, standing behind his father's back, miming out his own response – his head to one side, his tongue lolling and his right hand pulling upwards on an imaginary hangman's rope.

One mention of a boat trip cued Fraser's mother into a blur of cupboard opening and shutting. Bread was buttered and the Thermos filled in the time it took for Simone to go upstairs and change her bra into a bikini top. 'All under control,' Simone was told when she offered to help. Fraser had been seconded to assist with getting the boat onto the tow bar and there seemed to be a lot of shouting of commands coming from the front yard. By the time Simone got out there, the boat was ready to go, but Fraser's complexion had drained into ruddy rashes on each of his cheeks.

Just at the very moment when the car had been packed and everybody was ready to go, Fraser's mother pulled a fast one. She opened the door to get into the front passenger seat and then stopped and put her hand to her forehead. She overdid the feebleness in her voice as she announced she might have one of her migraines coming on. 'It might be better for everybody if I don't come after all,' she said, and there were murmurs of consent – perhaps even a whiff of relief – from the driver's seat. A few moments later, as the car pulled out of the driveway, Simone turned and watched her wave them off and thought she looked quite recovered already.

The boat ramp was only a few kilometres away, but with Fraser sitting so stiffly alongside her in the back seat it was like being seated next to an armed gin-trap. His father began whistling the tune to 'Camptown Races' as he chauffeured them down the hill and Simone reached across to take Fraser's hand, giving him a secret finger-tickle to the underside of his palm.

At the boat ramp detailed instructions were barked at Fraser but there was still a horrible scraping sound when the boat came off the trailer. Fraser's father frowned but didn't say anything as he got back into the car and drove off to park. 'Just wait, this will be all my fault,' Fraser said as he helped Simone up into the boat. When his father came back he nodded for Fraser to get in, holding the boat steady for him, and then swung himself up over the back while at the same time pushing the boat off in what Simone thought was an impressively competent manoeuvre.

He turned a key, the boat spluttered into life, and they were motoring out through the moored yachts, still in the five-knot zone, when he turned to Fraser and said, 'Reach down there and get the tackle box out, will you. You can get the lines ready for later. At least you remember how to do that, don't you kid?'

Fraser stared at him unflinchingly for a moment – looking for all the world like a challenged young bullock psyching up to headbutt his way to primacy – and then suddenly he stepped up onto the side of the boat and dived into the sea. His father throttled down as the boat rocked violently from side to side and they both heard Fraser shout, 'I'm not in the mood. See you back at home later.' He turned then, in the water, and began swimming to shore. The jandals he'd been wearing bobbed about, unclaimed, on the surface behind him.

'So ... looks like it's up to you and me to catch tonight's dinner,' Fraser's father muttered with an air of old disappointment as he slammed his hand down on the throttle. Simone sat in the back of the boat, clinging on to the handrail, not taking her eyes away from the back of Fraser's head as she was powered off towards the horizon. She wanted him, needed him, to turn around and at least wave at her, but he never did. 'Always was a quitter,' Fraser's father shouted into the wind. 'Now you know.'

Later, when they were back at their own place, and curled around each other in bed she didn't use words like *thoughtless* and *desertion*. She had, for reasons of tenderness and unity, colluded in Fraser's version of the events. It was all, they both agreed, his father's fault.

The course is often set, she decided, in what you don't do, in the words you don't say, in the things you don't ask for, and in the accumulation of actions you quietly permit. Fraser had the tendencies of a lazy spider, responding only when somebody else vibrated his orbit. He moved in with her basically because her flat was nicer than his. And he stayed because it was easier than not staying, he could convince himself he loved her just enough. And neither was his leaving particularly premeditated. Presumably he started having sex with the neighbour because it was offered, and he left only because he'd been given a profound reason.

But what did that make her? The quietly willing accomplice? Drawn in to the peril of his vicinity by a heart that secretly loves a hazard? She'd found Fraser's aloofness exciting. The effort to keep his attention was enlivening. She'd believed his lack of guarantees was somehow game-lifting for her. But that kind of running doesn't demand much from the one who receives it.

Joey lit up cigarette, not bothering to ask them if they minded, but rolling down his side window as a small concession. It was easy to detect in him the same lazy reluctance to lift himself.

If Joey was toying with any ideas of her at all, and she wasn't sure he was, it had only to do with her proximity. After today she ought to be done with anything less than equal regard. It would be difficult to ever again feel that unreserved surrender of the past, and ending up with Joey might be little more than repeating a pattern.

When they were about halfway home Ethan shifted around in his seat to face her.

'So . . .' he said carefully, 'arsehole or not arsehole?'

'Total arsehole,' she replied.

'Yeah, he looked like an arsehole,' Joey said.

32

The next morning Simone lay in bed thinking of something Lexie once told her about how she often tried to sneak some extra tonic into Anton's drinks at night so he wouldn't get too drunk and start repeating himself. All those years together had worn off some of the edges in their relationship and they tended to show only the smoothest surfaces towards each other. They fitted together so naturally, like two merging shades of blue, that they didn't often argue, but neither did they rise too much above a state of accepted neutrality. His nightly maintenance of this placid drift required some medication with vodka and tonic, and hers involved a significant intake of television. They accepted that this enabled them to be available parents, long-term lovers, but the thought of such routine boredom dismayed Simone. There was the quality of sleepwalking about it.

A long time ago she'd seen a film set in Marrakesh and it had made her ache with desire to go somewhere as surprising and bustling. At the time she hadn't thought of the possibility of simply travelling there, but now she saw that she could. Or she could find a place on a boat and travel aimlessly around the Pacific Islands if she wanted. She could study again. She could get a job she actually liked. She could go to some country where men found women like her exotic and sexy. She could shag herself stupid with a different stranger every night. If she wanted.

It was only a matter of how you looked at it all, she could see now. All this time she'd been anchored to the idea she was a failure, her whole life was a failure, when actually, if she chose to believe it, some unplanned quirk of circumstance meant what she had accidentally become was free. The opposite of commitment, the opposite of restraint, the essence of adventure, free.

She had only one responsibility and right now he'd propped himself up against a wall and was scroffling noisily around between his legs. It was one of his tricks to gain attention. Even with new choices in the house, Clouseau still spent his nights beside her bed. She had to be careful if she got up in the middle of the night not to put her feet on him. Occasionally she'd open her eyes to find he was resting his muzzle on the side of the bed and was silently staring at her, with what looked in the dark like gorilla eyes, willing her awake. If he was really impatient for her to get up, as he evidently was this morning, he would take to licking himself with excessive enthusiasm. This was guaranteed to attract a certain kind of notice, even if it was a low-flying pillow.

She'd developed a habit of talking to him about what they would do that day, although not if Ethan or Joey were within hearing. He'd sit and twist his head in a very human way, trying hard to understand, and at the mention of certain words his tail would thump on the ground – beach, walk, café, biscuit. He could identify all the names of the neighbours they would be walking past – thump, thump, thump, thump, thump – and he especially liked the sound of Ethan's name.

There was a possibility now of handing it all over, walking off. But as soon as she conceived that idea a reluctance pulled at her and all at once her thoughts began to migrate in another direction. It was that word *daughter,* she supposed, uttered in the garden so ingenuously. They'd both laughed but at the same time a seam of warmth had run through her. Without any particular mindfulness the barnacled old anchor rope she'd been trailing had snagged on something that, while not quite as contractual as family, still had some of its casually involved affection. And while travelling the world without any attachments might be an enticing notion, in the end that could probably only bring a short-lived kind of fulfilment, more suited to absolute youth.

After a time the heart quite likes its little involvements.

*

She was late getting up and Joey had already left the house. Ethan volunteered to accompany her to the café. As they were leaving Simone noticed the photo of him which used to hang in the hallway was missing. Presumably he'd taken it down. It hadn't been a flattering likeness, she could see why he might not be comfortable with it hanging there. If she was him she would've taken it down as well. When she asked him about it he said, 'I fucking hate that photo. I don't know why Mum hung it there.'

'Maybe she liked that idea of you,' she suggested. 'Dressed in a suit, your hair all brushed.' She told him that based on that photo she and Lexie had decided he might be an undertaker. He told her they were half right – it was taken on the day of his father's funeral. He said this in the same way he always told her anything – uncomplicated and plain. When he and Joey had first come she'd thought them similar but now she recognised that Ethan was much more knowable. She could ask questions, expect answers. So different from Joey, who seldom gave a straight answer to anything, and incited in her an urge to display something so unexplored and messy it just ended in a tangle where she could hardly speak at all, hardly be herself.

'What was your father like?' she asked Ethan.

'A bit of a bastard. Drank a lot.'

'What happened to him?'

He took his time answering her. They walked along side by side for a while and she thought perhaps he wasn't going to say anything at all. 'It was Mum's idea to come here,' he said. 'About six months after they moved he had a heart attack in front of the telly and that was that.'

That was that. That was what Dads did. They ate. They drank. They did all kinds of masculine stuff – developed phobias about going to the doctor. And then one day they dropped dead. 'Your poor mother!'

'I dunno – he was a bit of a miserable bugger. I don't think they made each other happy.'

249

'You didn't get on with him?' Simone asked, although she didn't need him to speak to know the answer.

'I wish I could say yes,' he said. 'Did you get on with yours?'

'Yes.'

'He probably didn't like to hit the piss and then tell you what a useless little shit you were growing into, did he?'

'No. That's true. He liked to drive me around in his car and make me sing while he whistled.' Was that terrible? She wanted to take it back as soon as it was out of her mouth.

'Lucky you then,' he said without bitterness. 'Do you want to know something funny?'

Simone nodded, but knew it wasn't going to be the kind of funny to make her laugh.

'I got my first tattoo to piss him off.'

'And did it?'

'Yes. But that's not the funny thing,' he said. 'It's gone now.'

'You had it removed?'

He shook his head – and then suddenly she got it. 'It was on the leg you lost?'

'Yup,' he said. 'On the back of my calf.'

At first she couldn't look at him. She walked beside him and thought for a moment she couldn't imagine anything sadder. But then she felt him turn his head toward her and she sneaked a glance and saw the corner of his mouth had the beginnings of an upward curl. For some reason it made her think of giggling. He nudged her with his shoulder and she said 'Owww' in an exaggerated way which made him laugh and set her off too. So the two of them carried on down the street, on the way to the café, with laughter rising out of them, coming from who knows where, as if they had never thought of laughing about such things before. And she thought perhaps this is what living is. You start out whole, intact, with every bit of you expecting to get what you deserve, but then pieces start to get chipped off. A father's love. A long-held expectation.

A piece of leg. A tiny arm. A corner of the heart. And the challenge is to start to feel formed by what is not there and what is left. She looked at big, buoyant Ethan and had an urge to jump on his back and make him piggyback her to the café, but just in time she remembered his leg. It was surprising how easy it was to forget.

'Those tools in the shed. They were his?' she asked.

'Yeah. He always had this idea he would make stuff but I think he just went out there to drink. Might've got himself onto it though.'

'Do you mean the boxes?'

'Yeah.'

'That was me,' she confessed, feeling herself redden.

'Oh,' he said. 'Clever you. I thought they were a bit too imaginative for him. What are you planning to put inside them?'

'I dunno. Those are boxes made without a plan.'

'Well, how very novel,' he retorted.

When they arrived at the café Joey was behind the counter with Hanife and they were talking animatedly. Both had one hip resting on the counter, each had their head slightly inclined towards the other. Standing close together like that they looked looser somehow, softer, as if the staunch force fields they presented to most other people had met and been rendered powerless. Hanife looked up and smiled widely when she saw Simone come in with Ethan. 'So today you are back at work?' she said.

Joey greeted them with a brief lifting of his chin. 'One for the road?' he said to Ethan. He made Ethan a coffee in a take-out cup and then said, mostly to Hanife, 'See you guys later?'

'Where are you off to?' Simone asked.

'Got a bit of man's business to take care of,' Ethan said.

When they went out the door she asked Hanife if she knew what they were up to. Hanife shrugged and said, 'Man's business? I don't know. I'm thinking they just like to keep up some stupid pretend mystery. Anyway look, we have some business of our own today!'

Hanife's idea was to make and hang ninety Chinese lanterns for Zita's party. She had spent the previous evening making the paper templates and the wire shells. Throughout the day she encouraged customers to help, and some of the regulars were so surprised to be asked anything from Hanife they put considerable effort into their creations, like it was a test of their future worthiness to take up a seat at one of her tables.

'Joey told me they took you to visit with your man,' Hanife said.

'Not my man any more,' Simone replied, liking to imagine the meeting yesterday might have taken place in an airport cafeteria and he'd had now permanently left her country.

33

Zita was escorted to the café by Toss, who'd persuaded her to leave the house on some pretence or another. She'd probably been expecting something, but she didn't let on, and when she walked into the room and saw her friends and family gathered there in the frittering light of ninety Chinese lanterns her eyes began to water copiously and a chair had to be fetched.

Zita's eldest son Benjamin was still in Hong Kong with his wife, but the rest of her family were there, including all her grandchildren, who were now adults and who had brought along their partners and offspring, the great-grandchildren. There was some confusion for a little while because the wayward grandson, the one Zita thought was an *artist*, who was now in his forties, had brought along a shy young girl who looked like she should've been his daughter, and she had a small baby.

'Is this the first great-great-grandson?' Clara asked excitedly. But no, it turned out the young woman was actually his girlfriend and the baby wasn't even his. The baby was called Vaughn and whenever the girlfriend said his name she had a way of chewing on the word so it came out in two syllables. 'Stop that Vaur–yaghn!'

Zita's daughter-in-law Mae kept anxiously telling anyone who would listen that they'd been planning to do something special for Zita themselves, 'But what with Tony being so unwell, and all the travelling Zita would've had to do to come to them . . .' Her husband, Zita's son Tony, did appear to have a yellowish pallor. He was in his late sixties and had a disfigured veined nose that told of a long career with alcohol. Overall he looked far less robust than his mother.

Skulky, shadowy Ravi had even come along with his host

family. When Simone saw him she dragged him over to where Clara was standing and said, 'This lady seems to think we had sex together. Do you know why?'

Ravi shrugged, and with his soft liar's mouth, said cheekily, 'Perhaps she has a good imagination.'

He skittered away and Clara laughed heartily. She patted Simone on the hand and said, 'I forgot to tell you that I got to the bottom of all that. Apparently he was brassed off with his host family for sending him off to stay at Zita's house so he made up a few little untruths to try and upset them. Worked a treat apparently!'

The presents were opened. Zita was sweet and thanked everybody effusively, but it was easy to see she wasn't much interested in all the lovely soaps and fluffy towels she'd received. She'd had enough of new things for now. Simone had given her one of the wooden boxes with some chocolates inside, but Hanife had given her the one thing that really tickled her – a fake tiara. Zita put it on her head and gave everybody in the room a royal wave. 'This reminds me of that time we got caught up in the royal cavalcade,' she said. 'Do you remember, Tony?' Her son shook his head unwilling or unable to remember, it was hard to tell which. She told a story about heading out on a visit to her husband's sister to see the new baby and they came to a corner where traffic officers were holding up the line of cars. They were running late and her husband was impatient to get on, and when two big Rolls Royces went past he saw his chance and pulled in quickly behind them. 'Next thing we rounded a corner and there were hundreds of people lining the road. And we saw an arm in the front car waving like this.' She did her royal wave again.

'Was it the Queen, Nana?' one of the grandchildren asked.

Zita nodded, 'Your granddad went bright red and I slid down the seat. The boys thought it was a great hoot and waved at the crowd until a police cyclist came up alongside and made us veer off. We all got a bit of a telling off and then we went and had a lovely visit with your Great-Aunt Aggie!'

'Dad, you never told us about that!' the granddaughter said, giving Zita a laughing kiss on the cheek.

'I'd quite forgotten all about that,' her father said. He looked as though he might have forgotten quite a lot.

Mae took that moment to note the occasion. 'I can feel tears spring to my eyes,' she said, 'when I look around the room and see the fine family you created darling. What a wonderful legacy you've provided to the world.'

There was a chorus of 'Hear, hear!' and a clinking of glasses and the sound of kisses landing on Zita. Hanife, standing just behind Simone's shoulder, whispered, 'Well that's one kind of legacy anyway.' And Simone thought another might be that of the impish young girl who once liked to give a now-famous schoolboy a little motivation by chasing him for kisses.

Ethan had set up Charlie's stereo in the corner and the two of them were playing some of Charlie's old 78s. Mostly show tunes, Gershwin and Cole Porter, giving the party a rascally, Tin Pan air. Simone noticed Ethan consulted with Charlie before each record was spun. When it came time for Zita to cut her cake they chose 'You're the Tops'. Ethan's eyes searched across the room for Simone. He'd shaved off his big gingery sideburns and she saw for the first time he had strikingly deep dimples when he smiled. As Zita took the knife and sliced down through the layers her son said, 'Fit as a fiddle aren't you, Mum?'

His wife added, 'Amazing. Still managing at your age.'

Toss came up to Simone with his slice of cake on a plate. 'I've been wanting to come and see you,' he said. 'Had my day in court today.'

'Oh, I didn't realise. Was it okay? What happened?'

There was a moment of hesitation and Simone drew him over to one of the tables, away from the others. 'Well I must admit I was a bit shaken up by it,' he said. 'I felt like such an old fool. Don't know how I would've got on without Ethan and Joey.'

'Ethan and Joey?'

'Yes. Didn't they tell you, lass? They came along with me.

Helped me find my way around the court system. I tell you, for an old man like me it was mighty confusing. The place was full of young kids in those hoodie things, milling about, drunk-driving charges it mostly seemed to be. I wouldn't have known where to sit meself but those two got me a lawyer. And he got me diversion in the end. Had to sit down with the police prosecutor and show remorse and agree never to touch the stuff again. And there's a donation to pay, I suggested IHC could use it.'

He shovelled a forkful of cake into his mouth and they sat listening to the music for a moment. 'So you still don't know how it all came about?' Simone asked.

'Yep. I do now.'

Simone waited.

'It was my boy,' Toss said sheepishly. 'It's not that he meant to get me in trouble, he just has a bit of difficulty with perspective sometimes. He likes to stand out in ways that you or I could never imagine. I'm not mad at him or anything. But that's why they sent the dogs in. The way he talked it up they were expecting a big haul. I think they thought they were going to uncover one of those big commercial outfits with everybody in on it – not just a couple of straggly plants and a bunch of old pensioners.' He looked a little crumpled so Simone asked him if he'd like a beer. He nodded and she went off to find a bottle and refresh her own wine glass. She'd wanted to say, *But why did the police believe somebody like Hughie?* but thought that might be too unkind.

When she came back Toss gratefully took up the beer and began to explain further. 'He had all the facts, see. I liked to show him how it worked – the hydroponics. A man ought to be able to do that kind of thing with his son. Course I never told him what it was, just said it was special cooking herbs. Not so far from the truth, eh. Anyway one day somebody shows him one of those anti-drug pamphlets and he works it out. Pleased as punch for a reason to take himself off to the police station, he goes in there and tells them all about where the plants are, how they're grown. All of it. Lots of realistic facts. Only when it comes to telling them how many plants he didn't make any distinction between that stuff and the rows of lettuces I had going. And on top of that he couldn't help exaggerating a little. Must take after his old man after all. I used to say it'd all be up to the ceiling before you know it, so no prizes for guessing what he said to them.'

'And the police knew he was talking about his own Dad?'

'Thinking it was their lucky day, I reckon. They asked him lots of questions and the funny thing is they asked him who I supplied the *crop* to. That was the word they used – *crop*. So he gets that a bit mixed up in his head and thinks of me handing you vegetables over the fence. And Zita. And Clara. So that's how he got you all in it too.'

There was a brief spike of laughter from across the room – somebody telling a funny joke, a circle of people responding.

'So after the disappointment of visiting all us old pensioners,' Toss said, 'they must've thought it was their lucky day when they found you.'

'Do you think that was why they were so thorough when they got to my house? The anticlimax of it all?'

'Maybe. Sorry, girl,' Toss said. A grey wretchedness showed on his face.

'S'all right. Just wish I'd had a chance to try one of those Anzac cookies before you vowed off it all.' They smiled briefly at each other and she clinked her wine glass against his bottle.

He nodded up towards Ethan and said, 'They're a funny lot, though, those two boys. When I tried to thank them for it all later they weren't having it. That one just said, "Well, mate, at last something good comes from a coupla misspent youths!"'

Ethan had his back to them, searching through the crate of records fetched from Charlie and Clara's living room. He was enjoying himself, Simone thought, taking the business of tailoring the music to the mood of his crowd as seriously as any urban DJ. It was only then that she thought to look around for Joey. She saw he was standing out on the front deck, having a cigarette with a group of the smokers from Zita's family, his left arm slung ever so casually around Hanife's shoulders.

'It's nice what you've done for Zita,' Toss said.

'It was Clara who did it really.'

'But still.'

A couple who were out for a stroll down the beach stopped and looked up at the café windows. They would've been able to hear the music from where they stood and they looked to be wondering if anybody was allowed to join in on whatever fun was being had in there. An unfamiliar sense of fortune came over Simone as she sipped at her wine, the homely sort of prosperity which comes from being admitted as a smallish cog in the central pursuit of happiness.

Marjorie came in through the door, went over to greet Zita, then after a while came to sit with Toss and Simone. Clara joined their table too. This was the first time anybody'd seen Marjorie since she'd gone off to collect Stanley, but he wasn't with her. 'Did you decide to leave him at home?' Clara asked.

'No, he's not at home,' Marjorie said, taking a sip of her wine and looking around the room.

Clara exchanged a look with Simone and then asked delicately, 'Is he still . . . ?'

Marjorie took another large gulp of her wine and then told them that as she was driving down to collect Stanley she felt herself fighting the urge to turn the car around and go back home without him. She stopped at the roadside several times and in the end decided to go on with it. But as soon as she saw his face she knew she couldn't possibly live with him again. She didn't want to wake up in the same house as him. She didn't want to share anything with him at all. They sat down together and talked it all through. He volunteered to go and live with his brother, so they sorted it out with the authorities and she drove him there, settled him in, and then returned home alone.

'Once the trust is broken . . .' she said. 'Silly old fool had taken me to a charity art auction the night before he was arrested, you know. There we stood with him bidding away

258

like some wealthy patron, and all the time he knew he wouldn't even be able to front up with the money. I've been so mad about the humiliation of that all this time. And you know what. I feel so much happier now. I've realised I'd been dreading it for months!'

Clara raised her glass and said, 'Well here's ta-ta to Stanley then.'

'And hasta la pasta,' Marjorie said, clinking glasses, but she looked a little remorseful. It was still a bit too fresh and sore to mock.

A new record was placed on the player and Simone saw Ethan give Charlie an encouraging nudge. Charlie came over to where they were sitting and with a surprising assurance put out his out hand to Clara. Zita's family were too busy to notice, occupied as they were with all the jostling and joviality of their reunion, with all the small factions and alignments of family, and the withholding of petty resentments that such a significant occasion as the ninetieth birthday of one of their members required. But at their table there was a round intake of breath and Clara stood up with a slightly stunned expression on her face. Charlie pulled her close to him, into the customary position, and then they were borne off around the room on the collective amazement of all their neighbours. Because while the mind might forget, the body doesn't. Dancing around the tables Charlie was elegance itself, and seeing him straight-backed and for once in full command, it was possible to see why Clara might have been inclined to forgive his sins over all those years.

Simone looked up and found Ethan was watching her, beaming across at her. She noticed again his uncontained grin and those dimples, and then their eyes locked for the briefest of moments, but that was all the time it took for the air in the room to change completely, for the shape of him to alter irrecoverably. It was as if the softness of the light from those ninety glowing candles suddenly made the entirety of him more visible. Now that she could see it, she wasn't sure why she hadn't noticed it earlier – it was all something to do with how he was from the inside out. He had the kind of moral compass that could be relied on to do the good and true thing in any situation, which was so different from relying on a person to do the unpredictable or difficult thing.

'You know who would've enjoyed all this?' Marjorie whispered into Simone's ear, 'Alice.'

At the end of the evening Simone was bending down rearranging plates in the bottom of the Hanife's fridge when she felt a hand on her bum. It was a man's hand, she could tell. A number of terrible possibilities ran through her mind. Ravi. Toss. The wayward grandson. When he leaned down and whispered in her ear, 'I've wanted to do that from the moment I first saw you', she knew it was the one she was hoping for.

Her bra was lost somewhere on the beach. By the time they got in through the door her lips were raw from kissing him. When they fell down on the bed she ripped off his shirt and made him flex his biceps while she ran the tip of her finger lightly around the tattoos which had always been hidden by his clothing. When she reached for his belt he put his hand on her wrist and masked what she thought might be a sudden bashfulness with a show of responsibility, unusual for a man. 'Wait, wait. Do we need to use anything?'

'Do we? I've been tested since my boyfriend ran off with a stupid hussy. What about you?'

'Yeah, after my last tattoo I got tested for everything. I'm clean. But what about . . . ?'

'Contraception? Well I have to tell you I'm so difficult to get pregnant that if it happened all the birds would probably fall from the sky in shock.'

Ethan brushed a lock of hair out of her eyes and looked at her with his sadsweet curly smile. 'Yeah?' he said. 'Well my boys like a challenge.'

Afterwards, while he was sleeping, she reached out and put her hand on his chest, and felt the warm, solid beat of his heart.

One day soon, she thought, she might go back to the city. One day soon, she might go and visit Alice. She wanted to lean down and whisper in her ear. She wanted to say thank you. Thank you for all this. This place to stay. The happy dog. And the rest. Oh and yes this, Simone thought. Especially this. These warm lips. This appetite. These haunted, kissing eyes. Who can think too far ahead when you have such nice things being offered up so tenderly? Such lovely heart-warming things.

In the end, there are only such moments, only what is in front of you. It could be so easy, this new thing, with Ethan. Here he is – strong and lovable, funny and direct. She could even see how they might be together when they were old – his gently caring manner grazing softly up against her. He'd whispered things that made her think a love might already be in progress. And if it was love it would be a trustworthy thing. And if she let herself love in return, it wouldn't be the sort of thing she'd craved in the past, with all its singular intensity. Not the kind that burnt up its own energy worrying about the quality and depth of it. Not the kind that closes everything else out. Ethan had a soundly loyal, reliable beam that landed absolutely on her. So unambiguously, so solidly that . . . well, she had to wonder, and she did think of the wondering as a kind of weakness, but where in all this, in this thing that came to her so swiftly and so easily, was the challenge for the heart?

ACKNOWLEDGEMENTS

Thank you to the wonderful team at VUP, Fergus Barrowman – a great believer, Heather McKenzie, Craig and Kylie. And special thanks to Sue Brown, much-valued editor.

Thank you to everybody at the IIML, particularly Damien Wilkins, and my classmates Pip, Kirsten, Emily, Deborah, Abby, Marty, Adrita, Tim and Nic. Also Kate Duignan. And especially Pip Robertson for all her additional help.

Thank you to Olivier Pellenard for his line of French, and Katherine Ivory for her photography.

For their support and generosity and some colourful little anecdotes which I hope I've used well – thank you to Jenny, Katherine S, Kate W, Janet, Bryce, Margie, Anna and Ken, Kate H, Jerome, Tom, Buzz, Tiger, Sally and Gordon, my lovely mother, and my father who I wish was still alive.